TWENTY INSPIRING
STORIES FROM
TOUCHED BY AN ANGEL

In the Words of Angels

Martha Williamson
EXECUTIVE PRODUCER

With Davin Seay

A Fireside Book
Published by Simon & Schuster

New York   London   Toronto   Sydney   Singapore

FIRESIDE
Rockefeller Center
1230 Avenue of the Americas
New York, NY 10020

For information about special discounts for bulk purchases,
please contact Simon & Schuster Special Sales:
1-800-456-6798 or business@simonandschuster.com

Designed by Joy O'Meara

Manufactured in the United States of America

1   3   5   7   9   10   8   6   4   2

Library of Congress Cataloging-in-Publication Data is available.

ISBN 0-7432-0368-2

Contents

Such a Time as This   9

Psalm 151   23

Mother's Day   35

Black Like Monica   50

Sins of the Father   65

The Man Upstairs   79

Clipped Wings   93

Reunion   107

Til We Meet Again   120

The Face on the Barroom Floor   134

The Wind Beneath My Wings   148

Pandora's Box   162

Life Before Death   177

Flights of Angels   191

Beautiful Dreamer   205

Buy Me a Rose   219

Trust   233

Into the Light   247

Lost & Found   261

Great Expectations   275

In the
Words of
Angels

Such a Time as This

Thomas lay slumped over the kitchen table as morning light poured through the window and over the sleeping figure of the ten-year-old boy. His head rested on an open file folder from which a sheaf of black and white photos spilled out, the images in stark and shocking contrast to the comfortable suburban affluence of the Cooper home.

The pictures displayed gaunt and hungry faces staring into the camera lens, their haunted eyes like windows on their tormented souls. A small child, strapped to its mother's back, seemed numb to the bleak landscape of the African desert through which it was being carried, one agonizing step after another. A man, wrapped only in a loincloth, was being prodded down a dusty trail by a guard wrapped in a turban and brandishing an automatic weapon. Behind him, a woman, her ebony skin as parched as the wasteland across which she trudged, had fallen to her knees. Her hands were lifted to the sky, as if pleading for death to put an end to her misery and the misery of her people.

Thomas stirred uneasily, his dreams reflecting the flickering images of naked human suffering so graphically portrayed in the photos. He had come across the file by accident, searching through his mother's briefcase for the gift she had promised him when she had called from her Washington, DC, office the day before. Thomas had gotten used to hearing his mother's voice on the far end of a telephone line—for as long as he could remember she was, first and foremost, a US Senator, her face on the evening news, speaking into a forest of microphones. And now that she was running for reelection, she seemed even more distant, more unapproachable. Thomas had tried hard to understand, telling himself over and over that his mother had an important job to do, working to help people, to make the world a better place to live. But sometimes he just couldn't help wishing that she cared as much about him and his dad, about their family, as she did about all the problems that she sometimes seemed to carry around like a weight on her shoulders.

Thomas stirred, opening his eyes to the morning sun and lifting his head from the table. As his eyes adjusted to the bright light, the letter that had accompanied the photos swam into focus and he read it again, struggling over the big words and trying to make sense of its urgent message.

The letter was written by a man named Dr. Joseph Akot—a name Thomas had immediately shortened to Dr. Joe—and it told the story of the people in the pictures, including one little boy with cuts and bruises all over his face, a boy who would have been about the same age as Thomas' brother Sam: if he had lived.

"Dear Senator Cooper," Thomas read. "I write to you today on behalf of innocent people who cannot speak for themselves: the slaves of the Sudan." Thomas didn't know where the Sudan was, but it sounded very far away. "Their villages have been destroyed by militia and soldiers," the letter continued, "the men murdered and the women and children taken into slavery where they are beaten and raped and even branded like cattle." The young boy's eyes filled with tears as he read these words, but he forced himself to continue. "They are used as currency, bought and sold like livestock. I enclose the testimonies of several redeemed slaves." Thomas didn't exactly know what "redeemed" meant, but he hoped that somehow, some way, the slaves would be set free; he was suddenly ashamed about the resentment he felt over his mother's work and the time she spent away from home. If she could do anything to help these people, to bring them food and water, clothes and shelter, then missing her was a small price for Thomas to pay. He had so much. They had so little. He felt a swell of pride. The work his mother did really mattered. She was making a difference between life and death and that was the most important job of all.

Monica stood in the corner of the kitchen, an invisible, angelic witness to the young boy's thoughts and emotions. Tess had warned her when they had taken on this assignment that it wouldn't be easy, that Thomas and his parents would be faced with choices and decisions that most people didn't have the courage to confront. It was their job to help, in any way they could . . . but there was so much to do. And so little time.

"Yes, Thomas," Monica whispered, wishing her words of comfort could be heard by the child. "It's true. There is a whole world out there, oceans away, where children just like you can't play or go to school or even say their prayers. They don't dream of going to the Moon one day, like you do. They only dream of going home."

A little child shall lead us. That's what Tess had told her when they had first come to this place and begun to learn about the Cooper family and their history. But lead them where? Monica couldn't help but wonder. After all, Thomas and his parents seemed more than a little lost themselves, good people caught in circumstances that were testing the bonds of their love and commitment.

It was true that James and Kate Cooper shared a past full of high ideals, hopes and dreams that stretched back to the tumultuous Sixties when they had both believed that the world really could be changed. But as time went on, that very belief had become a wedge between them. Kate, working within the system, had gone on to a high-profile career in politics, while James had taken a different road, dropping out to become a simple carpenter, expressing his disillusionment by refusing even to vote.

Yet somehow, they had managed to maintain a love and respect that kept them together over the years, even when faced with the most trying test of all—the death of Sam, their first child. Kate still wore a locket with Sam's picture in it, a precious memory that tore at her husband's heart every time he saw it. After all, they'd been too poor at the time to afford medical insurance and, although his wife never said as much, it was as if the locket around her neck was a constant reminder of James's failure as a provider.

But that was all a long time ago, and since then Thomas had been born, an unexpected blessing in both their lives, even as Kate tried her best to balance motherhood with a fast-rising Beltway career. It wasn't easy, and the time she spent away from her home sometimes weighed like a stone on her heart. It was in those times that she needed to tell herself, over and over, that doing the right thing came at a price. And there was no more convincing proof of that than the agricultural bill she was getting ready to introduce on the floor of the Senate. The farm families of her constituency needed her help and even though she had her doubts about some of the lobbyist and special interest groups that were promising their support, she had to reminded herself that, sometimes, the ends really did justify the means.

A little child shall lead us. That's what Tess had said. But Monica couldn't quite see exactly what the problems of one American family had to do with the plight of enslaved Sudanese villagers half a world away. It had been Andrew who had taken the pictures that now lay on the Cooper's kitchen table, summoned to be at the right place at the right time to help Dr. Joe in his lifesaving mission. But when Monica had seen for herself the terrible evidence of man's inhumanity, the only question she could ask was why they had been given this assignment instead of being sent to that barren desert where life was cheap and death was common. *A little child shall lead us,* was all that Tess would tell her and, for the moment, that would have to do.

Still groggy from sleep and thinking of nothing but her first cup of coffee, Kate Cooper was startled to wakefulness at the sight of her son sitting at the kitchen table with an expectant look on his face. She caught her breath as, in the next moment, she saw the terrible photos spread out in front of him. She bit her lip to keep her exasperation from spilling out. Those meddling people at the embassy party last night . . . she should never have agreed to take this packet of photos and documentation from them, never agreed to even consider looking into the Sudanese slavery question.

But they'd been so earnest, so persistent, beginning with the one who had pleaded their case in a lilting Scottish accent—Monica was her name. And her associate, Andrew, who claimed to have collected the evidence to prove what the government of Sudan had for so long denied . . . that its citizens were being bought and sold like cattle. But the most compelling thing of all had been the look of urgency in the eyes of Dr. Joseph Akot, whose determination to help his people had cut through the distractions of Kate's busy schedule to make a lasting impression. It was because of the doctor, because of the unspoken plea he'd conveyed to her, that she'd reluctantly agreed to take a look at their evidence, even as she hurried out the door to catch a red-eye flight back home. And now those same pictures, those haunting images, had fallen into the hands of her son Thomas, an innocent boy who had no way of understanding how inhuman human beings could sometimes be.

"What are you doing?" she asked sharply, as she hurried over to gather up the photos. "Haven't I told you never to go into my briefcase?"

"I was looking for my present," Thomas explained, his eyes wide. "Mom," he asked, "what does 'sexual chattel' mean?"

Kate turned to him, her anger draining away as she sat down next to her son. "Thomas," she began with a sigh as she pointed to the pile of photos. "There is a war going on in this country. Terrible things happen when people fight wars."

"I thought soldiers fought wars," Thomas replied, nodding at the pictures. "Those little kids aren't soldiers."

"I know," Kate answered, wincing at the pain and confusion her son felt. "But you don't fight fair in a war."

In reply, Thomas pulled out a photo of the young boy with the scarred face. "I think his name is Sam," he said, handing it to his mother. "Like my brother."

"You think about him a lot, don't you?" asked Kate.

"Can I see it?" was Thomas's plaintive response.

Kate smiled and, as she had done so many times before, opened the locket around her neck and showed her son the tiny photo of his brother.

Thomas looked at it, as if half expecting to find the answers to his questions in the infant's innocent face. "So," he asked after a moment. "Are you going?"

"Where?" replied his puzzled mother.

"To the Sudan," was his prompt reply.

Kate sighed again. "I don't think so," she told him. "It takes a lot more people to change the world."

"But if you went, you could get him free," Thomas insisted. "You could buy him and bring him home, and he could live with us."

Kate felt an ache in her heart. "Maybe he has a mommy who would miss him," she said softly.

"Maybe they killed her already," was her son's solemn reply as he looked up at his mother, his clear blue eyes searching her face. "All it takes is one person to make a difference," he continued. "That's what Dad says."

Suddenly aware of another presence in the room, Kate looked up to see her husband standing in the doorway. They exchanged a long and wordless look, as if trying to measure the distance that had grown between them.

It was show-and-tell time in Thomas's grade school class and the small boy stood solemnly at the front of the row of desks. "I've got something to tell you," he said with all the seriousness a ten-year-old boy can muster. Tess, substitute teacher for the day, hushed the children and listened carefully as Thomas began to share. This, she knew, was why they had come—the innocent expectation of a child that would bring redemption to a far distant land.

"Remember how we learned about slavery and how they abolished it a long time ago?" he continued. "Well, it's not true." Tess silenced the snickering students with a stern look and nodded for Thomas to continue. Pulling out the photo of the small Sudanese boy, Thomas held it up for the class to see. "This is Sam," he explained. "He costs fifty dollars." Suddenly, complete silence fell over the class and the children listened intently as Thomas began to read from one of Dr. Joe's testimonials. "I am a twelve-year-old girl," he began. "I was a slave for three years. My master was a cattle farmer. My master's wife threw boiling water into my eyes because she was mad that my master used me as a . . ." he hesitated, carefully sounding out the word, "concubine. Then he sold me to another master who would not give me food unless I changed my religion. I was very sad because I missed my mother and my father and my little brother."

Thomas stopped, looking up at the class as he held the picture of the small, battered boy. "I don't know if this is her brother," he said.

"But he's somebody's brother. I had a brother once. I never really knew him, but I miss him anyway. And I don't know this kid, but I think I know a way that we can help him."

Kate, with James by her side, moved briskly through the crowd across the school playground, surrounded by a buzzing throng of reporters. It was a bright and balmy morning and the banner over the school entrance announced PARENT'S DAY. But this was more than just a photo opportunity for a political candidate anxious to be on the right side of the education issue. This was the school Thomas attended and Kate was relieved that for once, she could combine her job with a chance to show her son that she cared, really cared, about him.

She scanned the crowd, smiling and waving as she saw Thomas running toward her and the cameras captured the action as the boy excitedly led his parents across the playground to see his class project.

"Mom," he said, breathlessly. "Remember when you said it took a lot of people to change things?"

"Not exactly . . ." Kate began, all too aware of the cameras following their every move.

"Well," Thomas exclaimed. "I found them! And we're going to help you!"

With a flourish he led them to a homemade booth set up on the playground that was manned by his classmates. Coffee cans covered with paper were on display behind a large map of Africa, and a banner overhead proclaimed 4th GRADE FUND-RAISER—FREE THE SLAVES OF SUDAN!

The reporters stumbled over one another as they crowded in to shout their questions. Was this Senator Cooper's idea? Did she support the Sudanese rebels? Would she be taking up the slavery issue in the Senate? As she tried her best to put a positive spin on the situation, without making any real commitment, Kate glared angrily at her husband. "Did you put him up to this?" she demanded in a harsh whisper, as her press secretary herded the reporters away.

"What are you talking about?" James shot back as Monica and Dr. Joe suddenly appeared through the welter of cameras and microphones.

"Senator Cooper," Monica began, "raising money was the children's idea. Maybe it won't solve the problem, but their hearts were pure and—"

"Don't lecture me about my son—" Kate interrupted furiously, then turned to see that her husband was about to put a ten-dollar donation into one of the coffee cans. "Don't do that!" she demanded. "The reporters are watching."

A long moment passed as James stared deep into his wife's flashing eyes. Then, with all deliberation, he dropped the bill into the can.

"What are you trying to do?" she asked, in shock and anger.

"Support my son," he replied evenly. "Do a good thing."

"And humiliate me," Kate spat back.

"It's not about you," her husband replied. "You can't take African slaves and make them about you." He paused for a moment, then softened. "You're a good Senator, Kate," he said. "Why don't you go to the Sudan?"

Kate breathed an exasperated sigh. "The Sudan has nothing to do with farming or education or any of the issues that—"

James held up his hand, stopping her mid-sentence. "Tell it to your son," he replied sadly and, turning, walked away.

On a television over the bar in an airport lounge, a newscast replayed the events on the schoolyard as Kate, waiting for the flight to Washington, nursed a glass of wine and watched glumly.

"The Senator's own son said he got the idea to raise money from reading his mother's intelligence briefings," the reporter was saying as footage of Thomas appeared on the screen, smiling broadly into the camera "All you have to do is send it to me," he explained. "And my mom and Dr. Joe will take it to Africa and buy some of the slaves back. Just remember that a girl costs more, but I'm not sure why . . ."

An anchorman picked up the story. "Although Senator Cooper claims to be proud of her son's initiative," he reported, "she would not comment on a possible fact-finding mission to the Sudan."

Suddenly Kate became aware of a presence next to her and, turning, found Monica settling onto a stool. "Why are you doing this?" was all Kate could say.

"Tell me, Kate," the angel replied. "When you were a child and you imagined the twenty-first century, did you ever imagine slavery?"

"You don't know anything about me or my work," Kate answered bitterly. "I'm not saying that what you care about isn't important, but I have to prioritize based on the realities of what I can actually accomplish. I have to make choices and that means I have to make sacrifices." But even as she spoke the words, she knew she was withholding the truth—from Monica and from herself. The reality was, she had powerful vested interests behind her campaign, interests who had no desire to see her embroiled in a controversial international issue. They were the ones she had to think of now, if she wanted the money it was going to take to win reelection. She looked Monica straight in the eyes. "Please give this up," she begged. "Why won't you give this up?"

Monica never flinched from her gaze. "Because," she replied, her voice ringing with authority, "you're the one, Kate."

Bob Sumner, founder and CEO of Sumner Candies, one of the biggest employers in her state and among Kate's most generous contributors, looked as if he had one of his own chocolate nougats stuck in his throat. His eyes bulging, his face red, he slammed his fist down on her desk and shouted, "There is no slavery in the Sudan! The government says it doesn't exist and I believe them. Now you get that boy of yours and your hippie husband off the evening news and get back to the job we paid you to do."

Kate looked calmly at the sputtering executive, even as her mind raced with the implications of what he was saying. Bob Sumner was not a man she could afford to offend, and without his support her whole campaign just might sputter out for lack of funds. But there was something in the man's eye, an evasive look as if he were trying to hide something, that put her on her guard. His outburst wasn't about Thomas and his campaign to buy back slaves. There was something else at stake and Kate had a pretty good idea what it might be.

"You believe the slaves don't exist," she said slowly, staring straight back at Sumner, "because the government told you so?"

The businessman suddenly looked very uncomfortable. A long moment passed as he considered his options. "Look," he said at last, sitting down across from her. "It's simple. The Sudan exports something called gum arabic. It's used in everything. Food. Soda pop . . ."

"And candy," interjected Kate.

Sumner nodded. "We keep the prices stable, I make my candy and your constituents keep working. It's that easy." He leaned forward. "You walk away from this thing, Senator Cooper. You tell your kid and the rest of the world you're not interested in the Sudan." He stormed out, leaving his unspoken threat lingering behind.

Kate sighed and, picking up the phone, asked her secretary to try her home number again. She had to talk to James, to try and heal the breach that had grown between them. It was at that moment that the office door flew open and a triumphant Thomas, trailed by his father, paraded in, pulling a rolling suitcase behind him. "You are really going to be surprised, Mom," he announced as Monica appeared in the doorway behind them.

"I already am," admitted Kate.

With a flourish the boy unzipped the luggage, revealing a mound of bills. "Three thousand two hundred and thirty-six dollars and seventy-six cents," he announced. "That's sixty-four people, Mom."

Kate looked over to her husband and Monica, realizing there was no one who could help her say what must be said now to her son. She knelt down next to him, capturing his wide blue gaze. "Honey," she began softly, "I think it's wonderful what you've done. But I can't take this money."

"But why?" asked the stricken boy.

"Because I'm not going to the Sudan," she explained. "There are people who don't want me there and, if I don't listen to them, I'll lose my job. Then I won't be able to do all the good things I want."

Thomas' eyes welled with tears. "But . . . what about Sam?" he asked. He pushed the suitcase at her, the money spilling out around them. "Please, Mommy! Please! There's got to be enough here for Sam!"

He sobbed as his father crossed the room and took him into his arms. Turning to leave, he felt his wife's hand on his arm. "Where are you going?" she asked.

"I'm going to register to vote," was his stinging reply.

Monica knelt, picking bills off the floor as Kate stood numbly, staring at the door through which her family had just walked. "If you think this is going to change my mind," she said at last in a tone of cold fury, "you're mistaken. I love my family, Monica, and they've paid a price because of this job. If I don't follow through now, then it was all for nothing. I've had dreams, too. Dreams of helping people. But it's not about dreams. It's about compromise."

"God doesn't compromise," Monica replied simply. "And it's God who wants you to go to the Sudan." She straightened, standing before Kate as a soft glow began to grow around her. "There's not much time left," she continued urgently. "A plane is leaving in a few hours. There's room for five: Dr. Joe, three angels, and you."

"Are you telling me you're an angel?" Kate asked, swallowing hard. "That's not possible. Why would God send an angel to me?"

"Because you're the one," Monica repeated. "You're the one who must pay the ransom to redeem human beings from the closest thing there is to hell on earth. You're the one who needs to come back and say, 'Yes, it's true. People are in slavery today, right now.' You're the one to tell them, the ones who take their freedom for granted. You're the one who can shape the policy of the entire nation, perhaps the entire world."

Kate shook her head, trying to block out the words. "You're asking me to give up everything," she protested, "everything I've worked for."

Monica nodded even as the light around her grew brighter. "You could lose those things," she agreed. "You could lose the election. Or you could lose your life in the Sudanese desert. It's not always easy to do what God asks of us."

"I am . . . so afraid right now," Kate admitted, tears flooding her eyes.

Monica smiled, comfortingly. "Do you remember the story of Queen Esther?" she asked. "Esther was the queen of Persia and she had a secret. She was Jewish. And she kept that secret until one day she discovered that her people were about to be wiped out. She had the power to prevent it, but she was afraid to come forward. She was afraid she would lose her throne, perhaps even her life, until someone said to her, "Who knows? Maybe this is what it was all for. Perhaps you were brought to the kingdom for such a time as this." A moment passed as Monica's words echoed, finding their own place in Kate's heart. "You are the one, Kate," Monica said at last. "And I'll tell you a little secret from heaven. Sooner or later, everyone is 'the one.' They just have to say 'yes' when the time comes."

A few months later and several thousand miles distant, the brilliant sun of the Sudan desert glinted off the polished metal of the helicopter as it settled onto the parched earth. From every direction people seemed suddenly to appear as slaves and the guards gathered around the small knot of people who emerged from the chopper and began handing out money in exchange for freedom. Monica, Tess and Andrew watched as Senator Kate Cooper distributed the last of the neatly bound bills and a woman stepped forward, a joyous expression attesting to her redemption.

Then, from behind a small knot of scrubs, Kate noticed one more slave—a small boy, his face covered with welts and bruises. The money was gone. There was nothing left to pay his ransom until Kate reached up and unhooked the gold chain that held the locket, holding the small picture of Sam around her neck. The image of the Senator was flashed across the world and onto television screens on a thousand streets in a thousand neighborhoods where families watched and felt a common hope stirring among them—the hope of a better world.

Psalm 151

Monica walked slowly down the pleasant suburban street in suburban Cleveland, on a bright and brisk day in late autumn. In her gloved hand she held an address on a slip of paper—the home of her one hundredth assignment, the one Tess had told her was the hardest thing an angel has to do.

"I've seen ugliness and pain," Monica thought as she moved down the avenue of modest homes. "I've seen treachery and vengeance and I've seen hope die in hundreds—no, thousands—of faces, only to see it live again at the sound of the words 'God loves you.' I have shared in the glory of the heavenly host, I have served in Search and Rescue and delivered messages for Annunciations. But being a caseworker for the Almighty has been my greatest joy, a journey, a privilege and a blessing." Whatever she would face this time, she thought, the certainty of her calling would carry her through. . . .

Approaching a tidy house halfway down the block she saw a man raking leaves, helped by a ten-year-old girl with eager eyes and blond pigtails. "Excuse me," said the angel. "I'm looking for three–four–seven–two."

"You just passed it," the man said. "The two fell off a couple of years ago."

"I'll show you," said the girl as she skipped alongside the stranger.

"Cornelia," her father called after her, "you're not finished here."

Monica's new companion frowned. "Daddy," she said, "my name is Celine now. And I'll be right back . . . promise."

"So," the angel said, as a two-story, wood-framed home came into view. "You changed your name from Cornelia to Celine. And why is that, may I ask?"

"Because of Celine Dion," the chatty youngster replied. "She's my favorite singer. She's from Canada and speaks French sometimes. So do I. *N'cest pas?*"

Monica smiled. "So you're a music lover," she asked, but the self-proclaimed Celine had already run ahead to the wide porch of the house. "Are you here to rent the room?" she asked and, without waiting for an answer, explained, "You can just go right in. Petey's taking a nap and Audrey's probably got her headphones on. But that's okay. I practically live here." She pushed open the front door as a hesitant Monica followed.

From down the hallway she could hear the sound of a clear, lilting voice singing a commercial jingle. "That's Audrey," Celine explained as she led the way. "She writes music for ads on TV. Sometimes she even writes her own songs." She frowned. "But not a lot since Petey got sick."

"And who's Petey?" was Monica's next question.

"He's my best friend," Celine answered proudly. "He has cystic fibrosis. You can't get that from germs. You have to be born with it. The mucus and stuff gets really thick in his lungs and then he can't breathe. He has to take a lot of medicine, and he's been in the hospital lots of times. Sometimes he misses school, but I bring him his homework. I guess I'll go up and see if he's awake." She pointed to a door. "Audrey's in there."

Monica entered and found an attractive woman with long, flaming red hair that matched her own, sitting at a small keyboard with a pair of headphones over her ears. Gingerly, the angel tapped her on the shoulder and when the woman turned, Monica could see in a flash that she was carrying a heavy weight of sorrow behind her large green eyes. "I've come to the right place," she thought, as she smiled and introduced herself.

Not more than ten minutes had passed before Monica felt as if she had known Audrey her whole life. A single mother who wrote and recorded jingles to make ends meet, Audrey had a way of making Monica feel right at home in the cozy confines of the house. As she showed Monica the small, sunny upstairs rental room, another song, sweet and vibrant and resonant with joy, could be heard from down the hall.

"That sounds like you," Monica remarked.

Audrey smiled self-consciously. "It's my son, Petey. He plays that old tape all the time. I guess you could say he's my biggest fan."

They stood for a moment, listening, as the words of the song seemed to mingle with the afternoon sunlight to create an aura of serenity and peace. "All the colors of the rainbow," Audrey's voice sang, "All the voices of the wind / Every dream that reaches out / That reaches out to find where love begins . . ." The song trailed off into silence.

"It's beautiful," said Monica. "But where's the rest of it?"

Audrey looked at her, the sadness in her eyes now overflowing. "I wrote that right after Petey was born," she explained softly. "I called it the Hundred and Fifty-First Psalm, because I looked in the Bible and out of the hundred and fifty in it, I couldn't find a single one that thanked God enough for the joy I felt." From the room down the hallway came another sound, a hoarse, hacking cough, and Audrey stopped and looked away, turning her face into the shadows. "But then things changed. And I can't think of a single reason to finish that song now." She sighed, then straightened and turned back to Monica with a brave smile. "I hope you'll be comfortable here," she said. "It's not much, but it's home."

Petey, a bright and precocious ten-year-old boy with deeply-dimpled cheeks and bangs that fell across the lenses of his round glasses, sat on the front porch wrapped in a blanket and writing carefully in a notebook. On a chair next to him was a large and placid iguana that seemed to watch over the boy with one eye as he searched for flies with the other.

On the street beyond, neighborhood children ran to catch the school bus and their happy cries brought a sting to Petey's lonely isolation until a familiar figure turned down the front walkway and hurried up to the porch railing.

"Aren't you going to school?" Celine asked.

Petey sighed. "No," he replied. "I've got to stay home and rest."

Celine thought for a moment. "You're not going to die today, are you?" she asked with a child's innocence.

"Nah," was Petey's equally open answer. "I don't think so."

Celine grinned and skipped off. "Okay, then," she cried. "I'll see you."

As Petey watched her round the corner, anger and frustration clouded his face, and with no other way to express his feelings, he threw his notebook into the bushes below the porch. A moment later, Monica appeared from around the hedge, dusting off the discarded pad.

"Morning," she said and holding it up, asked, "What's this?"

"Nothing," said Petey gloomily. "I was making a list . . ."

"What sort of list?" the angel persisted as she came up the steps and sat beside him.

Petey looked at her for a long moment, as if deciding whether he could trust this newcomer. "It's things I've got to do before I die," he explained at last.

"Ah," nodded Monica. "Everyone ought to have one of those."

She opened the notebook. "Do you mind?" Petey shrugged and Monica began to read. "Number One: Learn to play the piano." She smiled. "An excellent and perfectly achievable goal," she remarked and returned to the list. "Number Two: Find a good home for Fluffy." She looked at Petey. "Who's Fluffy?" she asked.

Petey pointed to his large pet lizard. "Celine named him," he explained. "She has a great sense of irony. Only she doesn't know it."

Monica nodded solemnly. "Number Three:" she continued, "Find someone else to sing with Mom."

"I like singing with her," Petey explained with a smile. "We sound good together. But when I'm gone . . . well, I hate for her to stop."

"That's very thoughtful," the angel remarked. "Let's see . . . Number Four: Get someone to shovel the sidewalk when it snows. Number Five: Help Mom finish the song." She looked up. "Is that the song I heard you playing in your room?"

Petey nodded. "She wrote that a long time ago. But she can't finish it. I know if she could just write one whole song, then maybe she'd write more and she wouldn't have to worry about money anymore."

"Good thinking," replied Monica. "Number Six: Operation You-Know-What." She looked up again, puzzled. "And what might that be?" she asked.

"It's a code," Petey replied. "In case Celine ever sees it. I want to do something nice for her before I die, and if she could meet the real Celine Dion in person, that would be just about the most awesome thing I could think of. But I guess that's impossible."

Monica shook her head. "I don't think there's a single impossibility on this list," she said. "You just need a little help, that's all. Number Seven:" she read, "You want to die at home."

"I want to be here, with my mom and Celine and Fluffy," the boy explained. "Not with the nurses in the hospital. But Mom says the insurance company is in charge of that."

The angel smiled knowingly. "You'd be surprised who's really in charge," she said. "Now, let's see. Number Eight: A giant flagpole."

Petey nodded emphatically. "I want a really tall one right here in the front yard." He looked at her, his eyes wide. "So that when I'm ready to die, I can put up a flag and the angels will know where to find me."

Monica turned away to keep him from seeing her brimming tears and, at that moment, a flatbed truck pulled up to the curb, hauling an old upright piano. At the wheel was Andrew and next to him was Tess, smiling and waving like a homecoming queen.

"Did I mention I was thinking of taking up the piano myself?" Monica said to the bewildered boy.

A few nights later, the angels had gathered with Petey and Celine in the parlor, where the boy happily picked out the chords of "Heart & Soul" to the enthusiastic encouragement of Tess. "Look at you, Petey!" she cried. "You're doing it. You're really doing it." The elder angel cast a hostile eye at Fluffy the iguana perched atop the piano. "Scat!" she hissed, shuddering at the sight of the large ugly beast.

Sitting on the couch with Celine between them, Monica and Andrew smiled as they consulted Petey's list.

"I think we're doing very well," Andrew said as he looked at the notebook. "Number One: Learn to play the piano."

"Cross that one off," crowed Tess, with one dubious eye still on the lizard.

"Snow shoveling?" asked Monica.

"Mr. Morgan across the street said he'd be happy to help with *la neige*," volunteered Celine. Then, turning to Monica, translated, "The snow."

"And the church choir says Mom can come and sing with them whenever she wants," Petey added happily from the piano bench.

"I've got the giant flagpole ordered," said Andrew.

"—And I'm going to make the flag," Celine piped in.

"Just make sure it's in English," cautioned Petey, then asked, "How many have we got so far?"

Andrew counted. "Four," he announced. "We're halfway there."

Petey grinned happily but in the next moment his face darkened as he felt a sharp ache in his chest and began a heavy fit of coughing. Celine jumped up and began pounding him rhythmically on the back to loosen the blockage while the angels exchanged solemn looks.

"My mom wrote a letter to the insurance company," Petey wheezed after the coughing fit had passed.

"Still pending," Andrew noted, then read, "Get Mom to finish her song."

"That's my job," said Monica and, leaning over, read the next item on the list. "Find a home for Fluffy." All eyes turned to Tess.

"Let me think about that," the elder angel scowled.

"That just leaves one more," grinned Petey, and he winked knowingly at the angels.

"Which one?" asked the mystified Celine.

Andrew and Petey led a blindfolded Celine through an excited crowd of concert-goers to the backstage door of the stadium.

"Where are we going?" the girl asked for the twentieth time that night.

"You'll see," said her friend as Andrew whispered to the security guard, who checked his list and stood aside.

Five minutes later, the star-struck Celine, her mouth hanging open, stood inside the dressing room of her namesake—the famed Canadian singer Celine Dion. The star's smile was dazzling as she greeted them. "AH, *ma petite* Celine!" she said. "Petey! *Enchante de faire votre connaissance!*"

"This is impossible," muttered the little Celine.

"Nothing is impossible," replied Petey proudly, then turning to the singer, explained. "You're all she ever talks about." A cough rattled in his chest and Andrew cast a knowing look at Celine Dion.

"Thanks for making time to see us," he said. "I know your time is precious."

"It is for everyone," the singer replied, then knelt down to talk to the children. "Tonight I am going to sing a special song, just for the two of you. It's about living the very best you can through a difficult time." She looked directly into Petey's wide eyes. "Sometimes you come through the darkness back into the sunlight. And sometimes you come through the light itself. But, whatever you do, keep your eyes on the light."

The front row center seats were the best in the sold-out house and the children watched spellbound as Celine Dion smiled and waved from the stage to her new friends as she sang a song which, in that moment, seemed to be performed only for them. "There ain't a dream that don't have a chance to come true," the song asserted, "It just takes a little faith, baby . . ."

In the audience, little Celine turned to Petey, her face brightly lit with joy. It was then that she saw her friend doubled over in searing pain, desperately gasping for every breath of air. A moment later, Andrew was by their side and, taking Petey in his arms, he rushed up the aisle while the security guard radioed for an ambulance.

Petey's head lay on the pillow, tubes and monitors trailing from his nose and mouth. His skin was pale and his breathing labored as his mother sat at his bedside, her head in her hands. Monica entered and gently touched her shoulder and as Audrey turned, the angel's heart felt as if it might break at the sight of this suffering woman. "The doctor says this is it," Audrey said, her voice catching. "Even if he were moved to the top of the transplant list, there's too much damage." She began to sob. "Oh, Monica. I'm going to lose my baby."

The angel reached out and touched her hand. "Not yet," she said softly. "Not yet."

Down the corridor, in the waiting room, a disconsolate Tess sat with Celine, holding a form letter in her hand. "Your request for in-home hospice care has been denied," she read. "The above-referenced patient does not meet the criteria, blah, blah, blah . . ." She threw down the letter and looked glumly at the small child.

"He's going to die in this stupid hospital," Celine wailed. "Just like he was afraid of."

With a shake of her head, Tess roused herself to action. "Now you listen to me, Cornelia," she commanded and, noticing the girl's surprised look, added, "That's right. You can pretend to be Celine on your own time. But right now we've got work to do . . . and it's going to take a Cornelia to do it." She reached down to pick up the letter and pointed to the letterhead of the insurance company. "Doesn't your daddy work here?" she asked and the girl's face brightened as she nodded. "Well, then," Tess said, getting to her feet. "I think it's about time we paid a visit to your daddy."

"It's impossible," Eric Casey, Celine's father, insisted, from behind the desk in his office. "If we did it for him, we'd have to do it for everybody."

"All he wants to do is die with a little dignity, Mr. Casey," Tess insisted. "With his family around him."

"Please, Daddy?" pleaded Celine.

Eric Casey sighed. "This is a managed care company," he explained. "We base our decisions on providing the most care to the most people at the lowest cost. I know it's confusing but . . ."

His voice trailed off and he watched with surprise as his daughter stood up in her chair and began singing at the top of her voice, "There ain't a dream that don't have a chance to come true . . ."

"You go, girl!" cried the delighted Tess as curious office workers began to gather at the door.

"I could lose my job for this," muttered the exasperated executive, as he realized he was fighting a losing battle.

"You could lose your daughter for this," retorted Tess. A moment passed until, with a sigh, Eric Casey pulled Petey's file from a pile on his desk.

Petey, still hooked to a battery of machines, looked around with satisfaction. He was home, in his own bed, where he wanted to be. Glancing down at his notebook, he crossed another item off his list. He was almost done. The flagpole had been erected outside. Celine was making the flag and Tess had agreed to take care of Fluffy, although Petey could tell from the look on her face that a big green lizard may be the hardest thing in the world for her to love.

That left just one piece of unfinished business. "Number Five: Help Mom finish the song." Despite all the miracles that had happened over the past few weeks, he still didn't know how he was going to accomplish this last task. But he was too tired now to think about it. Maybe after his nap . . .

Petey's eyes closed and the notebook, slipping from his hands, fell to the floor. A moment later, Audrey entered and, seeing the pad, picked it up. As she did, the pages fell open to her son's list. "My God," she whispered as she read, and when she saw the last unfinished task, she began to sob. "I can't do it," she cried in anguish. "I can't finish that song . . ."

"You must, Audrey," said a voice behind her. Monica stepped into the room, a gilded light beginning to form around her.

"What is . . . happening?" stammered Audrey.

"I am an angel," Monica replied. "So are Tess and Andrew. God has brought us here to bring Petey home."

"No . . . please . . . no," sobbed Audrey.

Monica took a step forward as the light around her became brighter. "Petey has been strong for so long," she said softly. "But now he needs to rest. He needs to be carried to the Father's arms, where there is no pain." She smiled. "But he's a tough little boy. And he won't go until everything on that list is finished."

"That's why I can't do it," Audrey cried. "When I finish that song, he'll die!"

Monica nodded with compassion and understanding. "But there's Someone else who wants you to finish," she urged. "You began it as a Psalm, a hymn of praise to God. Now God wants to hear it. All of it. You must finish what you began, Audrey, with the best that you have. Just as Petey is finishing the life he began with all the courage and love his little heart can give. He deserves nothing less from you."

"But I . . . don't know even know how to start," Audrey replied.

"Yes, you do," Monica insisted. "That's what inspiration is. God put in to your spirit things that could never come from our own minds. He'll help you write that song, if you'll let Him. It will be your gift to Petey, but it will also be God's gift to you. Because when the nights are long and too quiet and your arms are empty and the table is set for one and you think you can't bear another day without your little boy, that song of praise for his life will rise again in your soul and you will make it through another morning. The words will lift you higher every time you sing them. Just as every step that Petey took in this life brought him closer to heaven, he brought everyone in his life a little closer, as well. Tell him that. Tell the world that you won't forget. Be a witness to a life lived completely in love. Write it, Audrey. Write the hundred and fifty-first psalm."

The front door of the house swung wide as Andrew carried Petey on to the porch and into his chair, facing out on to the street. Monica stood beside him, holding his notebook in her hands. On the lawn in front of him was a large assembly of neighbors and friends, a local band from a downtown school and a church choir fully dressed in their robes. Eric Casey and his wife stood by their daughter and from in front of them all Tess took a commanding position, holding a conductor's baton aloft. "Okay, everybody," she announced. "Are we ready?"

The band began playing a familiar melody, as Audrey stepped from the throng, strumming a guitar. "All the colors of the rainbow," Audrey sang, "All the voices of the wind / Every dream that reaches out / That reaches out to find where love begins . . ." She paused for a beat, then continued triumphantly as the crowd behind her joined in.

" . . . Lives to testify! / For as long as we shall live / I will testify to love / I'll be a witness in the silence when words are not enough." Monica handed Petey the notebook and watched with tears in her eyes as he crossed off the last item. She turned to Audrey, who continued to sing with all the new strength and conviction that God had given her. With tears welling in her eyes and rolling down her cheek, she smiled back at the angel, certain now that the angels were comforting her son, and life slowly ebbed from his body. "All the hope in every heart," she sang, "Will speak what love has done!"

Petey's notebook dropped from his lifeless hand as Andrew gathered him in his arms to take him home.

Celine moved through the choir toward the flagpole, a bundle in her arms. With the help of her father, she raised a small handmade flag that flapped bravely in the breeze as the song played on and on. The words on it stood out boldly against the blue sky: PETEY LIVED HERE.

Mother's Day

Sitting alone in the kitchen, Audrey heard the doorbell as if from a distant country, summoning her from the haze of alcohol that had become her constant companion. She opened her eyes, wincing from the pain of sunlight, and got slowly to her feet, trying to keep her pounding head steady. Was it morning or afternoon? Weekend or weekday? She couldn't remember the last time it had really mattered. Making her way through the cluttered living room, she passed a cardboard box full of empty liquor bottles, evidence of how much she wanted to forget . . . and how hard it was to keep the memories at bay.

The faces that greeted Audrey at the door brought with them their own flood of memories and emotions too painful to bear. Standing before her were the three angels who had come a year ago, at the end of her son Petey's long battle with cystic fibrosis. Andrew had guided her son into the arms of God, while Tess and Monica helped Audrey through one of the darkest valleys any mother could walk—the death of a child.

Seeing them now, standing before her like witnesses to the suffering she had endured, brought back that time in an overwhelming flood of vivid recollections, a surge all the more powerful for the efforts she had made over the many months to hold it back. She heard Petey's voice again, as if it were yesterday, asking, "Mom, who's going to sing with you when I'm gone?" She could see the list he had made of all that he wanted to do before he died and experienced again the anguish that came from trying to fulfill her son's wish to write a song just for him. She remembered the terrible fear that if she were to finish that song, Petey's list would be complete and she would finally lose him. But, most of all, she remembered standing at the graveside of Peter Patrick Carmichael, lifting her voice high into the clear blue sky to tell the world "For as long as we shall live / I will testify to love."

It had been Monica who had urged her to finish those lyrics and put them to a melody to "be a witness to a life lived completely in love," and her words had filled Audrey with an unshakable faith that whether Petey was with her or with God, she would never truly lose him. But, in the dark and lonely months that followed, her faith had been shaken and the pain of missing him ate away at her spirit until only the bottle could soothe the ache inside.

She stared coldly at the smiling faces of the trio that now greeted her on the doorstep. She was hardly in the mood to entertain angels. In fact, she couldn't remember the last time she been in the mood for much of anything, except sitting alone with the shades drawn and a glass in her hand.

"That song you wrote for Petey," Monica said, "I expected to hear you singing it on the radio by now. It was wonderful."

"I don't write music anymore," was Audrey's guarded reply.

"Oh," sighed Tess, "now that's a shame. God gave you a real gift."

"God gave me a son, too," Audrey snapped back. "Then He took him away. So I took the music away." She stepped back into the gloom of the house, swinging the door shut on them as she said, "I hate to be rude, but go away. All of you. I really—really—don't want to see you again."

"I didn't expect that," admitted Monica as the angels stood on the sidewalk outside Audrey's gate while neighborhood kids on scooters and bikes passed by them along the shady street. "I thought we'd done our job."

"We did, baby," replied Tess. "We told her the truth and helped her say good-bye to her son." She shook her head sadly. "And she still hasn't forgiven us for that." She looked from Monica to Andrew as she continued. There was much for the angels to learn in the midst of this tragedy, and the lessons wouldn't be easy. But that's what came with the territory—angels could only accomplish as much as humans would let them. "A funny thing happens sometimes when people find out that God exists," Tess explained. "It should make them happy. It should give them hope. But some people don't want God for that. They just want somebody to blame."

"Well, she's made it very clear," replied Monica. "She doesn't want any angels around."

Tess shook her head in disagreement, a familiar twinkle in her eye. "She said she didn't want *us* around. But she didn't say she didn't want an angel."

Even as she spoke, a figure approached from around the corner, a sprightly woman in her late sixties with an old suitcase in her hand and a spring in her step. "Emma!" Tess cried delightedly as she spotted the veteran angel, and for the next few moments, the two caught up on old times and renewed an enduring friendship. A bit eccentric, a little flighty, but warmhearted and good-natured, Emma concealed an angel's compassion and a hard-won wisdom beneath her simple veneer.

"Do you know why you're here?" asked Tess, as the pair finished talking.

"I have no idea," Emma replied blithely, as she began her march to Audrey's front door. "But I'm ready." She nodded at the ROOM

FOR RENT sign in the front window even as she straightened the crooked mailbox and blew dust from the windowsill.

Emma's cheerful face and sunny disposition contrasted sharply with Audrey's bleary eyes and irritated frown as she answered her door for the second time that morning. "My name is Emma," the angel announced, "and I don't smoke, drink, use foul language or play loud music after nine o'clock."

Standing invisibly on the sidewalk, Tess, Monica and Andrew watched as Emma, not wasting a minute, promptly moved herself into Audrey's house . . . and into her life. Somehow things seemed brighter, a little more hopeful, than in the moments just before the indomitable angel had appeared on the scene. The trio turned to walk down the street, soaking in the warm sunshine and the smell of newly mowed grass.

"I don't think anyone but God can understand the pain of losing a child," Tess ventured.

"Except someone who's lost a child, too," interjected Andrew, who spoke with the conviction of an Angel of Death.

"Exactly," said Tess with a knowing smile. "And that's why you're going to Atlanta."

Liz Knight moved through the radio station studio like a tornado, leaving quaking staffers in her wake as she pulled together a dozen last minute details for the evening show. The flurry of activity was nothing new for the beautiful redheaded air personality— she hadn't gotten to the top of the talk radio game by being laid back. And tonight her commanding presence had an extra element of urgency to it. She'd fired the latest in a string of on-air producers the day before, proving to herself once again that if she wanted to do something right, there was only one person she could depend on—Liz Knight. The station's new hire was due any minute, but she couldn't afford to wait. The show had her name on it, and that's exactly where the buck stopped.

Watching unseen from a corner of the broadcast booth, Tess let out a low whistle and said, "She's all yours, Angel Boy," to Andrew, who took a deep breath and stepped directly into the path of the whirlwind.

"You must be the new producer," Liz remarked without breaking stride, and before Andrew could reply, she continued in a clipped and no-nonsense tone. "I don't ask much," she continued, as the angel hurried to catch up. "Keep the calls coming, screen out the weirdos and coordinate the guest appearances."

"I can do that," Andrew replied a little breathlessly.

"Good," Liz shot back, then stopped suddenly to face him. "Let's get this straight right up front," she said. "I'm tough and demanding, but I'm not unreasonable and I'm always willing to listen to a good idea."

Andrew, sensing what might be his only opening, jumped in. "Great," he responded enthusiastically. "How about a series on addiction? Drugs, gambling . . . alcohol?"

Liz shook her head adamantly. "Too depressing," was her snap judgment.

"I disagree," Andrew persisted. "Someone who's recovered from addiction herself can offer a lot of hope."

Liz started at his words, looking Andrew over with a new respect. "I can see you've done your homework," she said. "But that's ancient history."

"Maybe," Andrew replied, "but maybe you're so tough and demanding because you're still punishing yourself . . . for your drinking." He paused, taking a deep breath. "And because you lost a child."

Back at Audrey's home, Celine watched with a mix of interest and trepidation as Emma stood on a ladder scrubbing the ceiling of Audrey's kitchen. The eleven-year-old couldn't help feeling happy that this friendly, energetic old lady had made a sudden appearance, but, at the same time, she couldn't help but worry about how Mrs. Carmichael—Petey's mother—might feel about the intrusion. After all, she'd been through so much since her son died. Sure, Petey had been Celine's best friend, ever since her family had moved in next door, but friends and family were two different things and it was hard for her young mind to grasp the sorrow and grief that Audrey struggled with from day to day.

Celine had done her best to help, coming over every afternoon to cook and clean for Petey's mom, but there was nothing she could do to keep the liquor bottles from piling up or wipe away that look of bitterness and anger that had settled on Audrey's face. And now, suddenly, Emma had arrived and the young girl could only hope that all this busy spring cleaning would reach through the dirt and dust of the house to renew the hope in Audrey's heart.

"Does Mrs. Carmichael know what you're doing?" Celine asked hesitantly.

"I thought I'd surprise her," was Emma's cheerful reply.

"Maybe you better check before you do any more," Celine cautioned. "She's been through a lot already. Her little boy died. And now . . ." she paused, looking over the box of empty bottles in the kitchen corner, "she's kind of taking some time off."

At that moment, a sound, so long absent from the house, could be heard down the hallway where Audrey had set up a small home-recording studio. With a twinkle in her eye, Emma signaled for Celine to follow her.

Audrey strummed her guitar thoughtfully, as Emma and Celine entered the studio and began busily straightening and dusting. "What are you doing?" she asked, trying to keep the irritation from her voice.

Emma's sunny smile offered the answer. "Don't mind us," she explained and, continuing her work, added, "a little spring cleaning makes you strong."

Audrey stared at her, an elusive memory stirring inside her as she repeated Emma's words to herself.

. . . *Makes you strong . . . makes you strong . . .*

All morning long she had been chasing down the fleeting images of a dream she had had the night before, a strange, unsettling encounter with Petey's pet iguana, Fluffy. Only, in her dream, Fluffy could talk and the words he said, uttered in a tough New York accent, suddenly flooded back to her now. "When you love somebody, you need somebody," the dream lizard had said. "And when you need them, that's what makes you weak. But knowing you're weak, that's what makes you strong."

Audrey was enough of a songwriter to hear the beginnings of a good lyric in Fluffy's message, and ever since getting out of bed, she had heard it echoing in the back of her brain, just out of reach. But now, as Emma spoke, it came flooding back, and with it, a simple yet resonant melody. "That's what makes you strong," she sang, then stopped and started again, feeling her way through the lyrics and their meaning. "That's what gives you power / That's what makes the meek / Come sit beside the king / That's what let's us smile / In our final hour . . ."

Absorbed now in the creative act, she didn't notice as Emma, with a wink to Celine, managed to press a button on a nearby tape deck, recording Audrey's song even as it began to take shape. The spools kept turning even after Audrey, suddenly overwhelmed by what she was singing and the memories it stirred, abruptly stood up and left the room.

Later that afternoon, Celine found herself alone in the makeshift studio finishing the dusting and cleaning she and Emma began earlier that day. She had a funny feeling about that old lady, the same kind of feeling she had when she'd first met Tess and Monica, back when Petey was still alive. They were angels and Celine wouldn't have been the least bit surprised if Emma turned out to be an angel as well. As she wiped the recording equipment clean, half-listening to the radio turned low to keep her company, she found herself hoping that it would be true. Mrs. Carmichael would need a lot of angels around her, especially now, since Celine had found out that her dad was being transferred out of town to a new job. She'd be moving away soon and, when that happened, who would be left to take care of Petey's mom?

As she thought about these things, mulling over the problems that life seemed to bring with it, a voice on the radio caught her attention. "We're going out live tonight coast to coast," the talk-show host was saying, "and we want to hear from you on the important subject of alcoholism." It was that word, "alcoholism," that caught Celine's ear and, putting down her dust rag, she turned up the volume and leaned in close. "I know there's someone out there tonight," the woman's voice continued, "who's staring at a bottle and trying their best not to pick it up. Well, maybe we can give you a little support." She gave the station's phone number and cut to a commercial break even as Celine, her eyes bright with sudden inspiration, grabbed a nearby telephone, repeating the number under her breath as she quickly dialed.

Liz Knight randomly punched one of the blinking lights on her console and through her headphones heard the voice of a child over the line, a voice high with excitement and hope. Her name was Celine, the voice told Liz, and she was calling all the way from Illinois, because she had a friend, a very special friend named Audrey, who was very sad and was always trying to make herself feel better by drinking tequila.

"Do you think Audrey has a drinking problem, Celine?" Liz asked with a look through the studio's glass booth to where Andrew was now standing. She had to admit, this new producer had come up with a real ratings grabber.

Celine hesitated. "Maybe," she admitted after a moment, "but I was thinking that maybe you could help her." Liz started to reply, the standard speech about support groups and local outreaches, but the excited girl didn't seem to be listening. "See," Celine continued, "Audrey is a really good songwriter and I was thinking that if you maybe just played one of her songs on the radio and people liked it, well, then, maybe they'd ask her to write more and then she'd be too busy to drink tequila all day."

Liz sighed. "That's a sweet idea," she said in the mike. "But, you see, Celine—"

"Just listen," the voice over the air insisted. "I know you'll like it!" There was a moment of silence before another voice, clear and pure and more than a little sad, could be heard, accompanied by a guitar and singing words that sent a sudden shock of recognition through Liz's body. "That's what makes you strong / That's what gives you power—" Suddenly the sound of an opening and closing door was heard in the background and, as quickly as it began, the music stopped.

"I gotta go," Celine said in Liz's headphones. "Sorry . . . 'bye!"

"No! Please!" Liz cried. "Wait!" A loud click was followed by a dial tone as she turned to Andrew, a stricken look on her face.

"What is it?" Andrew asked urgently, pushing open the door to the sound booth.

"That song," Liz replied, her voice barely above a whisper. "On the radio." She looked up at him, sorrow and confusion in her eyes. "I wrote that song. And there's only one person who's ever heard it." She swallowed hard. "My little girl. The child I lost . . . thirty years ago."

"What are you doing?" demanded Audrey, her voice slurred and her bleary eyes glaring at the cowering Celine.

"That song you wrote today," the girl responded with a tremor in her voice. "About being strong. I let the lady on the radio hear it . . ." She began to cry as she saw the look of rage spreading over Audrey's face. "I was just trying to help."

"I don't need your help!" Audrey spat back.

"Yes, you do!" shouted Celine, more bravely than she felt. "You're turning into an alcoholic and you've probably got a drinking problem, too! That's why you sleep all the time and that's why you won't go see Petey!"

"Shut up, you little brat!" Audrey shouted and took a menacing step forward.

"You need help, Mrs. Carmichael!" Celine said, tears streaming down her face, but holding her ground. "Because I can't do it anymore. My dad got transferred and we're moving away."

"I don't care!" was Audrey's drunken reply. "I don't need you! I don't need anyone!" With a stagger she lurched toward the front door and, throwing it open, plunged into the gathering darkness of evening.

"Mrs. Carmichael!" Celine sobbed, but the only answer was her echoing cry in the now-empty house.

An hour later, Audrey found herself with her head resting on the cold wood of the long bar in the half-empty saloon that had become her second home. The jukebox played a mournful country tune and her eyes were heavy with grief and exhaustion. She would just close them for a minute, she thought. Just long enough to pull herself together, to gather the strength to go on . . .

Suddenly, her thoughts were interrupted by a familiar voice. Raising her head, she found Monica standing behind the bar, pouring out an endless drink that spilled over the sides of the glass and across the bar as she spoke. "Where were you?" the angel asked, her voice echoing in the suddenly empty room. "Where were you last Mother's Day?"

Audrey thought for a moment, trying to clear the alcohol fumes from her mind. "I had flowers," she recounted. "I had my guitar. I was going to sing a song for Petey. At the grave. Then I saw a bar on the way." She spoke slowly, as if describing the actions of another person. "I pulled in . . . for a drink . . . to stop the pain . . . but I never made it out . . . I got stuck at the bar."

"What are you waiting for, Audrey?" said another voice behind her, and she spun around to see Petey's iguana Fluffy staring at her like a pugnacious Brooklyn cabdriver. "It's almost Mother's Day," the lizard snarled. "You're going to be late!"

Audrey's eyes snapped open. The dream was over and the slow routine in the bar continued as if nothing had happened . . . as if nothing would ever happen.

Emma sat beside Eric Casey, Celine's father, as he drove the dark streets of the small town, his daughter asleep between them. The angel had knocked on his door earlier that evening, after Audrey had failed to come home for dinner, and now the threesome was scouring the taverns and saloons on the wrong side of town, hoping to find her. Emma kept up an aimless chatter to pass the time and buoy their spirits, but even she had just about run out of things to say when she noticed the dials of the car radio. "Do you mind?" she asked, as she switched it on and, with a few deft turns, found a clear and powerful signal, all the way from Atlanta, Georgia.

The pleading voice of a woman filled the car as Eric and the angel listened. "Celine," said Liz Knight. "If you're out there please call me back! And if you're just joining us, we're looking for a young girl named Celine, who called in a little while ago with some news about her friend Audrey, a songwriter from Illinois."

Eric, a look of amazement on his face, turned to Emma, who only smiled and suggested, "I guess we'd better find a telephone."

The night had passed and brilliant morning sunshine poured through the lace curtains in Audrey's bedroom. Somehow she had made it home from the bar last night, but she had no recollection of how. In a corner of the room, Monica sat silently in an old straight-back chair, a silent guardian over the long night. She watched now as the insistent sound of a doorbell roused Audrey from a deep and alcohol-drenched sleep. With a groan she stirred and, after several more rings, she slowly rose and shambled into the hallway.

At the bottom of the stairs, Emma's beaming smile was like the beacon of a new day, a beacon shining a little too brightly in Audrey's impaired condition. "What are you doing here?" was her surly question.

"It's a lovely morning," Emma replied, unfazed. "And you've got company."

Audrey peered into the living room where Andrew stood near the fireplace. "I thought I told you—" she began, but stopped in the next moment as a smartly dressed Liz Knight stepped into view.

"Hello, Adrienne," said Liz. "I'm your mother."

For a long moment, Audrey stared at the stranger, trying to put the shreds of her memory back together. But the effort was too much, and her pounding head pushed away the reality that suddenly faced her in the bright morning light. "I don't have a mother," she said, her words cutting and cruel.

"That song," Liz replied gently. "The one Celine played on the air last night." She took a step forward. "I wrote that song, Adrienne. I used to sing it to you every night and I've been looking for you ever since."

"My name is Audrey," she insisted, shaking her aching head

stubbornly. "And, whoever you are, why don't you just leave me alone? I don't need your help."

"I think you do," was Liz's soft answer. "That's why I'm here."

The anger in Audrey's eyes sparked and ignited. "Where were you when I really needed you?" she shouted. "Where were you when my husband left me and I lost my little boy?"

"You . . . have a child?" Liz asked with a catch in her voice.

"Not anymore," Audrey spat back. "And neither do you. You abandoned her, remember?" With trembling hands she reached out to pour herself a stiff drink from a bottle on a side table. Gulping down the burning liquid, she sputtered then shouted, "I want you people out of here! This is my life! Stay out of it!"

As Andrew guided Emma and Liz into the kitchen, Audrey hurled the glass after them. It shattered on the door and, with it, she felt something shatter inside of her, as well. With a sob she sank into a chair and put her head in her hands. A long moment passed until, sensing another presence in the room, she looked up. Monica, dressed in white, was kneeling on the floor, carefully picking up the shards of broken glass.

"I saw you in a dream," Audrey said, trying to make sense of the angel's appearance. "Am I going crazy?"

Monica shook her head and smiled. "No," she replied. "God makes His voice heard, one way or another. But whether you listen, that's up to you." She stood, carefully placing the broken glass on the table. "You wrote a beautiful song," the angel continued. "It helped Petey die in peace, with a joyful heart for the life he had lived and great hope for the life he wanted you to keep living." She smiled, as a glow began to grow around her. "God loves you and He gave you a gift, Audrey," Monica continued. "He gave you the blessed assurance that your son would be with Him forever. And He gave you a promise: that He would mend your broken heart if you gave Him all the pieces." She picked up a jagged chunk of the shattered glass and held it out in the palm of her hand. "But you didn't," Monica said sadly. "You held on to them—to the guilt, to the anger, to the loneliness. And those pieces are sharp and dangerous, Audrey." Her fingers closed over the broken glass in her hand, gripping it so tightly that blood began to drip from her clenched fist as Audrey looked on in horror. "This is what you're doing to yourself, Audrey," the angel explained. "It is wrong and it is ugly and it is suicide. Alcohol may block the pain of it, but it won't save you." She paused. "Only God can do that." She opened her hand. The skin was unmarred, the blood was miraculously gone. "Sometimes," she whispered, "He sends angels to show you how. And sometimes He sends mothers."

Monica looked up and Audrey followed her gaze to the kitchen door where Liz stood, silently, expectantly. Monica smiled and joined the other angels, leaving the mother and daughter alone together for the first time in many long and lonely years.

"I don't blame you for hating me," Liz began softly. "But I want you to know that I've always loved you." As Audrey stared silently, Liz took a deep breath and pushed on. "You were four years old when your father and I got divorced. I got full custody, but one day he came and begged to take you to the zoo." She choked back a sob. "He never brought you back. He must have told you that I abandoned you."

Now it was Audrey's turn to fight back tears. "Maybe it was just easier to hate you," she said, "than to miss you."

"Adrienne . . . Audrey," Liz continued. "I am an alcoholic. I started the day I lost you and I couldn't stop until I turned my life over to God. I believe He brought me here to help you do that, too." She took her daughter's hand and leaned close, looking deeply into her eyes. "It's okay to admit that we're weak," she said. "That's what makes us strong. I wrote that song for you and I'm so glad that somewhere, deep inside, you were still singing it."

The tears fell freely now as the two women embraced. "Mama," Audrey wept, "when I lost my baby I felt so alone."

"But you're not," replied Liz. "You've got God and you've got me and we're going to get through this one step at a time. Starting today." She lifted her daughter's chin, wiping away her tears. "Do you know why?" she asked and the child in her arms shook her head.

Liz smiled. "Because it's Mother's Day."

Liz nodded and gave her long-lost daughter a hug. Inside her arms, Audrey felt the aching pain begin to subside, and for the first time in as long as she could remember, a sense of security and safety seemed to envelop her. With her mother by her side, she felt that now, at last, she might have the strength to return to Petey's grave. There, she knew, the healing would continue as she and her mother would sing in perfect harmony, as if they had known the song their whole lives, "Every word of every story / Every star in every sky / Every corner of creation / Lives to testify!"

Black Like Monica

Monica lay her head on the thin pillow, stretching her weary body out on the narrow cot bolted to one side of the small jail cell. The pale light from a street lamp outside cast a barred shadow across the floor as she felt her eyes growing heavy. It wasn't normal for an angel to feel fatigue. But, then again, there had been nothing normal about this day from the very beginning. Alone, frightened, and with more questions than answers, she replayed the strange and tragic events that had unfolded in this sleepy Illinois town over the past few hours—events that had landed her in a prison cell and put the conscience of a community on trial.

Monica knew immediately that something was terribly wrong when she saw the stricken, angry expression on Tess's face that morning. Sitting by the side of the road on a bright clear morning, the senior angel held a sinister object in her trembling hand—a length of rope, crudely noosed and stained with blood.

"How many times?" Tess asked in quiet despair. "How many times will He ask me to do this?"

Monica noticed the familiar figure of Andrew standing in a clearing just visible through the trees. At his feet was the crumpled, lifeless body of a black man, his hands tied behind his back, his face bruised and battered beyond recognition.

"Enough is enough!" Tess cried out, turning her face to the cloudless sky. "No more, Father! I'm coming home."

"But, Tess," Monica protested. "What am I supposed to do? I don't know what my assignment is." She watched helplessly as her mentor walked silently up the road and out of sight. Whatever the reason Monica had come to this terrible place, she would now have to discover it on her own.

It was supposed to be an exciting time in the little town of Aynsville, Illinois, a community where excitement was hard to come by. But all that had changed not long ago when it was discovered that one of Aynsville's founding fathers, a man named Elijah Jackson, had made his home a stop for runaway slaves on the famous Underground Railroad, one of the network of abolitionists who helped fugitives to freedom in the tumultuous days before the Civil War. Elijah Jackson's courage and resourcefulness was going to put their town on the map—at least if the city fathers and leading citizens had anything to say about it.

Several of Aynsville's leaders had gathered in the square that morning to insure that their moment in the spotlight would go according to plan. Thanks to their tireless efforts, a gala celebration had been planned to honor the town's newly found place in American history. The high school band would perform a concert, the local middle school was staging a pageant and news crews from as far away as Chicago had been invited to the festivities. But by far the biggest event of the upcoming weekend was the arrival of Aynsville's special guest of honor, Rosa Parks, the mother of the Civil Rights movement, who forty years before on a Birmingham, Alabama, bus, sparked a revolution when she refused to give up her seat to a white man. Ever since that act of extraordinary bravery, Rosa Parks has come to symbolize the spirit and determination of her people's struggle for equality. And now, this living legend was coming to their town, and bringing with her the attention of the whole state and, perhaps, even the whole country.

It was the kind of public relations money couldn't buy and Mayor Ed Polk, for one, was determined to capitalize on this once-in-a-lifetime opportunity. He'd shown up early that morning to watch the pageant rehearsal, overseen by the brisk and efficient LaVonda Sawyer, one of the town's most active black citizens, whose tireless efforts had secured the appearance of Rosa Parks.

As he approached across the courthouse lawn, Mayor Polk could hear LaVonda barking orders to the town's affable Sheriff, Tom McKinsley, who had been corralled into playing Elijah Jackson in the upcoming extravaganza. At that moment, the Sheriff, dressed in a stovepipe hat and fake beard, was standing on the makeshift stage while his deputy, the quiet and sometimes brooding James Robinson, stood at the sidelines, a rare smile on his broad black face as he watched his boss fumble through his cues. The assembly of Aynsville notables was completed by Charlie Ryan, the high school principal who was conducting the school choir and marching band for the musical segment of the program.

Drawing LaVonda to one side, Mayor Polk nodded approvingly. "Everything looks good," he said, "but I have one concern." He lowered his voice and in a conspiratorial whisper asked, "Is it still appropriate to say 'Negro spirituals' when I introduce the singers or should I say 'African-American spirituals?' I want to be historically accurate but I also want to be politically correct."

LaVonda stared at him in disbelief but before she could answer, the Sheriff approached, still in costume. "Sorry to interrupt," he said, "but we've got a problem with the scenery up there, LaVonda."

They all turned to look at the stage set, leaning dangerously to one side. "Mooney was supposed to finish building those supports," LaVonda complained. "Where is he, anyway?"

It was at that moment that a stranger approached from across the square, an auburn haired woman with a soft Irish accent, holding a length of blood-stained rope in her hand. "Excuse me," she said to Tom as they all turned to look at her. "Are you the Sheriff?"

"That's me," he replied as he took off the top hat and beard with a smile. "What can I do for you?"

"I want to report a murder," Monica replied as the others stared in shock and disbelief.

The body of the man once known as Mooney lay where Monica and Andrew had left it, a shoe missing from one foot and a rope tied around his ankles. His dusky skin was bruised and bloodied and his sightless eyes stared into the brilliant blue sky.

Standing at his car a short distance away, Sheriff Tom paced nervously, while Deputy James Robinson and LaVonda stood in stunned silence and Monica watched, a witness to human beings trying to come to terms with evil in their midst. "I just saw him yesterday," LaVonda was saying. "He was so excited. He wanted to show me something he'd found at the old cemetery." She choked back a sob. "I told him I didn't have time."

From down the road the mayor's car approached, followed by an ambulance. Ed Polk surveyed the scene as a dapper black man in his fifties emerged from the ambulance. "That's Cyrus Taylor," James told Monica. "He's the city manager. He also owns the local diner and the only ambulance service in town."

Accompanied by the Sheriff, Cyrus and the Mayor inspected the dead body, sharing in the uncomprehending horror of the others. "It's Mooney," Tom informed them. "And somebody definitely wanted him dead." He turned back to his car. "I was just on my way back to call the FBI. Hate crimes are a federal offense. This is their jurisdiction."

"Now hold on there," interjected the Mayor. "I think we'd better get the lay of the land, so to speak, before we involve anyone else."

"What are you talking about?" a mystified Tom asked. "This is murder, plain and simple."

"Can't you figure it out, Sheriff?" his deputy replied with a bitter tone. He looked around at the assembled citizens. "Looks like the Mayor has called himself a little meeting of the town council. I'd say he's about to take a vote."

"James," Mayor Polk warned. "You and the Sheriff here are employees of the city and county of Aynsville."

"Ed's right," remarked Cyrus. "We've got a problem here. For a hundred and fifty years, no one noticed us. Now, because of the Underground Railroad connection, something good's about to happen to put us on the map . . ."

"And Rosa Parks arrives tomorrow," added LaVonda. "A true hero is coming here and someone murders an African-American man the day before she shows up."

"This is a good town," insisted the Mayor. "We've never had a race problem. But if the media gets a hold of this, we'll never live it down."

"There's only two people that could have done such a thing," Cyrus continued. "We're all thinking it, so why not say it? It was those Foley boys."

"I already got the Foley's figured for this," said Tom. "But if you think I'm just going to leave poor Mooney lying in the road here—"

"Of course not," interrupted Mayor Polk. "Cyrus can take him back in the ambulance. You can investigate, Sheriff. Just don't tell anybody . . . yet."

"Don't you get it, Tom?" said James, his voice heavy with sarcasm. "There's too much riding on the next few days to let a little thing like murder stand in the way."

"You better believe it," the Mayor spat back vehemently. "The Governor's coming and I'm going to hit him up for funding on that new bridge. Cyrus here is counting on the diner business and poor

LaVonda has been working her fingers to the bone." He turned back to the Sheriff. "This isn't a cover-up, Tom," he insisted. "We're just . . . postponing things for a while."

"I can think of at least four constitutional amendments we're violating," Charlie observed.

"For heaven's sake!" snapped the Mayor. "The man is already dead. Why kill the town along with him?"

"He lived out in the woods," LaVonda offered. "He doesn't have any family. No one is going to miss him, I'm afraid."

"LaVonda," Tom said in dismay. "Are you seriously considering this?"

"I worked three years to make this weekend happen, Tom," she replied, not daring to look him in the eye. "I discovered Elijah Jackson. I invited Rosa Parks." She swallowed hard. "I even got Mooney to build the stage."

"Mooney would have wanted it this way," intoned the Mayor solemnly.

"You didn't even know Mooney," shot back James.

"I don't appreciate your tone, Deputy," Ed Polk huffed.

"That tone is the righteous indignation of a black man," James seethed, "who's watching the mayor of this town sell us down the river."

A long, pregnant silence followed as Monica witnessed the struggle of their conscience and the dark implications of their decisions. "Well," sighed Mayor Polk, after a moment, "shall we take a vote?" Slowly, one by one, the council members raised their hands, until all that were left were Charlie and LaVonda. Then they, too, cast their lot with the majority.

"Do James and I have anything to say about this?" demanded Tom.

"No," was the Mayor's flat response. "That way you can always say you were just following instructions. The next two days will go on as planned, with nothing to poison the celebration." He paused,

taking a deep breath. "Which brings us to one last piece of unfinished business."

All eyes followed him as he turned to look at Monica.

"What are you going to do?" demanded Tom. "Violate
someone's civil rights to celebrate civil rights?"

They called it "protective custody" but Monica knew better.
What the good people of Aynsville were protecting was themselves
. . . from the truth. That's why they had thrown her in jail and that's
why, one by one, they came to see her the next morning, as they
tried to find a way to soothe their guilt, as if by trying to convince
her they were trying convince themselves.

LaVonda was the first, slipping into the Sheriff's station, while
outside, the bright and colorful preparations for the pageant continued. "You know who she is, don't you?" LaVonda asked Monica,
and the angel nodded. The name of Rosa Parks was well known,
even in heaven. "She's been my hero since I was a little girl. Now
she leads something called Pathways to Freedom, which takes children on buses all across the country, tracing the Civil Rights movement. My whole life I've tried to follow in her footsteps. And I've
dreamed of this moment for so long."

"This is how you want to meet Rosa Parks?" was Monica's pen-
etrating reply. "Like this?"

LaVonda could only shake her head. "I'm truly sorry you've
been detained," she said with a sigh. "But it's for the best . . . believe me."

It was not too long afterward that the Mayor Ed Polk made an
appearance at the jail, spouting platitudes and half-truths that Monica knew must have sounded threadbare and worn, even from him.
Next came Charlie Ryan, then Cyrus Taylor, each in his own way
seeking absolution for the guilty secret they shared, each assuring

her that it was all for the best, each ignoring the simple truth that justice delayed is justice denied.

It was Tom McKinsley who brought Monica her dinner that evening, sitting down outside her cell like a penitent in confession as she ate. An awkward silence ensued until Monica set her fork down and asked, "Who was Mr. Mooney, Sheriff?"

"A nice old guy," Tom replied. "He came to town about fifteen years ago. He said he was looking for some family that used to live around these parts. Went through the records at City Hall and down at the church, then he ended up going door to door and even wandering around the graveyard."

Monica nodded. "He told LaVonda he'd found something at the cemetery," she reminded him.

Tom sighed. "He got a reputation for being a little crazy. But he wasn't crazy. He was just trying to figure out who he was."

Evening fell as Monica lay down on her cot. The town was silent now and the only sound to be heard in the empty station was the angel's soft prayer. "Why am I here, Father?" she asked. "What good can I do behind bars? I feel tired and hungry and afraid. Test me, Lord, and know my anxious heart, for I am so confused."

Comforted only by the thought that God is not the author of confusion, Monica closed her eyes, realizing that, for the second time in as many days, she was feeling the all-too-human need for sleep. Perhaps, she thought, as she drifted off, it wasn't really sleep that angels needed. It was dreams . . .

Yet had she known the nightmare that would haunt her that night, Monica would not have let herself slip away so easily. In a strange, twilight landscape, she saw the man they called Mooney kneeling by the headstone in a neglected cemetery. As he lovingly cleared away the dead leaves and weeds, a rope was suddenly and savagely thrown around his neck. Voices, angry and hateful, could be heard as Mooney was dragged backward, one of his shoes falling off in the struggle. The sound of a revving engine was deafening, and through Mooney's terrified eyes, the dreaming angel saw the grill and tires of a truck bearing down until, with a sickening crunch of shattering bone, Monica woke with a short, stifled scream. Morning light poured through the cell window, but the dark images of her nightmare were not so easily dispelled.

Rising from her cot, Monica immediately saw that the door to the cell had been mysteriously left ajar and, still dazed from the horrific events of her dream, she reached out to push it open farther. It was then that she noticed that the skin of her hand, instead of its familiar pinkish hue, had taken on a dark and dusky tone. She stared at it, wiggling the fingers as if to convince herself that they were her own, then caught sight of her face in a mirror hanging outside the cell. Her straight red hair had become a mass of tight dark curls, her face a rich chocolate brown. Monica had been transformed into a black woman.

Stunned at the face that stared back at her, she whispered a questioning prayer to God, wondering aloud if this strange change of color had something to do with her mission in this troubled town and, if so, what? Still pondering the puzzle, she walked out onto the nearly empty town where a banner had been strung across the street reading WELCOME ROSA PARKS. Certain that her new color would stop citizens dead in their tracks, she was surprised to see Mayor Polk rush past her without a glance. Who, after all, would have time to give notice to a stranger . . . and a black stranger, at that?

As if invisibly guided, Monica moved down the main street and through the doors of a diner, just opened for business, where the patrons greeted her with a mix of indifference and thinly disguised suspicion. She crossed to the counter and asked for a glass of water, realizing for the first time how thirsty she was. Like sleep, it was another unfamiliar, human need for an angel to feel. When Monica opened her mouth to speak, another startling change was revealed. Instead of her distinctive Irish lilt, she now spoke with a flat American accent. God had left no stone unturned.

The looks of suspicion that greeted her inside the diner made her feel still more uncomfortable and disconcerting emotions. It was as if, because she was now in a black body, she were treated with an indifference bordering on disrespect. She could feel the eyes of the customers on her, but none would meet her gaze. It was as if, suddenly, she had become an invisible presence.

It was at that moment that a commotion could be heard on the street outside, as townsfolk and a contingent of reporters began hurrying toward the town square. "She's coming!" Monica heard an excited voice proclaim. "Rosa Parks is coming!" Exiting the diner, she followed the crowd, noticing for the first time an anxious knot of familiar faces gathered near the courthouse.

Sheriff McKinsley and his deputy, James Robinson, had just broken the bad news about Monica's disappearance to Mayor Polk, whose own face quickly turned beet red. "The biggest day in this town's history," he sputtered, "and that woman is running around loose! You find her, you hear me," he hissed at Tom. "I don't care what it takes."

James cleared his throat. "Sure," he said bitterly. "It's not like we have murderers to catch or anything." He ignored the Mayor's reproachful look and continued. "By the way, Bud Foley and his brother were in the hardware store the other day and bought a brand new rope. Just in case anyone's interested."

The tense exchange was suddenly interrupted as a cheer went up among the crowd. A bus rolled down the street and LaVonda, a radiant look on her face, stepped to the curb to be the first to greet Rosa Parks. A hush settled over the assembly as a procession of children and escorts filed out, forming a double row down which a frail old woman with bright eyes behind thick glasses stepped off the bus and made her way to the grandstand where the city fathers were waiting. She smiled, her wrinkled face beaming as she caught sight of the tears streaming down LaVonda's cheeks, then nodded at James as he held back the crowd. Her gaze even seemed to linger for a moment on Monica, who watched from the side of the court-house lawn, a woman who, even in the midst of this celebration, couldn't help but wonder what God's purpose had been in making her black.

Later that same morning, and still asking herself that same ques-tion, Monica found herself walking down a dusty country road on the outskirts of town. Once again the unfamiliar feelings of hunger, thirst and exhaustion rose up in her as she turned into a ramshackle roadhouse in hopes of escaping the blazing sun that beat down on her dark skin.

As soon as she pushed open the door of the dive she felt a sud-den and sharp pang of fear. All eyes had turned toward her, includ-ing those of two brothers, sitting at barstools in front of several empty beer cans. She knew immediately who they were—the Foley boys, the ones the Sheriff had immediately suspected in the murder of Mooney. She fought the urge to turn and run and only after the other patrons had turned away, distant and disinterested, did she have the courage to walk back into the bright sunlight and hurry down the road.

Only a few nervous minutes had passed before Monica heard an ominous sound growing louder behind her. She turned to see two men in a pickup bearing down on her. Picking up her pace she continued down the road as the rumble of tires got closer and closer until she suddenly bolted, running with all her strength through the thick underbrush of the forest. Back on the road, the truck door slammed and the sound of running footsteps echoed in the angel's mind. Blindly she kept running as fast as her legs would carry her, until she emerged at an old and overgrown graveyard, the same one she had seen in her nightmare. She caught a glimpse of a moss covered headstone and, nearby, a single shoe. A cry of pure terror rose in her throat. So this was what it was like to be human . . . to thirst and hunger and fear. She hid behind the gnarled branches of a tree, her heart pounding so loudly she was sure it would give her away. Sure now that her only-too-human flesh would suffer the same agonies as Mooney's, she began to whisper a prayer while, in the graveyard beyond, she could see the Foley boys emerge, shotguns in their hands.

"Oh Father," she begged. "Dear God in Heaven, help me. I'm so afraid. Please . . ." the words came without volition, rising up from her fear, "make me white again." At the sound of her own voice, a shudder of shame and revulsion racked the angel's body. A breathless moment later, her pursuers burst through the trees, stopping dead in their tracks at the sight of a trembling white woman, half hidden behind the truck of a tree.

"Please . . . no . . ." Monica whimpered.

"Relax lady," said the older of the brothers. "We're not going to hurt you. We're looking for a black woman that came by this way."

It was then that Monica realized what had happened. Her prayer had been answered and, with a choked sob, she sent a silent cry up to her creator. "My God, my God," was the angel's anguished prayer. "Why have I forsaken Thee?"

Rosa Parks sat alone in the empty bus that had brought her into town. It was in a bus that her struggle for equality had begun and now, able to sit in any seat she wanted, she reflected on the long and eventful road that had brought her to this evening. Painted on the outside of the bus was a sign that read PATHWAYS TO FREEDOM, the organization she had formed to help carry on her mission of freedom and equality. But at this particular moment, she was content simply to rest her weary bones. It had been a long day, full of ceremony and celebration, but the weariness brought with it the satisfaction of a job well done. Maybe her presence in this little town, like so many other little towns across this country, would help to heal the hatred and suspicion that divided the races from one another. She hoped so, and it was that hope that kept her going.

A figure moved up the stairs and stood in the aisle, her face darkened in shadow. Mrs. Parks smiled. She had known, somehow, that her work here wasn't quite finished. Perhaps this stranger needed her help . . . and she was always ready to lend a stranger a helping hand.

"Mrs. Parks?" Monica said softly, stepping out of the shadows. "What are you doing in here?"

"I like to sit in here sometimes and think," the old woman replied. "But tell me—who are you?"

Monica took a deep breath. Where to begin? How to explain? "My name is Monica," she said after a long moment as the air around her took on a golden hue. "I am an angel sent by God as a messenger of hope and peace."

On the dark street outside the open door of the bus, Tom and James listened as she spoke—two men, one black, one white, sharing the same look of astonishment at the words they heard. They stood motionless and silent as the angel related her story, sparing none of the terrible events of the day just past, or the agony of shame and doubt left lingering in her heart.

"I know I don't belong in heaven and I don't belong on earth," she concluded, tears welling in her eyes. "I've betrayed both. I know in my heart that if I had been white and those men were chasing me, I wouldn't have begged God to make me black." She broke down and wept, overcome by the human feelings of failure that racked her with guilt.

"God is good, Monica," Mrs. Parks said softly. "He forgives and heals. Even angels."

"Especially angels that have been human for a day," came a resounding voice.

"Tess!" Monica cried and in the next moment she was in her mentor's arms. "I'm so sorry . . . I'm so ashamed."

"Baby," Tess said in a soothing voice. "I gave up on this world yesterday and I let the Father down. I'm not proud of that either. But our God is a great God. And He forgave me. Just like He forgives you. Why do you think He made you black? To change this town? To change these men? No. He did it to change your heart. Because you can't go around preaching against the darkness in this world until you've seen it in yourself first. You've got to dig real deep and face yourself first. You've got to dig real deep and face yourself. And you did that, baby."

Monica nodded as understanding flooded her heart and mind. "For one day I knew how it felt to be tired, to be a frightened, weak and earthbound human. And I discovered that hiding deep inside of me, there was a dark corner of fear. In my weakest hour I trusted that fear instead of God. But by His mercy, He shed light in that corner." Her voice rose, knowing now that the two men who needed to hear her most were standing just outside. "The people of this town must seek out the same dark corner and, as hard as it will be, they have to confess it to one another and to God. Because the color of racism is fear."

Sheriff Tom McKinsley and his deputy, James Robinson, stood by a small, weed-choked headstone in a cemetery deep in the forest. To any outsider, the two men appeared as they always had—one white, one black; one in authority, the other following orders. But to the angel standing beside them, it was as if a veil had been lifted from their eyes, a veil that had kept them from seeing the common humanity they shared.

"I've tried to hide it, even from myself," Tom admitted in a choked voice. "But, when I shake your hand, James, it feels like . . . got to wash something off afterward."

James held out his hand. "I know that feeling," he acknowledged. "It's not something I'm proud of either. But, maybe, the two of us . . . we can change that."

The two men shook and in that moment, the new respect, the new dignity each gave to the other had begun to change their lives forever. Their duties for today were done: the Foley boys had been arrested and the town informed of the crime that had been committed in its midst. But the real work had only just begun.

"This is what Mr. Mooney was searching for," Monica told them as they looked down at the headstone. "Elijah Jackson, the hero of the Aynsville Underground Railroad, wasn't a white man. He was black. And he was Mooney's great, great grandfather. You see, he not only found the truth. He found his family."

Sins of the Father

It's been said that at the moment of a man's death, his entire life flashes before his eyes. For Willis Thompson, a handsome but hardened black man whose face was etched with the bitterness of a wasted life, that moment was fast approaching. When the clock struck midnight, he would be led from his cell to the prison execution chamber to pay for his crimes against society. But what he had done, the sins he had committed, were of no consequence to him anymore. What mattered now was what he would choose to do with the precious few hours he had remaining. As that handful of minutes ticked away, he faced the most important decision he had ever made. It was a decision that would make the difference between life and death . . . but not his own. It was too late for that now. Yet it wasn't too late for Willis and Samuel, the sons he had left behind so long ago and whose destiny he now held in his hands. The choice he made now could bring him peace, even as he faced his death. He knew it was true because a real angel from God had told him so.

He hadn't known she was an angel, of course. At least not at first. When she had first arrived on death row, the redheaded white woman with the soft Irish accent had seemed as out of place as feathers on a fish. Johnson, the death row guard, had brought her in to talk to the prisoner in the cell next to Willis, a punk kid named Luther who reminded Willis of himself at that age—talking trash and strutting around with a chip on his shoulder, just daring anyone to knock it off.

The angel posed as a journalist, a newspaper reporter who had come to do a story on Luther, the youngest inmate on death row, a gangster and a cop killer and one more casualty from the streets of the same ghetto that Willis had once called home. Lying on his cot, he listened as this lily-white woman, who'd introduced herself as Monica, tried to get the hardened and angry young inmate to open up. It was useless, Willis told himself. The punk was proud of what he'd done, proud to have earned the respect of his homeboys back in the set. That's what life on those mean streets had done to him. Just like they'd done to Willis.

"How much chips you getting for telling my story?" Luther had asked with a sneer.

"Chips?" was Monica's puzzled reply. "I don't understand . . ."

"You come a little closer and I'll make you understand," Luther had snarled. "Just like I made that cop understand. Shot him dead and watched his blood run out on the street."

From the even tone of her voice, it didn't seem that the reporter was fazed by Luther's threats. "You told the judge you weren't the one who pulled the trigger," she countered.

Luther snorted with disgust. "Lady, if you ain't got no chips, then give me a Snickers."

Willis had to laugh at that. "Candy!" he mocked. "Baby boy wants candy!"

"Shut up old man!" shouted Luther in a sudden and frightening explosion of rage. Then, turning to Johnson, the guard, he added, "This woman be crazy. Get her outta here!"

As Monica rose to leave she smiled at Luther. "If you had a Snickers," she asked, "where would you keep it? Under your pillow perhaps?"

Luther ignored her, throwing himself on his cot. Putting his hands behind his head, he felt a small lump on the mattress and, a moment later, pulled a Snickers bar from beneath his pillow.

Tess, her characteristic salt-and-pepper hair setting her apart in the crowd, had arrived on assignment at a community meeting in a local church. The angel sat listening as the parents and concerned citizens of the neighborhood noisily argued amongst themselves. She understood their frustration only too well; the frustration of common, decent people trying to find a way to stem the flood of drugs and crime and despair that threatened to destroy the fragile families that they tried so hard to keep together in the face of seemingly insurmountable odds. Pastor George, a tall, well-built black man, was trying his best to restore order, but feelings were running high and answers were running short. The man of God knew that, for all the solutions they might come up with, there was only one that would give them the strength to keep fighting.

"When you go home tonight," he said, after managing to quiet them down, "pray for strength. Pray for the power of God to come down and lead the way. With the Lord's help, we will begin to take back our streets and our children."

Tess turned to the woman sitting to her right, her beautiful features so worn with care and burdened with sorrows that the angel could read her as plainly as a book. Her name was Valerie. "Are all your meetings like this?" Tess asked.

"No," Valerie replied tersely. "Some of them are even more useless."

"Trusting God doesn't seem useless to me," said Tess.

"Haven't you heard?" Valerie answered bitterly. "God doesn't live in this neighborhood."

Tess sighed and stood up, her strong presence and mane of salt-

and-pepper hair commanding immediate attention. "Protecting our children starts at home," she began. "We've got to tell them the truth. And we have to keep telling them until they hear us. All your plans—the neighborhood watch, the street canvassing, the citizen and police committees—are all fine. But they're not enough. We have to fight these gangs, not with our fists, but with the power of God."

"What do you mean 'we'?" Valerie interrupted vehemently. "You're not from this neighborhood. My husband was, and he's on death row. My son is gone, too, and I'm about to lose my baby. Praying is a waste of time. This is a hopeless situation."

"If it's so hopeless than what are you doing here?" asked Tess gently.

A look of pain crossed Valerie's face, but before she could answer she was interrupted by the sudden and insistent wail of an alarm. "My car!" shouted someone and a moment later the entire meeting had rushed into the parking lot, led by Pastor George.

A small, furtive figure sat in the driver's seat of the vehicle, visible through a broken window, trying desperately to shut off the blaring alarm. As Pastor George reached in to grab him, Valerie froze in her tracks. "Samuel!" she shouted and then ran instinctively to protect her twelve-year-old son.

"If you try to save him now," Pastor George warned her, as he pulled the boy out and held him by the collar, "you won't be able to save him later." A police siren could be heard approaching in the darkness as Valerie stared helplessly at Samuel, a good looking boy whose eyes reflected the innocence of his tender age.

"Mama, help me!" her son cried, his voice cracking with fear.

Valerie shook her head, choking back her tears. "God help him," she whispered.

"He will, baby," Tess replied softly. "He will."

Back in the prison, Monica, talking intently to the defiant young inmate, asked, "Tell me about your brother," as she sat outside Luther's cell, holding up a small tape recorder. "Samuel, isn't it?"

"First you tell me how you did that thing with the Snickers bar," he demanded. "That's the only reason I let them bring you back in here."

Monica smiled. "You tell me the truth now," she countered, "and I'll tell you the truth later. Now, about Samuel?"

Luther shrugged. "I taught him what he needed to know. Got him corded on real good."

" 'Corded on?' " replied a mystified Monica.

"In the gang," snapped Luther. "You gonna listen to me, or what?"

"Sorry," said the angel. "So Samuel is in the gang?"

"You in the set, you in the gang," was Luther's exasperated answer.

"And the set is . . . ? " Monica ventured hesitantly.

"The hood!" he snapped back. "Lady, you wearin' me out."

"Just tell me," Monica pressed. "Why does everyone want to be in a gang?"

Luther rolled his eyes. "No gang, no respect," he said, as if talking to a child. "Got to start jackin' what makes you the big green."

Monica looked puzzled. "You think your friends still respect you, now that you're on death row? And what about Samuel?"

"They respect me even more," Luther sneered. "Specially Samuel."

"What about your mother?" Monica asked quietly.

A look of sadness flickered in Luther's hard eyes. A long pause ensued. "It ain't her fault," he said at last. "Mom's tried to keep me outta the gang, but all the preachin' in the world ain't gonna change the way it is out there."

Monica thought for a moment, trying to find the right words for her next question. "If Samuel respects you," she finally said, "then maybe he'll want to act like you. And maybe he'll end up sitting in there, just like you." She leaned forward, ignoring the anger flashing in the young man's eyes. "Haven't you ever looked up to anyone, Luther? Your father, perhaps?"

"My father was a dog," Luther snapped back. "He had a family and responsibilities. But he took off. He wasn't no man."

"Maybe so," the angel admitted. "But he was still your hero. Just like you are Samuel's hero. And because he looks up to you, he may end up making the same mistakes you made."

Luther shook his head. "Sam's my boy," he said affectionately. "Ain't nothing gonna happen to him. He's got the stripes."

"Stripes?" echoed Monica and when Luther looked away, she added, "I can't understand you, Luther, if you don't talk to me."

The angry inmate sighed with frustration and a sadness he couldn't hide, and leaned up against the bars. "Sam's fierce," he explained. "Like my pops. See, pops had these scars on his shoulder. Like some big cat had clawed his skin. I remember him telling me they didn't hurt half as bad the other guy looked." He laughed, a quick, harsh sound. "The other homies used to say my pops had the stripes. When I was little I thought he was so hard. I was gonna be just like him. But . . ." his voice trailed off.

"But he left you," Monica said.

Luther nodded. "Shook the spot when I was six."

"And you miss him?" Monica asked, her voice barely above a whisper.

The look in Luther's eyes this time was a mix of memories and emotions too painful to bear. "Next question," he said, turning away.

Valerie's heart sank when she arrived home with a bag full of groceries and saw Samuel, released from jail, sitting on the front porch with an all-too-familiar figure from the neighborhood. His

name was Dre and he had been a friend of Luther's, before her eld-
est boy landed on death row. The fact was, Dre had been an accomplice to the botched robbery that had ended in the murder of a
policeman. But somehow Dre had evaded all responsibility for the
crime while her son had been tried and convicted as the sole perpe-
trator of the crime.

But her main concern now was Samuel and for the moment she
suppressed her anger at the intrusion of Dre once again into the life
of her shattered family.

"Can you help me with these bags, Samuel?" she asked tentatively.

"I'm busy," her son spat back in reply.

"Now don't be disrespecting your mama," Dre scolded. Then,
with a meaningful glance at Valerie, added, "'less I say different."

"You better hope that day never comes," she replied with a
scowl as she moved past him and through the kitchen door. Samuel
followed and, calmer now, his mother said, "Welcome back, son.
How does spaghetti sound for dinner?"

"Why did you leave me in jail?" Samuel replied in a sullen accu-
sation. "Why didn't you come to get me? You always picked up
Luther."

"I know," replied Valerie, swallowing hard. "And maybe if I'd left
him there for the night that first time, he wouldn't be in there now."

"What kind of mom are you?" Samuel demanded, his dark eyes
flashing.

Valerie took a deep breath, trying to control herself. "The kind
that loves you," she replied. "The kind that makes hard choices because she wants what's best for her son. I want you to be so scared of
prison, baby, that you'll never go back!"

"Scared?" Samuel echoed. "You think I was scared? The scariest
thing I seen is you!" He rushed out the door ignoring his mother's
plea and leaving her in the same house where, for so long, she had
been so alone.

Still pumped up with anger, Samuel walked rapidly down the street until, from an alleyway, Dre fell in next to him. "That Pastor man been messin' with the brothers for too long," he said and, lifting his shirt, he revealed a semi-automatic handgun tucked in his waistband. "His time is up."

Samuel looked fearfully at the weapon. "You sure about this?" he asked.

Dre snorted. "I shoulda known better," he sneered. "Your brother was the one with stripes."

"I be just as bad as my brother!" the boy sputtered, walking fast to keep up with Dre's stride.

In reply, the gang leader simply pulled out the gun and handed it to Samuel. "Prove it," was all he said.

In the barbed wire confines of the exercise yard, Willis did a long series of push-ups with single-minded determination, as if each thrust could somehow slow down the final hours he felt fast approaching. His eyes closed, his forehead beaded with sweat, he suddenly felt a presence beside him in the empty yard and, looking up, saw the woman reporter who had been interviewing Luther.

"It seems a little strange, doesn't it?" Monica asked. "A man exercising on the last day of his life."

"How did you get in here?" the condemned man asked, looking around for a guard. "Who are you?"

"I'm an angel," Monica replied. "But the real question you should be asking is how will you die? Will it be as you lived? Or will you leave some truth behind for the sake of your sons? There's still time left, Willis. Not for you, but for your children."

"You're no angel," Willis responded bitterly, "and my kids are long gone."

Monica smiled as a strange golden light began to form around her. "Your son is in the cell right next to you," she revealed. "He may have to spend his life on death row, but he doesn't have to be alone. And Samuel has a chance to live a long life, instead of dying on the streets. But it starts with you, Willis. God loves you and He's given you a chance to do something with your life, before it's too late." The glow around the angel was intense now as Willis Thompson struggled to understand the depth of the words she spoke. All this time his son, right in the next cell, had been so close and yet they were separated by more than thick prison walls. It was the legacy of disappointment and betrayal that had kept them so far apart. "Reach out to your son, Willis," Monica urged him. "Tell him who you are. Be the father you wanted so desperately to be when you first held Luther in your arms."

He closed his eyes, trying to shut out the thoughts and memories that welled up in his mind. When he opened them again, she was gone and he was alone. A guard stood at the gate. "Time's up, Willis," he said, as he led him from the yard and back into the cellblock. It was there, at the prison door, that he met Luther, being led out for his own hour of exercise.

"Hey old man," the youth taunted. "Last piece of sky you'll ever see."

Silently, Willis stopped and, removing his sweat soaked T-shirt, revealed three deep stripes across his shoulder, like the scars of a big cat's claws. Luther recognized the marks immediately. This was his father.

Dre lured Samuel into a dark alley down the street from a small convenience store in the heart of the neighborhood. The gun felt cold and heavy in the boy's small hand and he had a sick feeling in the pit of his stomach, but when Dre pointed out the figure of Pastor George heading into the store, Samuel pulled himself a little straighter and tried to assume the same look of studied cool that he saw on the older boy's face.

"That's his daddy's store," Dre said in a low tone. "He's gonna be a while. You just wait here. He'll be out. Then you do what you got to."

Willis, meanwhile, was taking the last bites of his last meal. It was eleven o'clock, one hour before his scheduled execution. All appeals had been exhausted. All clemency denied. Tonight he was going to die. As he stared at the empty tray in front of him, a now familiar light began to fill his cell and, looking up, he saw Monica standing beyond the bars.

"Talk to your son, Willis," she pleaded, in a voice that only he could hear. "And when you need me, I'll be here." The prisoner turned away in anguish, trying to find the courage in himself to do what he knew was right, and when he looked up again, Monica had vanished. Without giving himself time to think, or time to doubt, he grabbed the shiny metal tray and, dumping the plate and utensils on the floor, held it outside the bars, casting his own blurry reflection into the cell next to his.

"Hey," he said, then swallowed hard. "I'm sorry."

"For what?" asked Luther, approaching the bars and looking at the dim reflection of his father.

Willis hesitated. "You know that white lady been hanging around? Monica?" He laughed nervously. "She told me she was an angel." Luther snickered, but Willis pressed on. It was too late to turn back now. "I think she is," he continued earnestly. "I think she come straight from God."

"Man, you must be trippin'," was Luther's incredulous reply.

"I didn't listen to her at first," his father told him. "But my time's running out. And now, I got somethin' to say to you . . . son . . ."

"Shut up!" Luther spat back. "I ain't your son no more!"

"Yes, you are!" Willis insisted, trying his best to convey the truth through the dim reflection in the tray. "You're my son and I gotta tell you something . . . something you got to pass on to your little brother. Those stripes I got that you think make me so bad? I got those runnin' away from a gangster I couldn't put down." The shadow of a memory clouded his eyes. "Funny thing is, I met an angel back then, too. White dude hanging around the hood. Never could figure out why until I realized who he was." He paused. "It was the angel of death, Luther."

The same strange shadow now passed over Luther's face. "I seen that dude myself," he said softly. "Night that cop was killed. We was running away and this white guy walked right past us like nothing was happening."

"You sorry?" Willis asked after a moment. "Sorry that cop is dead?"

Luther stared at the reflection in the dull light. "I'm sorry those kids ain't got no daddy," he answered. "'Cause I know how that feels."

The hollow clang of a steel door announced the arrival of the warden. "You ready, Willis?" he asked, as Johnson opened the cell and began to escort the condemned man down the hall.

"I am now," he replied, then turned back to his son. "Next time you meet an angel," he said, "you listen, hear me?" Luther nodded and Willis saw the figure of Andrew suddenly materialize beside him. "You see him, Luther?" was Willis's awe-struck whisper. "The dude in white. You see him here beside me?" Luther nodded, sharing the angelic vision of death with his father.

"God can be with you here tonight," Andrew said. "It's up to you."

Willis nodded. "Show me the way to go home," he replied simply, as the guards led him away.

Monica's work was almost done. Everything now depended on a simple choice and, even as she realized that the result was out of her hands, she sent up a silent prayer, asking God that somehow, some way, the truth would be revealed to Luther.

"I think your father is going to die in peace," she said to him, in the silence of the cellblock after Willis had been led away. "It's too bad he couldn't live that way."

"Who cares about him, anyway?" countered Luther, as he clung to his bitterness.

"You do," Monica replied calmly. "You won't admit it, but you loved him. And when he betrayed you, it filled your heart with bitterness and hatred. And now you're about to do the same thing to Samuel."

Luther started, stung by the angel's words. "I take care of my bro," he insisted.

"And who's going to take care of the family of that policeman you killed?" Monica said, anger finally flashing in her green eyes. "I have listened to you for days," she continued urgently. "I've tried to learn some of your language. Yes, it's all very impressive, your secret codes and dead homies. And where has it gotten you?" She gestured at the prison walls. "Alone in here, for the rest of your life, with no one, Luther, except God. He loves you and will stay with you, and with your little brother, if you'll just let Him. Your body may be in prison, but your soul doesn't have to be." She took a step toward him, the light beginning to shine from her body. "Samuel loves you, Luther. But right now he's holding a gun that Dre gave him and in a few minutes he'll murder someone with it."

The words were like an electric shock racing through his body. "No!" shouted Luther. "You got to stop him!"

"Only you can do that," Monica replied. "By loving him enough to tell him the truth."

From his hiding place in the alley, Samuel could see Pastor George leaving his father's store. Taking a deep breath, his face drenched with sweat, he pulled back the trigger and, taking aim, was suddenly startled to see his brother standing between him and his target. "Luther!" he cried incredulously. "What are you doin' here? How did you get out?"

"Don't do this," Luther begged. "Don't make my mistakes. Don't be like me."

"But you down, Luther," his brother insisted. "You got a rep. I want to get respect just like you!"

"I killed a man," Luther replied, tears welling in his eyes. "Dead. Gone. His babies are crying at night. I wish I hadn't done it. I wish to God I could take it back."

From the shadow of the alley, another figure emerged. "So this is how you got out of the pen," Dre snarled. "Singin' your regrets. Sellin' out your honor . . ." He turned to Samuel. "Come on, little Sam. You got a job to do. Show your brother you ain't a punk like him."

Luther's eyes narrowed. "You ever wonder why Dre beat the rap and I got sent to the row, Sam?" he asked. "I'll tell you why. 'Cause Dre turned over on me, that's why. He talked to the cops. Told them where to find the gun."

"He just be woofin'," Dre interrupted nervously.

Samuel looked back and forth between the two young men fighting for his soul and, with a slow and deliberate motion, raised the gun and pointed it at Dre. "That ain't the answer, Sam," Luther said in a commanding tone. "Listen, little brother. I want you to do what no man in our family has ever done. I want you to live. And I want you to remember how much I love you." Staring hard into his brother's eyes, he sensed a shifting of the scene around him as the alley disappeared and he suddenly found himself back in his jail cell.

"No!" he shouted to Monica. "You've got to send me back. I got to help him make the right decision."

"You can't make the decision for him," Monica replied. "But because of you, Samuel now has a chance."

Samuel stood on the quiet street outside his house. Through the kitchen window he could see his mother, sitting at the kitchen table, alone with a heart broken for her lost sons and shattered family. He looked down at the gun in his hand, the gun he hadn't fired, a weapon that suddenly had no power over him anymore. Lifting the lid of a garbage can he threw it inside and crossed the lawn to the porch.

"Mama?" he said as he came through the front door, and a moment later felt her strong loving arms around him as she rushed to welcome him home.

"I'm here, baby," she whispered through tears.

"Mama?" he asked. "Will you make me some spaghetti for dinner?"

His mother smiled and kissed the top of his head. She had her son back and together, with the help of God, they were going to make it. She had it on the very best authority.

The Man Upstairs

Gus Zimmerman had the gift of gab, one of that rare breed of silver-tongued charmers. It was said amongst the fraternity of salesmen to which he was a member in good standing, that he could sell iceboxes to Eskimos in the middle of winter. It was a talent, inbred and inborn, and if Gus never exactly considered where it came from, he never exactly took it for granted, either. God was up there somewhere, he believed in a vague and hazy sort of way, and every time he sold a policy or got a fat commission check in the mail, he threw a "thank you" up to the heavens the way some men would throw dice across a green felt table.

Gus wasn't really sure to what he owed his singular salesmanship, but he was sure of one thing—without that silver tongue, he'd never be able to survive in the cut-throat business that gathered like moths around the bright lights of Las Vegas. His specialty was selling insurance policies to the big casinos all along the Strip, and the managers and businessmen and silk-shirted executives who ran those glittering establishments had heard every line in the book. In fact, they'd probably written a few of the best themselves. It took all his powers and persuasion and persistence to make a sale, and in recent months there were more times than Gus cared to recount when he'd walked away empty-handed, defeated by the slick new breed of casino operators who only wanted to trim expenses and cut corners, the ones who saw him and his policies as a holdover from a fading era, when your word was your bond and you got what you paid for.

Those were the rules that Gus Zimmerman lived by. In a town where everyone wanted to get lucky, as if their very lives depended on red or black, the number twenty-one or the way a steel ball bounced along a spinning wheel, he worked hard for his money, patiently selling his policies year in and year out, making a decent living and earning every dollar with his own sweat and blood. He did his job with integrity, because it was all he knew how to do. And Esther was depending on him.

Gus and Esther had been husband and wife for thirty years, and, in a town of instant weddings and even more instant divorces, that was an accomplishment all by itself. Through it all they had stuck it out, for better or worse, richer and poorer, in sickness and in health; but more than just staying together, they had stayed in love, a love that seemed only to grow stronger, even as the tenuous circumstances of survival became harder and harder to endure.

Because, if there was one thing Gus Zimmerman knew, it was that love, no matter how enduring, doesn't pay the bills. It sure hadn't satisfied the hospital or the HMO when Esther got diabetes. And, although he tried to keep up a cheerful front and worked twice as hard, just to keep up with the prescriptions and weekly doctor visits, it was almost as if Gus had given up a piece of himself when his wife had eventually lost her leg. Somehow they had weathered that storm, but now it had gotten to the point where Esther needed full-time care. Very expensive care, with a full-time nurse, a lot of physical therapy as well as special medical equipment and medication.

And suddenly Gus found himself facing the most difficult predicament of his career. Just at a time when he was going through a dry spell, the inevitable curse of every salesman, no matter how experienced, Esther's doctors had told him he would need ten thousand dollars, just to meet her immediate needs. There were no prospects on the horizon and all his old customers had bought all the insurance they needed, and then some.

Monica, Tess and Andrew had come to Las Vegas uncertain of what their mission in that vast sparkling desert oasis might be. At first it had seemed a strange place for three angels on assignment, adrift in a city where it seemed that the only god worshipped was Lady Luck. The denizens of Las Vegas might have prayed every once in a while, but the prayers were weighted down with greed and the lust for money. If ever there were a repository for lost souls, it would have to have been in the noisy, smoky and sleepless confines of the casinos, where neon enticements flashed and flickered against the velvety desert sky.

Andrew looked trim and elegant in his guise as a bellman, welcoming guests to the sumptuous Paradise Grand Hotel and Casino, and Tess's sweet and soulful voice could be heard this night above the idle chatter and clinking cocktails in the hotel's dimly lit bar, entertaining customers as a lounge singer. It was late one evening, as she delivered her resonant rendition of "Taking a Chance on Love," that Monica, sitting at the bar, was introduced to their assignment, one that would test the courage and faith of all three angels to the utmost.

As the last notes of the classic torch song faded in the smoky air, a brash, gregarious and infectiously enthusiastic little man with a brush moustache and a sparkle in his eyes stepped out of the crowd and sat on a bar stool next to Monica. It was his favorite song, he told the angel, the tune that he and Esther had danced to the night they had met at the community center, all those many years ago.

Monica couldn't help liking Gus the minute he sidled up beside her, ordering himself a club soda and telling the bartender to pour her whatever she wanted.

"I'll have the same, thank you," said the angel in a soft Irish accent. Smiling at Gus, she couldn't help offering up a quick prayer that whatever it was that seemed to be burdening down this gentle soul—in spite of his best attempts to hide it—it would soon be lifted. But, even as she prayed, a dark sense of foreboding was starting to take shape in a corner of her heart. It wasn't just the insatiable hunger to get rich, which seemed to infect this casino, and not just the lonely lives wasting away in front of the slot machines and roulette wheels that gave her a distinct feeling of dread. No, there was a *presence* hovering over the Paradise Grand, a presence of evil that was as pervasive and inescapable as the surveillance cameras constantly scanning the games and their players.

The more she became aware of this menacing shadow of dread, the more it seemed to grow and, with it, the conviction that this gentle and unassuming man was in some kind of terrible danger. She just didn't know what it was or from what direction it would come, and as he told her his story, puzzled all the while by the sudden need he felt to confess everything to this sympathetic redhead, she grew more and more concerned for him. It seemed to Monica that any man who needed money as badly as Gus, money to save his wife's life, might just do anything to get it. And that was a dangerous place to be, made all the more perilous in a city that lived and died for the love of money.

Desperation can blind a man to danger, especially if the man in question had as much confidence in the persuasive power of his words as Gus Zimmerman did. And why shouldn't he be self-assured? After all, he had sold insurance to Mac, the general manager of the Paradise Grand, for going on ten years now and, if they weren't exactly best buddies, at least they had learned to respect and depend on each other. Gus's policies were the best in the business and, with the commission he would get from Mac's business, Esther would be sure to have the care she needed.

But a rude shock was awaiting the sincere salesman as he made his way to the elevator that would take him up to the penthouse offices of the hotel. The newfangled security system that required a special code was only the first clue that things were not as they had once been. But it was when he was brusquely informed by the guard that the Paradise Grand was under new management and that Mac was no longer the establishment's general manager, that Gus felt his confidence leaking away like water through a cracked glass.

Returning to the bar, he related this ominous turn of events to his newfound friend. "Things are going from bad to worse," he told Monica with a desperate edge to his voice. She felt her heart breaking as she watched the despondent look spread across the little man's face. "I've simply got to get that ten thousand dollars and Mac was my last hope." He was the only casino operator on the Strip who might be inclined to listen to Gus's plea. As if actually watching his options draining away at the bottom of his club soda glass, Gus shook his head and scowled. Suddenly, with a single violent motion, he pushed it away and sent his fist crashing onto the shiny surface of the bar.

"A double scotch," he demanded. "Straight up." From that moment on the evening became a blurry chain of disastrous events. Within minutes of swallowing the liquor, Gus began playing the roulette table, and within a few turns of the wheel he was not only shy the ten thousand dollars he so desperately needed, he had also lost another five thousand on the casino's line of credit.

"Gus is a good person, but he's opened the door to compromise," Tess told Monica as the two sat in a booth and watched the salesman plunge ever deeper into debt. "He's not a drinker and he certainly has no business in a casino. He keeps hoping his luck will change, but it's not about luck. It's about believing in the goodness of something greater than him, and so far, our Gus is still trying to get it done his own way." She shook her head sadly. "Trouble is, he's lost faith in himself and he's yet to find faith in the only One who could really help him. There's no telling what a man in his situation might do next."

"There's not much more he can do," Monica said as she watched another pile of chips disappear from Gus's dwindling stash. "He's lost everything he has."

"Oh no, Angel Girl," was Tess's grim reply. "He's still got something to lose. Something he can never get back again." As she spoke the words the dejected salesman returned to the bar to swallow another drink, steeling his nerve to wager his last few dollars on a hopeless roll of the dice. It was at that moment that the menacing figure of a man dressed in the hotel livery appeared as if from nowhere, and striding up to Gus, tapped him on the shoulder. "The manager will see you now," he said, bending low beside the salesman's ear. Then, turning to Monica, added pointedly, "Alone."

The angels followed Gus with their eyes as he crossed the casino floor and walked into the open elevator door, pulsing from inside with an eerie glow. The door slid silently shut as he rode with a rush of wind high above the neon blaze of the city. In what seemed like seconds, he was deposited in the foyer of an ornate office suite, so completely different from the wood-paneled and trophy-lined one in which Mac had done business.

It was there that Gus watched with an unaccountable shiver of fear as a shapely, shadowy figure spun slowly around in the plush leather desk chair, her silhouette eerily etched against the distant vista of the Las Vegas skyline, visible through the floor-to-ceiling window behind her. Gus smiled nervously, clutching his battered briefcase tightly as he swallowed hard.

"Steady as she goes, Gus old man," he muttered to himself. "Just remember, you've got the gift of gab. You can sell the Brooklyn Bridge if you had to." But the words sounded hollow in his ears. The liquor had left his senses dulled and it suddenly felt as if he had a mouthful of cotton instead of the smooth words he had depended on for so long.

The strangely beautiful woman introduced herself as the new general manager of the casino, and the face that greeted Gus with a chilling smile would have been only-too-familiar to the angel waiting helplessly in the casino downstairs. Monica had seen it before, a haunting mirror image of herself, the uncanny image of an identical twin, whose heart had turned to darkness instead of light. It was Monique, a fallen angel who could assume any shape, even that of Monica herself, to accomplish the destructive missions on which she was sent into the world. It was as if Monica's evil alter ego had emerged to wage war against the purposes of the Father, whenever and wherever she could, using human beings as her hapless pawns, stealing their souls and wreaking havoc with their lives.

What followed had all the tragic inevitability of a traffic accident unfolding in slow motion. Monique knew more about Gus and his dire situation than he knew himself. She knew that he would do anything to save his wife's life, and she also knew that the fatigue and desperation and fear of failure had taken their toll on this good man.

But she also knew, with chilling certainty, that here and now was the moment appointed for the greatest test of Gus Zimmerman's life . . . a test that she would do everything in her power to make sure he failed. Smoothly and subtly as a snake, she circled her victim, careful not to reveal her intent too soon, deftly playing off his hopes and fears until the moment came to strike the final bargain.

It all started out innocently enough. Monique, aware of the crushing debt Gus had piled up during his reckless round of gambling downstairs, made what seemed a generous and compassionate offer.

"I am going to make a little wager myself," she purred, as she sat down across from him on a luxurious sectional. "I'll take off half your debt to the casino," she continued, seemingly pulling a deck of cards from midair, "if you win on a single cut."

Gus swallowed hard. "One cut of the deck," he repeated, hardly able to believe what he was hearing. "And you'll forget twenty-five hundred dollars. What are you running here . . . a home for over-the-hill salesmen?"

Monique laughed, a sly and insinuating sound. "Tell you what," she replied. "I'm feeling generous tonight. One cut of the cards for the whole debt. What do you say?"

Gus' eyes narrowed suspiciously. "And what happens if I lose?" he asked, watching as the cards flipped back and forth between her slender fingers with magical dexterity.

"Oh, let's see," was Monique's stealthy answer. She pointed to his hand. "How about that ring you've got there? It couldn't be worth much."

"But," Gus replied, his voice cracking, "it's my wedding ring."

"Take it or leave it," Monique demanded as the cards seemed to stack themselves on the coffee table in front of Gus.

Hardly able to breathe, he closed his eyes and cut, pulling up the king of spades. Monique took her turn and produced a seven of hearts. The salesman crowed with delight, but the fire in Monique's eyes seemed to burn even brighter. He was falling into her trap, as predictably as every one of these weak and foolish humans had always done. It was almost too easy. The wedding ring, of course, had meant nothing to her, no matter the sentimental value. And if Gus's debt had been ten times what it was, it wouldn't have made the slightest difference. She was only luring him in; closer to the trap that would ensnare the true prize she sought. She could tell by the eager gleam in his eye exactly what his answer would be when she proposed a second wager, with stakes much higher this time.

"I'll sign that insurance policy contract," she told Gus, "sight unseen, if I lose the next round of the cards. But if I win——" she paused, letting the tension build.

"What," asked Gus. "What happens if you win?"

Her voice took on a subtle hiss as she spoke the next words. "Then I would require you to sign a contract of my own, Mr. Zimmerman."

"What kind of contract?" he wanted to know.

"It is a simple legal document," she continued. "Nothing to it, really. 'One human soul, intact, no lingering spiritual attachments, to become the exclusive property of the undersigned.' "

Gus could hardly believe his ears. This was crazy. Selling his soul to the devil? That kind of thing only happens in fairy tales. Did she actually think he would take her up on it? But lodged in the back of his mind was that magic number of ten thousand dollars and if this strange woman was foolish enough to make such a bargain, he asked himself, then who was Gus Zimmerman to turn down a sure thing?

He nodded and Monique dealt a hand of poker. One game, winner take all, she told him. Within moments the cards told the tale—a pair of queens against three sixes.

It was all over. He'd lost his soul. Nothing had changed. At least not that he could see. But there was no denying the empty feeling that suddenly opened up where his heart used to be. Whether he believed in it or not, Gus Zimmerman had just gambled away the most important thing he ever owned.

Monica knew immediately that things had gone terribly wrong when Gus returned to the bar later that night, his face ashen and his hands trembling. And, as he choked out the story for her, a small detail caught her attention. His hand, two queens, had been beaten by three sixes. Six. Six. Six. The very mention of that number had brought a sinking feeling in the pit of her stomach. There was no question now as to whom their opponent was, and what was at stake in the battle they were about to fight.

But it wasn't important what she knew. What mattered was that Gus understood what he had done, and how it could be undone. And for that to happen, he would need to see, in a way that he never had before, that the words he spoke, and the conviction with which he spoke them, had the power to create or destroy . . . to build up or tear down . . . to give life or to take it away.

The last round was played out against the vast Las Vegas skyline, on the roof of the Paradise Grand, where Gus stood, inches from the ledge, looking down into an abyss of death and despair.

For the hapless salesman, there was no place to run and no place to hide. Gus, with no options left, had tried to get another shot at winning that ten thousand dollars. But, this time, Monique was ready with yet one more proposition, one that would give her the chance to collect on the bet she had already won. The bet for Gus's soul.

The dark angel already knew that Gus had taken out a two hundred and fifty thousand dollar life insurance policy, with Esther as the beneficiary. It didn't take much to plant the suggestion that the salesman would be doing his wife the biggest favor of her life, one that would literally save her life, if he were to meet with a "tragic accident."

And Gus had believed her. As he made his way up to the roof, intending to jump off and deliver his soul into Monique's clutches, a figure emerged from beneath the starry sky, a figure wrapped in a soft golden glow. Monica knew that if she were going to stop what was about to happen, it was going to be then and there. She would only have one chance to deliver Gus from the consequences of his desperate act.

As she stepped forward and began to speak, she prayed, asking God to give her the words to say even as she trembled against the cold desert wind that blew across the roof.

"Gus," she shouted against the wind. "God wants you to know that no matter what you have done, He still loves you."

Startled, Gus turned to face her. "How could He love me?" the salesman asked. "I've given my soul to the devil."

"Yes," replied Monica, "but there's one thing the devil doesn't want you to know. That you can get it back."

"I can?" Gus asked, tears streaming from his eyes.

"It's your words that got you into this," she continued. "And it's your words that will get you out. You said the words 'I do' when you got married, and those words changed your life forever. The words you say right now can have the same effect . . . for eternity."

"But . . . how?" Gus took a step away from the edge and Monica's heart leapt. Maybe, just maybe, there was still a chance.

"Gus," she continued urgently. "It doesn't matter if you give your word to a customer at work, to Esther at the altar or to the devil over a poker game. Words always mean something. And when you say them, you give them life."

"Then, please," Gus begged. "Tell me . . . tell me what to say."

The answer, when it came, was spoken with a sweet certainty, as if God Himself had answered Gus's question through the voice of this angel of light. But it was not an angel sent from above. It was Monique who answered, disguised now as a heavenly being, more dazzling than any of the neon displays far below them, brighter and more brilliant that anything Gus's earthly eyes had ever beheld.

"Ask and ye shall receive, Gus," she said. "What do you want? You want shooting stars?"

With a wave of her hand, an awesome display of light erupted into the night sky overhead.

"How about fireworks?" the deceptive Monique continued, as, at her command, roman candles exploded in brilliant colors. "Maybe you'd like money. Tell me how much and it's yours. Anything you want, I can give to you. And all you have to do is ask."

Gus turned to Monica, a haunted look in his eyes. "Help me," he said. "What do I do?"

"Ask God to forgive you," the angel replied. "Ask Him to get your soul back for you. Say, 'I do not have the power to fight, but You do. Fight this fight for me!' "

Monique's haughty laugh could be heard even over the bursting fireworks. "He doesn't have to go through all that mumbo jumbo," she sneered. "You want your contract back?" she said, turning to Gus. "No problem."

The contract appeared from out of nowhere and Gus stared at it in his hands, hardly daring to believe that his soul was his again.

"Go ahead," continued Monique. "Tear it up. But I don't think you'll be happy if you do. I know Esther won't."

"Why not?" asked Gus, startled by the sound of his wife's name.

"She'll say anything to confuse you," Monica warned. "Don't listen to her. Listen to God."

"Listen all you want, Gus," Monique spat back. "But you'll never hear God guarantee that you and Esther will spend eternity together. But *I* can. That's why Esther signed this contract. The same one you did. Because she loves you."

"She signed it?" Gus whispered in horror.

"That's her signature, isn't it?" Monique asked, pointing to the trembling scrawl across a dotted line.

"The devil can counterfeit anything," Monica shouted. "Speak, Gus! Before it's too late! Pray . . . pray to God!"

"What about Esther?" Monique demanded in turn. "You're nothing without Esther!"

"You're nothing without your soul!" Monica countered.

"Think of Esther!" the dark angel shrieked. "Esther!"

Gus turned to face Monica. "She's right," he said. "I have to think of Esther."

"Gus, no . . ." Monica pleaded. There was nothing more she could do. The outcome hung in the balance, dangling by the thinnest of fraying threads. Slowly and calmly, Gus turned back to the demonic creature hovering in the darkness. He took a deep breath, then, opening his mouth, began to speak.

"As much as Esther loves me," he said, "she loves God more."
Monica's heart leapt. "Yes," she cried. "That's true!"

Gus threw back his head and shouted as loudly as he could into the night sky. "Please God," he proclaimed. "Forgive me and take back my soul." Then, in a voice that wavered at first but soon grew in strength and conviction, he began to sing. It was a song he had suddenly remembered from thirty years before, a song he and Esther had last sung together on their wedding day. "This little light of mine," he recited, "I'm gonna let it shine / This little light of mine / I'm gonna let it shine . . ."

The song, the most beautiful thing Monica had heard this side of heaven, continued, rising up even above the anguished scream of the thwarted demon, who, stumbling backward, stepped off the precipice and was swallowed in the darkness below. In her place, the contract fluttered to the roof where it disintegrated into a pile of dust that was blown into the desert night.

Monica smiled at Gus. "They were just words, Gus," she said. "But they were the right words, spoken with all your heart. And with all your soul. Esther will be very proud of you." Her eyes twinkled as she added, "Now I think you've got some unfinished business to attend to."

A familiar face sat behind a familiar desk as Gus entered the offices of the Paradise Grand's general manager.

"I thought you were fired, Mac," the salesman remarked incredulously.

"Me?" laughed the executive. "Not a chance. Car broke down in the desert. Cell phone died. Took me all day to get a tow. Gus, I've had the day from hell."

"I know the feeling," Gus replied with a smile, then swallowed hard. "Mac," he continued softly, "I was wondering—"

"Funny you should turn up here tonight," Mac interrupted with a wave of his hand. "I was just getting ready to call you. We're thinking of expanding this place and we're going to need some more insurance. I wouldn't buy it from anyone but you." He stood up. "What do you say we go down to the bar and grab a ginger ale while we work out the details?"

"Just the words I was hoping to hear," Gus replied as the manager laid a friendly arm across his shoulders.

"They take good care of you while I was gone?" Mac asked as they headed to the elevator.

"Sure thing, Mac," he replied. "I was in good hands." From out of the window, a dove flew across the dawn panorama of the city, as the rising sun faded the luster of the flashing neon signs.

Clipped Wings

Tess sat nervously in the anonymous waiting room, glancing every few seconds at the clock on the wall and muttering to herself under her breath. She stared at the frosted glass window of the reception area, dreading the moment it would slide open and the summons would come. No matter how many of these performance reviews she she'd been part of, there was something nerve-wracking about the whole process that set Tess's teeth on edge.

And today, of all days, Monica was late. That wasn't going to make a good impression on the judge, as Tess knew only too well.

"Where is she?" the angel asked, turning to Andrew, who sat beside her.

"She'll be here," Andrew replied. "She knows how important this is."

Tess shot him an irritated look. "I hope she does. Because Ruth is not going to cut her one bit of slack."

"Who's Ruth?" asked Andrew.

Tess sighed. "She's the judge, of course. She and I go way back . . . waded through the Great Flood together."

"No kidding," replied Andrew. "Well, I'm sure an old friend like that—"

"Who said anything about an old friend?" Tess snapped back.

Andrew's eyes widened. He's never seen Tess quite so nervous, quite so unsure of herself or the circumstance.

Monica stepped out of the elevator, immaculately dressed and clutching an appointment slip tightly in her hand. Looking at the numbers on the doors, she began moving down the hallway at a brisk pace. If she hurried, she'd make it just in time. And she knew how important promptness was, today of all days. As she rounded a corner, she glanced again at the paper in her hand, repeating the number to herself. "Two–four–two–five." When she looked up again she almost collided with a familiar, and none too welcome, face. "Kathleen!" she exclaimed. The fallen angel, her adversary on so many cases, was the last person she expected to see that morning, the last person she would have wanted to see.

"Monica," Kathleen purred, her eyes lit from within by a strange, cold light. "You're looking . . ." she gave her a long appraising once-over, "angelic as usual."

"I wish I could say it's good to see you Kathleen," Monica replied. "But I don't have time for a chat. I've got an appointment and—"

"Yes," Kathleen interrupted with a knowing smile. "Your evaluation. I'm here for mine, too. A few floors down, of course."

Monica hardly had time to reflect on how the dark angel might have known about her performance review, or to consider the possibility that her adversary was also subject to an assessment of her job. "You'll have to excuse me," she said. "I've got to find suite two–four–two–five."

Kathleen glanced quickly over the angel's shoulder. A sign on a door behind her read SUITE 2420—DR. R. J. BOMBAY—PSYCHIATRY. Her eyes narrowed as she concentrated on the numbers, magically morphing them, the last one from a "0" to a "5," then turned and smiled at Monica.

"There it is," she said. "Right behind you."

"Oh," Monica said, ignoring a sudden uncomfortable flash of intuition. "Thank you."

"My pleasure," was Kathleen's silky smooth reply, and she watched as Monica opened the door, unaware that as she closed it behind her, the suite number returned to its previous designation.

For the fifth time in as many minutes, Tess checked the clock on the wall, then turned to Andrew, the annoyance on her face now transformed to clear concern. "This isn't good," she said and Andrew nodded, sharing the foreboding she felt.

"Where is she?" he asked.

"I wish I knew," replied Tess, shaking her head. "I wish I knew."

At that moment, the frosted glass window across the waiting room slid open to reveal the dour, unsmiling face of an old man. "Monica," he intoned solemnly.

Tess and Andrew looked at each other and the veteran angel drew a deep breath and, standing up, moved to the window. "Hello, baby," she said, her voice dripping with charm. "I'm Tess." She put her hand on the glass and leaned forward with her sunniest smile.

"Hello, baby," was the receptionist's deadpan reply. "I called for Monica."

"Monica's not here yet," Tess replied, her smile never faltering, "but—"

"The glass?" interrupted the receptionist, looking askance at her fingers, smudging the immaculate surface of the frosted partition. "I hate it when anyone touches the glass. Do I go around touching your things? I think not." He slid the glass closed on Tess's surprised expression.

"Well," she said, turning back to Andrew. "That went well."

Monica looked approvingly around the lavishly decorated waiting room. Beautiful oil paintings hung on the walls, all tastefully coordinated with the exquisite furnishings. With delight she noticed a gleaming silver espresso machine in an alcove and, sitting down next to it, began to thumb through a stylish magazine.

But her thoughts were far distant, lingering on the disturbing presence of Kathleen in the hallway outside. Wherever the fallen angel appeared, trouble was not far behind, and Monica shuddered to think back on the many times she had had to confront this embodiment of pure evil in struggles for the souls of those she had been sent to help.

So distracted was the angel by her memories that she didn't notice when a petite blond woman, whose clear blue eyes seemed to carry some secret sorrow, entered the waiting room. Taking a seat next to Monica she smiled and said hello. The angel didn't seem to notice. "Are you all right?" the woman asked again, and at the question, Monica snapped back into reality.

"I'm sorry," she said and smiled. "My name's Monica."

"Jodi," the woman replied, returning the smile. "You seemed a little distracted."

"I was thinking about someone I used to know," said Monica. "I just ran into her."

"An old friend?" asked Jodi.

"Once," Monica responded, as other memories began to flash across her mind. "But that was a long time ago. We've . . . gone our separate ways."

"It's hard to lose an old friend," said Jodi sympathetically.

"Yes, it is," Monica agreed, looking at the woman as if noticing her for the first time. "I don't remember seeing you before," she continued. "Are you a caseworker, too?"

"No," replied the slightly puzzled Jodi. "I'm a file clerk."

Monica nodded. "I didn't know they had file clerks," she said. "Of course, I've been away for a while. I've had fifty cases on Earth so far, but I've been told they don't usually call you in until you've reached a hundred. Do you think maybe they're going to give me a new human form?" she continued, not noticing the increasingly perplexed look on Jodi's face "Or maybe they're going to transfer me to Acts of God. What do you think?"

"I think it means you've come to the right place," was Jodi's cautious response.

"I think so, too," Monica replied happily. "It's taken me some time to get used to this job. But I think I'm finally getting the hang of it."

"I'll bet you change jobs a lot," Jodi said, picking her words carefully.

"Indeed I have," Monica answered. "Some very interesting ones, too."

Twenty minutes later, Jodi sat fascinated as Monica filled her in on the full spectrum of roles she had assumed for her work as an angel on assignment—baseball player, policewoman, singer, waitress, veterinarian, the list went on—"I think my favorite was delivering babies," she concluded.

"You're very . . . versatile," remarked Jodi, as if she were not exactly sure what to believe about this strange woman.

"Thank you," Monica replied. "And how many jobs have you had?"

"One," was Jodi's mystified reply. "File clerk." Hadn't she already told her that?

Tess's fretfulness had reached a new peak of intensity as the minutes continued to slip away and Monica had still failed to appear. Hoping to distract her for at least a moment, Andrew cleared his throat and asked, "This judge. Ruth. You go back a long way with her?"

Tess sighed as her own flood of memories began to rise. "Ruth wasn't always on the High Court," she explained. "She used to be a supervisor, like me. As a matter of fact, she was my supervisor, back when I was a caseworker."

"You didn't . . . get along?" asked Andrew hesitantly.

"We got along just fine," was Tess's terse reply. "Back then, anyway, but then . . . well, Ruth changed. And now she plays everything by the book. Cut and dried. No excuses, no apologies."

Andrew pursed his lips and shook his head. "Monica's got trouble," he admitted.

"But not if we tell Ruth about all the good things she's done," Tess replied, with sudden enthusiasm. "All my years as a caseworker, I never saw an angel more dedicated to her work."

Andrew nodded. "She's terrific," he agreed. "I'm sure Ruth will understand and give her a break."

Tess's face dropped. "Ruth doesn't give anybody a break," she said. "Not these days. Not since . . ." she stopped.

"Not since what?" Andrew asked insistently. "Come on, Tess. What are you holding back?"

A long moment passed as Tess turned to look straight at the Angel of Death, her bright eyes clouded, as she remembered events long since passed but still resonating with meaning and consequence. "A long time ago," she began in a low voice, "Ruth had her own special angel. Kind of like I have Monica. She taught that little angel everything she knew. But one day, only a few centuries ago—"

She stopped as the frosted glass window once again slid open and the same stern face poked out into the waiting room. "The judge will see you now," the receptionist announced dutifully.

"But Monica's not here," objected Andrew. Tess put a hand on his knee to silence him.

"Let's go," she said, rising slowly. "And, whatever you do, don't mention the words 'free will.'" As she walked through the door, she deliberately left a trailing line of fingerprints across the glass partition. With a shocked expression, the receptionist whipped out a spray bottle and a rag and began furiously cleaning the window.

Jodi watched as Monica carefully prepared a delicious cup of espresso from the waiting room machine and, sitting down, savored her first sip with closed eyes.

"You seem to take your coffee very seriously," she remarked.

The angel nodded. "I take everything pretty seriously," she admitted. "It's both my best and my worst quality, I suppose." She looked across at Jodi, noticing for the first time the troubled look in her eyes. "So," she asked gently, "what brings you here today, Jodi?"

Jodi looked away, as if trying to hide her feelings. "It's a long story," she said softly.

"Those are my favorite kind," Monica replied with a smile, taking another sip of coffee.

With a catch in her voice, Jodi began. "I've been having a hard time lately. With a lot of things."

"Helping people through hard times is what I do," Monica interjected. "It's my greatest joy. And, if I do say so, I'm pretty good at it."

"Well," Jodi continued, seemingly encouraged by Monica's kind words and willing ear. "I'm so unhappy at my work, but I don't know what else to do."

"God must have had a reason for putting you in the filing department," the angel replied. "Surely He has something else planned for you down the line. You need to ask Him." She leaned forward. "Tell me, Jodi," she asked. "Have you prayed about it?"

Tess and Andrew took their places at one end of a long conference table in a room lit with bars of slanting light through a half closed Venetian blind. At the other end of the expansive table sat a prim stenographer poised over her machine and an older woman with close-cropped hair dressed smartly in a business suit and exuding an intimidating, no-nonsense air.

"The High Court is now in session," she announced in a measured tone, then with a barely perceptible tip of her head, added, "Hello, Tess."

"Ruth," was Tess's icy reply, then turning, she introduced Andrew. The Angel of Death rose nervously. "It's, um, very nice to meet you, your—"

"Sit down, Junior," Tess ordered, and Andrew quickly obeyed.

"You are Monica's supervisor," Ruth continued with a hard stare at Tess. "Are you not?"

"You know I am, Ruth," Tess replied sharply.

"I only know what's on the record," Ruth snapped back, then turned to the stenographer. "Make a note that Monica is not present for her performance review."

The Judge began to shuffle through papers as Tess turned to Andrew. "She's going to rip us a new halo," she whispered.

Ruth looked up and cleared her throat. "In addition to her tardiness," she began, "Monica's work has shown marked irregularities, especially in regard to Statute Apple-Baker-Delta. I direct your attention to Sub-section Two-Backslash-Six. Her work leaves, shall we say, something to be desired."

"Who says so?" bristled Tess.

"Why you do, Tess," the Judge replied triumphantly, as, from thin air, a thick sheaf of files suddenly appeared in front of Tess. "These are your case reports," she continued. "You're harder on her than anyone."

Tess swallowed hard as she thumbed through the reports, remembering the numerous occasions she had called Monica on the carpet for one or another violation of angelic protocol, most often in connection with letting her heart become too involved in her cases. "Look," she said, a pleading tone entering her voice. "Sometimes I get a little carried away. I only want her to be the best that she can be. But Monica is a great angel, with great promise. I'm sure if you—"

"I don't think you understand the gravity of the situation," was Ruth's imperious interjection. "Since Monica has failed to appear in her own defense, as of this moment, she is officially suspended. All angelic privileges have been revoked and she is stripped of her credentials and her access to power. Wherever she is, she's on her own."

"But," Tess objected, gesturing at the files. "These were nothing more than minor infractions!" She picked up one from the top of the pile. "Here," she continued, shaking it at Ruth from across the table. "In this one all she did was to mistake Jacksonville, Illinois, for Jacksonville, Florida." She shrugged. "It could have happened to anyone."

Ruth shook her head. "The record speaks for itself," she continued implacably. "Monica has completed fifty assignments. In twenty-eight of those I see errors in judgment. That represents a failing grade according to Code Seven, Section—"

"If I may?" Andrew's voice sounded tentative above the clash of the angelic titans. As the others turned to stare at him, he took a deep breath and continued. "I was thinking about Jacksonville," he said. "You know, Florida and Illinois." He turned to Tess. "You know, sometimes Monica does occasionally get her directions a little . . . mixed. Maybe she . . ."

"Go!" commanded Tess, pointing to the door. "Start looking! Now!"

As Andrew rose and hurried out, Tess turned to Ruth. "Let's put our cards on the table here, Ruth," she said. "God gave Monica a heart. And, after two and a half years on the job, she's just starting to learn how to use that precious gift."

"Well," replied Ruth with a hard glint in her eye. "Her time is up."

Monica and Jodi sat huddled in intense conversation when the door to the waiting room suddenly flew open and Andrew charged in. "Monica!" he cried, clearly relieved. "You're in the wrong place. The evaluation is down the hall. And you're really late."

A look of shock passed over the angel's face. "I . . . I am?" she stuttered, and stood suddenly. "I'm sorry, Jodi, but I have to run."

"Now?" Jodi replied, a pleading note in her voice. "No. Please. I mean, the doctor is good and all that, but I was just beginning to feel like you really understood what I was trying to say."

Monica turned back to Andrew. "I can't go," she said. "This woman needs me to stay."

Andrew shook his head, uncertain what to do. "Okay," he said at last. "But we're right down the hall. So hurry up!"

As he rushed out, Jodi took Monica by the hand. "Thank you," she said, tears welling in her eyes. "You're an angel."

"Yes, Jodi," Monica replied, "I am an angel." With a smile she waited for the customary golden glow that marked her unveiling to human eyes. Yet, after a long moment, it failed to appear. Everything was as it had been and for the first time, Monica felt the absence of the divine power that had come with her job. She sighed as Jodi looked on uncomprehendingly. "Listen," Monica continued. "It doesn't matter whether you believe I'm an angel or not. What matters is that you believe God. Believe that He loves you."

"God . . . loves me?" Jodi whispered and began to cry. Yet, even as Monica held her in her arms and stroked her head, the sobbing began to turn to laughter . . . wicked, triumphant laughter. Pulling away in horror, Monica watched as the face of Jodi transformed into that of Kathleen. "Sorry you have to miss your evaluation," the fallen angel said with a sneer. "But at least I've passed mine."

"But . . ." Monica said, her eyes wide, "I don't understand."

"It's simple, Monica," Kathleen replied, standing up and straightening her hair. "My evaluation was based on ruining your evaluation." She walked to the door and, opening it sort of repetitive, threw a last barbed remark behind her. "You may have won our battles," sort of repetitive, was Kathleen's parting shot, "but it looks like I've won the war."

The first thing Monica saw as she rushed breathlessly into the waiting room with its bare walls and frosted glass partition were the dejected faces of her fellow angels. One look at Tess's eyes told the whole story.

"Oh Tess," she cried, "I've been so foolish. It was Kathleen who kept me away. Her evaluation was based on keeping me from mine." She lowered her head in despair. "I guess she won after all."

Tess's eyes flashed indignation. "She most certainly did not!" she exclaimed. "God has a plan. He always does." She rose and put her arm around Monica. "We've been in tougher spots than this before, Angel Girl."

Monica's eyes, filled with tears, looked up at her mentor imploringly. "But I was never the one who got myself out of trouble, Tess," she confessed. "It was God." She looked at the shut door to the conference room. "If only I could get in there and explain myself."

Tess smiled. "You don't need to be in that room to talk to God, Angel Girl. Don't forget about His mercy. It lasts longer than any trouble you're in. You talk to Him. He'll listen." Straightening her shoulders, she moved toward the door. "But there's somebody I've got to do some talking to myself, in the meantime."

Sensing a presence in the room with her, Ruth looked up from her paperwork and saw Tess standing in the fading light at the far end of the conference table. "We're going to talk about what happened back then," Tess asserted in no uncertain terms. "And we're going to find out what changed you from a glorious angel to a pencil-pushing, rule-spouting bureaucrat who forgot why she's here." She leaned across the table, her eyes ablaze. "I want to appeal to the Angel of Angels. Monica was tricked by Kathleen."

At the sound of that name, Ruth's face went pale. "Kathleen," she repeated in a hoarse whisper.

Seeing her stricken countenance, Tess's own face softened. "Ruth," she said softly. "You were the best angel I ever knew. But you were done in by free will."

"Free will?" said Ruth, as if she had heard a sentence of death pronounced. "Did you say free will?"

"You were Kathleen's supervisor," Tess continued relentlessly. "She chose to go over to the other side. It wasn't your fault. She made the decision. And the day she made her choice, you made yours, too. You couldn't trust your heart anymore so you replaced it with rules and regulations. And now you're making every good-hearted angel who comes through that door pay for the one who got away."

Ruth's haughty expression began to crumble and her eyes filled with tears. "I failed," she sobbed. "I loved Kathleen so much, but she just walked away. I lost her forever. It was my fault!"

Tess shook her head. "No it wasn't," she insisted. "But if you don't call in the Angel of Angels, Monica is going to be Kathleen's latest victim."

Ruth looked at her, the tears slowly drying on her cheeks. "I owe you one," she said.

Tess smiled. "That's what friends are for," she replied.

As Monica paced the length of the waiting room, the hallway door opened to allow Kathleen to slink inside. "You still here?" the fallen angel asked with contempt. "No one is going to listen to you, you know."

"It's not them who need to listen," Monica replied with calm certainty as she got to her knees. "It's God."

"Go ahead," Kathleen sneered. "Beg Him for your job."

"Dear God," Monica prayed. "I'm not in the habit of asking for favors, but I need to ask you for one today. Please forgive Kathleen."

"What?" shouted Kathleen. "No! Stop!"

"She lost her way," Monica continued, "and walked away from Your grace. But, no matter what, I know she can't forget Your love and Your mercy."

"Stop it!" shrieked Kathleen. "Stop it!"

"Do with me what you will, Lord," Monica prayed. "But forgive Kathleen."

As the fallen angel rushed from the room, the frosted glass window slid back and the face of the receptionist, awestruck this time, appeared. "He'll see you now," he said in a reverent tone. "The Angel of Angels will see you now."

Monica stood before a large mahogany desk in a vast office lit from some unknown source, as a deep, majestic, yet somehow reassuring voice spoke to her. "Today I've heard many reasons why you shouldn't pass your evaluation," the voice said as Monica looked into the infinitely wise and compassionate face of the Angel of Angels.

"I know," Monica replied, hanging her head.

"But you have presented me with the evidence of your heart, Monica," the Angel of Angels continued. "You put someone before yourself. You did it twice. To help a friend and then to help an enemy. You made a good choice, Monica. Because love is always a good choice."

"So," Monica ventured timidly. "What does this mean?"

"It means you have failed many times," the voice continued. "But you have also loved every time. This would be a dilemma if

God were one to keep score. But He doesn't do that." The Angel of Angels paused as a white dove lit on the windowsill behind the desk. "You have passed your evaluation and we're expanding your duties. You have proven yourself to be a worthy angel."

"Thank you," Monica replied joyfully as she turned to leave.

"One more thing," the voice said as she stood at the threshold of the door. "One cup of coffee in the morning is plenty . . . and try a water process decaf."

A few minutes later Monica rejoined Tess and Andrew in the waiting room where, it seemed, a lifetime had passed in a few short hours. The smiles that passed between them reflected the relief and joy the trio shared as they walked down the hall toward the elevator and out into the burnished afternoon light of the city.

Reunion

The strains of an authentic Dixieland jazz band wafted through the thick branches of the oak trees as the mourners turned curiously to the country road that wound past a stately home on the outskirts of the small town of Wood Ferry. As the strolling musicians came closer and the melody of "When the Saints Go Marching In" became more raucous, a figure emerged around the bend—an attractive black woman, leading the band in a bright yellow dress and holding a bouquet of bobbing balloons.

On the front porch a distinguished lady dressed in dignified dark clothing stared at the approaching revelers with a mix of amusement and irritation. Clarice Mitchell knew at once who was at the head of the noisy procession. It was Megan Brooks, the daughter of her best and oldest friend, Dottie Brooks, in whose memory they had gathered today to honor. She shook her graying head ruefully—Megan always had a little of her mother's mischievous side and today was no exception. Clarice couldn't help but smile to herself. If she knew Dottie—and no one knew her better—a New Orleans–style send-off would have suited her just fine.

As Megan and the band came down the driveway, past the swinging wooden sign that read, CLARICE'S BED, BREAKFAST & BOOKS: HOME OF THE ANNUAL CLARICE MITCHELL POETRY WORKSHOP, another figure appeared on the porch, Clarice's son Sam, handsome and poised with a winning smile and a deep respect for his mother's international face as one of her generation's most influential poets. He returned home from Phoenix, Arizona, where he had moved after college, not just for this sad occasion, but to rekindle an old friendship.

From across the yard, as the prancing Megan looked up to see Sam's familiar face among her mother's mourners, some deeply buried memories began to stir in her heart. Seeing him again was like coming home, and suddenly she remembered a hundred scenes of their shared childhood, recalling with a pang the girlish dreams she had had, that one day they would be married, have children and maybe even live in the little town of Wood Ferry, happily ever after. But that was a lifetime ago, and so much had changed. There was no way she could find her way back to the innocence and simple joy they had once shared.

Sam, too, felt a familiar stirring at the sight of Megan and hurried down the steps to greet her. "Megan," he said, his face breaking into a broad smile. "You look beautiful."

"I bet you say that to all the mourners," she quipped wryly, but behind the irreverence, Sam caught a glimpse of the deep sadness that had brought them together again after all these years. After Megan's husband, Matthew, had died of cancer a few years earlier, her mother was the only family she had left. And now, she, too, was gone, and Sam could see the loneliness etched in the dark skin of his childhood friend.

As they turned to walk up the stairs together, two strangers suddenly approached from across the lawn, one with head of salt-and-pepper hair, the other a wisp of a woman with a ready smile and a melodious Irish accent. Assuming they were among the guests at the memorial service, Sam respectfully introduced himself.

"I'm Tess," said the big woman with the expressive eyes. "And this is my friend Monica. And we're here to register for the Clarice Mitchell Poetry Workshop."

"I'm sorry," replied Sam, "but the workshop has been post-poned. We tried to contact everyone, but, you see, there's been a death. But please, you're welcome to stay a while."

Smiling graciously, the angels accepted and followed Sam through the open door into the well-appointed parlor and book-shop of the famous lady poet.

An hour later, Tess and Monica sat on the sofa talking quietly, as around them, the well-wishers shared their memories of Dottie Brooks.

"You know," Monica mused, "I've always fancied myself some-thing of a poet."

"Oh really," replied Tess with a raised eyebrow. "Well, for your in-formation, Clarice is my assignment."

"Then why am I here?" asked the angel-in-training.

"I'm not sure," shrugged Tess. "But I was told to bring you along."

"Then if that's the plan, it sure can't be wrong." She giggled. "That rhymes."

"Stop that now," scolded Tess. "This is a very solemn occasion for Clarice. Her poetry has transformed souls and inspired entire na-tions. God has given her the words and I've often had the privilege of delivering." She watched as, from across the room, a silver-haired man pulled an envelope from his jacket pocket and began to walk to-ward Clarice. She sighed. "However," Tess continued, "I'm afraid the next message she's going to receive will not come from God . . . but from the grave."

Howard Boyle, the family attorney and longtime friend, ap-proached Clarice cautiously, an envelope held gingerly in his hand. "I just need a minute of your time," he said, drawing the poet away from a small knot of well-wishers and into a corner of the room. "Before she died, Dottie gave me this to give to you," he said, handing over the letter. She specifically told me to wait until after the memorial service. I'm not sure why she didn't give it to you herself, but . . ."

Clarice's dark eyes glittered with tears as she nodded and took the envelope. "Dottie knew I wouldn't have the patience to wait," she said, tucking it away. "But this time, I think I'll do just as she says." She looked around as guests began gathering in the parlor. "I've promised to read a poem for Dottie," she said to the lawyer. "I guess I better get along."

Howard nodded and moved in with the others as Clarice took her place by a bay window and, pulling out a sheet of paper, began to read in deep, rolling tones. "Future days / Promises dreamed / On the whisper of hope / Hold us forever / In your gaze . . ."

As the audience listened, spellbound, Sam caught Megan's eye and gestured for her to join him in the foyer. "I fixed up a very special room for you," he told her in a low voice.

"Anywhere but the attic," she replied.

"Bingo," grinned Sam and, lifting her suitcases, led the way up the stairs.

Sunlight slanted across the pitched roof of a small attic room, comfortably made up with a bed and an antique chest of drawers. On the bedstand a framed picture of teenage Megan with her mother shared space with a photo of Clarice and Dottie, smiling happily into the camera. As Sam set down the luggage, Megan looked up to one of the rafters where a carved heart held the initials, "S.M. + M.B."

"I missed you, Meg," said Sam softly, as he came up behind her.

"Really?" she asked as she turned to face him. "I guess that's why you stopped writing."

Sam shook his head ruefully. "I was a stupid kid then, Meg."

Megan sighed and sat on the edge of the bed. "When Matthew died, I had my mother to talk to," she said. "Now she's gone . . . and . . ."

"You have me," Sam interjected, sitting next to her. Reaching up, he brushed a lock of hair from her face. As Megan tentatively laid her head on his shoulder, he kissed her hair and let a long moment of silence pass. He could feel her sorrow, her loneliness and something else—a deep exhaustion that seemed to drain away her once vibrant energy. He would make it all right, he promised himself. He would bring happiness back into the life of the only girl he ever really loved.

The next morning, Tess and Clarice sat on the terrace, the remains of breakfast on a small table before them. Clarice, for reasons she couldn't quite put her finger on, was immediately taken with Tess—there was something so familiar about her voice. So she had invited Tess and Monica to stay over a few days at the bed and breakfast. The angels, in turn, had convinced their hostess to go on with her renowned poetry workshop, if for no other reason than to honor the memory of Dottie. But Monica had another reason, as well: A chance to prove her dubious poetic abilities to Tess. Even as they enjoyed the bright sunshine of a new day, they noticed Sam and Megan strolling across the verdant lawn together.

"Megan told me she and Sam were once high-school sweethearts," Tess remarked.

Clarice nodded, a smile breaking through the lingering sorrow of yesterday's memorial service. "Sam's always been a little hard to pin down. Maybe he's ready now." The smile faded as she tried to hold back a fresh flood of tears. "Dottie and I always talked about sharing grandchildren . . ." She stopped, trying to collect herself. "I'm sorry," she continued after a moment. "Dorothy and I went through forty years together. School, careers, husbands, children . . ."

Tess rose and put her arms around the grieving woman. "You go ahead and cry, baby," she said soothingly.

After a moment, Clarice took a deep breath and, reaching into her pocket, pulled out the letter Howard had given her the day before. "This is from Dorothy," she said, her voice barely above a whisper. "I know I should read it, but I don't think I can do it alone." She handed the envelope to Tess. "Would you read it for me?"

Nodding, Tess took the letter and began reading. "Dear Friend," she began, "Thought you'd heard the last of me, I'll bet. But don't you ever think I've gone away for good. We've shared too much in this life. And that's what this letter is about, the life I've left behind. I need you to look after my girl, Clarice. Don't let that happy face of hers fool you. She's in a lot of pain and not just because of me. Her husband didn't die of cancer. He died of AIDS. And now Megan has the virus, too."

A gasp escaped Clarice's lips and a fresh sob expressed a heart filled to overflowing with sorrow. Tess, also stunned by the news, looked up. "Do you want me to stop?" she asked, but Clarice shook her head and the angel returned to the letter. "Clarice, please don't let her know that I've told you. Megan's very private. When she's ready, she'll let you know herself, but I want you to be prepared. She thinks she can do it alone, but she can't. I need you to be her guardian angel. You were there when I delivered Megan into this world. Now, I deliver her into your care, once again. Love, Dottie."

In anguish, Clarice looked out across the lawn, where Megan and Sam stood talking. She turned to Tess with an expression that mingled grief with another overpowering feeling . . . that of fear.

Sam and Megan looked admiringly at the classic '57 T-Bird they had unwrapped from under its car cover in the garage. "Isn't she a beauty?" Sam asked as he opened the door and sat behind the wheel. "It hasn't been driven in years. In fact, the last time was—"

"The prom!" Megan interjected and they both laughed. Sam put the key in the ignition and the engine rumbled weakly. "Oh well," sighed Megan. "We'll have to take a ride in the country some other time."

"Why don't you let me give it a try?" came a voice from behind them and they turned to see Monica standing in the driveway. Opening the hood of the car, she closed her eyes as a warm light brightened around the motor. "Edsels are old and Packards, Jurassic," she recited, still practicing her paltry poetic skills, "but never lose faith, 'cause your T-Bird's a classic!" She signaled to Sam who cranked the car to life. "Have a good drive," she said, waving, as he pulled the car onto the tree-lined country road.

An hour later, the pair sat on the fender of the old T-Bird, parked by the side of a lush green pasture where cattle grazed and birds chirped in the low-lying branches of a spreading oak.

"I'll need to be going back home to Phoenix as soon as things get back to normal with Mom," Sam was saying, then turned to Megan with a glint in his eyes. "Maybe I'll take this old buggy back with me." He paused, then hinted heavily, "Of course, I'd need a co-pilot for a trip that long."

Megan turned away to hide the troubled expression on her face. "I'm getting hungry, aren't you?" she said, trying to change the subject.

Sam sighed. "That's what I love about you, Meg," he said. "You're such a romantic."

"That's what you said fifteen years ago," she reminded him.

"What?" he countered. "That you're a romantic or . . . that I love you." He reached out to draw her close but she resisted his embrace.

"You left me, Sam," she said bluntly. "I'm not blaming you, but . . . we can't go back."

Sam nodded understandingly. "I know you still miss Matthew," he said. "But you've still got your whole life ahead of you." He waited for a response and, when it didn't come, added softly, "Meg, I want us to be together." He turned and took her by the shoulders. "I knew when you'd married Matt that I'd made a huge mistake."

He searched her eyes, but she avoided his gaze. "Okay," he said at last. "I get it. Maybe this is all too soon."

"No, Sam," Megan replied, her anger and frustration rising. "It's too late! Too damn late!" She stopped and took a deep breath. She owed him an explanation. "Matthew didn't die of cancer," she continued in a low voice. "Before we met, he'd gotten into drugs and used needles. He'd kicked the habit long before we were married, but what he didn't know . . . what I didn't know . . ." she turned away, unable to face him as she spoke the next words. "Sam, Matt died of AIDS." She turned back now, to gaze directly at him. "And I've tested HIV positive." Sam, a stunned expression on his face, took an unconscious step backward. "I only have the virus so far," she continued. "Sometimes I can even forget about it for a while. Like today." She stopped, still searching his eyes. "Sam, please say something."

"Meg . . . ," he stammered, "I . . . don't know . . . what to say . . ."

"That's okay," Megan replied with a bitter edge to her voice. "Nobody ever does." She straightened, stepping away from the car. "Why don't you drive back?" she said quietly. "I feel like walking for a spell." She moved off quickly to keep him from seeing the tears in her eyes.

The house was dim with afternoon shadows when Megan returned to find Clarice sitting alone working on her poetry.

"We were worried about you," the older woman said, setting down her pen as her old friend's daughter entered.

"I'm fine," Megan replied. Then, looking around, asked, "Did Sam get back all right?"

Clarice paused, searching for the right words. She sighed. There was nothing else to do but tell it straight. "Child," she said. "Sam left. He came back and said he was taking the car to Phoenix. He was . . . in a hurry."

Megan blinked back her pain, but only nodded at the news. She wasn't surprised. Nothing surprised her anymore. "I guess I better start sorting through my mom's stuff," she said and, turning quickly to hide her face, left Clarice to her unsettled thoughts.

Outside, Tess and Monica watched as Megan moved with grim determination through the boxes of her mother's belongings in the garage. "How could Sam leave her like that?" Monica asked the elder angel.

"Did he leave?" Tess replied. "Or did she let him go?"

Monica shook her head sadly. "Either way, the result is the same. Two broken hearts." After a moment, her face brightened as she was struck with an angelic inspiration. "Unless . . ."

"No way, Angel Girl," Tess warned her. "Don't you go around flapping your wings and scaring people into living happily ever after."

"I just want to do something constructive," pleaded Monica.

"You can talk to Megan," Tess relented. "Just make sure you keep that halo hidden."

Monica nodded and, saying a silent prayer, approached Megan where she knelt, holding a pair of plaster of paris hand molds, one etched with her name, the other with Sam's. "You and Sam have a lot of memories, don't you?" Monica asked.

Megan nodded. "I was going to be Queen of the United States and Sam was going to be an intergalactic pirate." She shrugged and tossed the hand molds into a box of discards.

"Megan," Monica said quietly after a long moment. "I know about . . . your condition."

Megan looked sharply at her. "I don't want anyone else to find out," she warned.

"Are you sure that's—" the angel began.

Megan cut her off with a wave of her hand. "It's better if every-one finds out when it's over," she insisted.

"But is that fair to the people who love you?" persisted Monica.

"They can't handle it," Megan replied bitterly. "Sam couldn't. But I can. It's better going through this alone."

"No," the angel replied evenly. "I don't believe it is."

The sound of an approaching car turned both of their attentions to the driveway where the familiar grill of the T-Bird caught a glint of late afternoon sunlight. In the front passenger seat were several books detailing the diagnosis and treatment of AIDS. "I got as far as the Pennsylvania Turnpike," Sam said sheepishly as he climbed out of the car and approached a stunned Megan. Monica, suddenly, was nowhere to be seen. "Meg," he continued as he stood before her, cupping her face in his hands, "I was stupid to let you get away once. But it's not going to happen again. I loved you since the second grade, and I still love you. I'll always love you." He paused and, taking a deep breath, plunged on. "Will you marry me, Meg?"

His words seemed to rock her on her feet. "How can I say yes?" she asked, her voice trembling.

"Tell me this," Sam replied. "If you didn't have this illness, what would your answer be?"

She looked deeply into his eyes. "It would be yes," she said emphatically.

He grabbed her and held her tightly, then pulled back and captured her with his frank gaze. "Then what are we really talking about?" he asked. "There's no telling how long any of us have. I could be hit by a bus tomorrow. The same day you'd be leaving town on because I'd throw myself in front of it. I know there's going to be tough times ahead. But I love you and I want to be there for you."

"If you want to be there for me," Megan replied in a whisper, "then just be my friend."

Sam shook his head. "A friend can't be there like a husband," he retorted. "Marriage is a commitment . . . a declaration to the world that this is the one person I've chosen above all, over others. You're that person, Meg. I will love you and care for you . . ."

"Until death do us part?" she asked in a small voice.

He nodded, smiling. "That's the vow I want to make."

The two angels sat at the dinner table with a distracted and distant Clarice, the evening meal over and a bright full moon just beginning to rise over the tops of the trees. Tess and Monica exchanged a worried look. The distinguished poet, so gifted with words, seemed to be having trouble finding words to express the swirl of emotions that had overcome her in the past few days. It was only when the loud pop of a champagne cork sounded from the next room that Clarice seemed to snap back into the present.

A moment later, Sam and Megan burst in, one carrying a foaming bottle, the other, two handfuls of long-stemmed glasses. "I want to propose a toast." As he poured out the bubbly, Sam announced, "To Megan Brooks, who today has made me the happiest man in the world." He turned to Clarice. "Mom," he continued. "You can give us your blessing now. We'll take the poem at the wedding."

Clarice set her glass down with a loud clink and stood up, "No," she said loudly and the word echoed through the room like a gunshot. She turned to Megan. "I know you have the AIDS virus," she said, her voice dark with anger. "Your mother wrote me a letter. How can you be so selfish? You know I can't condone this. I've lost your mother and I'm going to lose you. But I will not lose my son as well!" Her voice resounded through the house as, tears streaming down her face, she turned and rushed up the stairs.

A long and painful moment passed. "Meg," Sam said, at last. "This doesn't change a thing."

"No," Megan said, her voice flat and the light in her eyes flickering dimly. "She's right. This will never work. I should never have hoped it would." Silently, she, too, turned to leave.

Clarice sat alone in her study, dark except for the moonbeams streaming through an open window. The poet had no words left to shape or explain the strange twists taken by life and death. And in the silence that ensued, all she could feel was the emptiness that had taken up residence in her heart.

Suddenly, she sensed a presence behind her and, turning, saw Tess, lit in an unearthly golden light. "There was a poem you tried to write once," said the angel, "when you were sitting alone in your daddy's barn. But you were missing a word. Then you tilted your head and listened to the wind through the rafters. And I whispered that word."

Clarice's eyes lit up at the recollection. "Joy," she breathed. "It's you. You're the voice I've heard all my life."

Tess nodded. "I've only been the messenger. The words have always come from the Poet." She took a step forward. "I am an angel, Clarice. And it has been my privilege to deliver God's inspiration to direct your work and fulfill your gift. Words have flowed from Him to you and on into the hearts of the meek and the mighty. You have used your gifts to lift up and restore. But now, when God wants to restore your family, you've closed your heart. I could yell God's words at the top of my voice, but you won't hear them until you let go of your fear."

"But I have a right to be fearful," Clarice insisted. "This is a matter of life and death."

"No," countered Tess. "This is a matter of life *or* death. There is a time to live and a time to die. This is Sam and Megan's time to live and to love. And you must let them."

"I don't think I can," Clarice sobbed.

"You must stop listening to fear, Clarice," Tess urged gently. "Open up those ears of yours and listen to the Poet. Maybe you don't want to give your blessing to those two, but He does." She pointed to the table where a beautiful fountain pen had appeared. Then, as Clarice watched in amazement, a piece of parchment and length of beautiful satin ribbon floated softly down from the heavens.

Clarice closed her eyes, then, opening them again, picked up the pen and held it, poised over the blank parchment. For a long moment the world seemed held in perfect silence until she heard the sound of wind stirring the trees outside. She looked to the window, where a white dove had alighted. Slowly she lowered the pen, writing out first one word, then another and another, all in the elegant hand of a master craftsman.

The day broke bright and clear as, once again, a crowd of friends and special guests gathered at Clarice's Bed, Breakfast, & Books, where a New Orleans band played a celebratory tune on the front lawn.

Megan, radiant in her bridal gown, stood next to her new husband, holding his arm as, before them, her mother-in-law carefully slipped a satin ribbon from a parchment scroll and began to read the words written there. The poem echoed the feelings of everyone who heard it on that very special occasion, as each stanza brought into being the truth and beauty that found their truest expression in the love of a husband and wife. It was poetry in its purest form—the vocabulary of the heart, spoken in a universal language.

"I don't know why we can't stay for some cake," Monica complained as she and Tess headed for their trusty Cadillac after the ceremony.

"You know very well why," Tess retorted. "So nobody has to hear any of that so-called poetry of yours."

"It's not such a bad poem," Monica protested as she began to recite, "Roses are red / Napkins are handy / Weddings are nifty / 'Cause they give you free candy . . ."

"Dear Lord in heaven," Tess sighed as she steered down the winding road and over the crest of a hill.

Til We Meet Again

Monica stood at the front door of the modest suburban home watching the autumn leaves from a large oak fall gently to the ground and listening to the fading echo of the doorbell chime. She was about to begin her new assignment, and as she waited, she remembered what Tess had told her earlier about the Carpenter family.

They had been sitting on the front stoop of the house, she and Tess and Andrew, the Angel of Death, watching as a doctor with a black bag hurried up the walkway and was quickly ushered inside. "There's going to be a death in his family," Tess was telling them. "No doubt about it. It is Joe Carpenter's time."

Monica looked puzzled. "But Andrew is here," she said. "Why did you call for me?"

"You have been called to attend the death of a good man," was the senior angel's reply. "Andrew can handle his transition. But there's a secret in this house that must be swept out before he goes. It's one of those 'family secrets' that colored every part of their lives and they didn't even know it. You'll find out soon enough what it is. But there's a problem. This secret must be put to rest before that man is, or the family he devoted his life to building will shatter to pieces the very minute he leaves this Earth."

Andrew looked around at the peaceful setting. "Is this how he wanted to go?" he asked.

Tess nodded. "Yes," she replied. "At home. With his family gathered around him." She turned to Monica. "Your job is to see that they don't kill one another first."

Inside the Carpenter home, three children had gathered, summoned back by the impending death of their father. The oldest, Kate, was dressed in a no-nonsense business suit, her hair perfectly in place and a briefcase close by her side. Her brother, Chris, was a tall, affable man in his early forties, whose good-nature seemed undercut not only by the solemnity of the occasion, but other, troubling and more personal worries.

The youngest was Kim, an attractive blonde causally dressed in jeans and a leather jacket, who had only arrived a few minutes before from one of the far distant locations that her work as a journalist took her to. Kim, too, seemed troubled—by the quickly deteriorating condition of her beloved dad, by her return, after so many years, to the house where she had grown up and by the feelings that stirred inside her as she gazed at the family piano in the parlor. It was there, on so many evenings, that the Carpenter clan would gather to sing the songs her father had loved so well, especially the melancholy air, "Til We Meet Again." Each of them would take a different vocal harmony and they blended beautifully. All, that is, except for Kim. When they sang in four-part harmony, there was no part for her to sing, and she would feel left out of these family gatherings. She would listen from under the piano where she sat, with her knees up under her chin, wondering why she felt so distant and separate from her brother and sister, her mother and father.

It was a feeling that returned now as Dr. Chappell, the family physician for as long as she could remember, came down the stairs, his eyes lighting up as he saw her. "Kimberly Ann," he enthused. "I thought you were on your way to some distant world conflict."

"I turned around in New York as soon as I got word," she explained as she embraced Dr. Chappell. "I thought I'd see you at the hospital." She searched his eyes. "How is he?"

"Well, he's dying, honey," the doctor replied. "But he's not at the hospital. He's here. You see, when he had that stroke last year, he made out a living will. No extraordinary measures. No intravenous feedings. And he wanted to die here, at home, with some dignity."

"He belongs in a hospital," said Kate, from between tight lips. "I think we should wait for Mother to come home, before we make any decisions about this will of his." Kim turned to look at her sister. The years had not been kind to her, with lines of disapproval and disappointment beginning to etch her face. "That's what comes from trying to control the whole world and everything in it," Kate thought to herself.

"There're no decisions to make," the doctor gently reminded her. "This is his choice and the living will is a legal document."

Kim turned to her brother. "Where is Mom?" she asked, so preoccupied until that moment she hadn't noticed the absence of her mother's strong, sometimes overpowering, presence.

Chris shrugged. "She picked this, of all weekends, to visit Aunt Laura in Florida. Who knew he'd get worse?" He lowered his eyes, as if he found it hard to say the next words. "I volunteered to stay with Dad. I've . . . been staying downstairs for a while. Carol and I separated a few weeks ago."

"What?" replied a shocked Kim. "Nobody told me."

"Mother told me," Kate interjected primly. "But then again, I try to stay in touch with this family."

Dr. Chappell cleared his throat. "I requested a nurse from the hospice service," he explained to them as, in that moment, the doorbell Monica had rung began to chime. "I'll get that," he said and returned a minute later with the angel in tow. "Perfect timing," he continued as they walked into the parlor. "This is Monica, the visiting nurse."

"Hello," Monica said with a smile. "I'm sorry to be here. I hope I can help." Seeing the discomfort and tension on their faces, she added, "The doctor tells me your father is going to die and that he knows it. You have an unusual opportunity to make this occasion something special. Most people never have that chance." A long silence trailed her as she turned and followed the doctor up the stairs to her patient.

Joe Carpenter lay motionless on his deathbed as an oxygen generator hissed softly and the autumn sun leaked through blinds drawn down over the window. Monica sat by his side, watching his face intently, when Kim appeared at the door and stepped inside. "Asleep?" she asked and Monica nodded. Sitting carefully at the edge of the bed, Kim spent a long moment staring at the wasted countenance of her father and then turned to Monica. "What did you mean," she wondered, "when you said we have an opportunity to make this special."

The angel thought carefully before responding. "Death is the most real thing that ever happens on Earth," she said at last. "It's awesome and profound, like birth. A soul passes from one realm to another. You can welcome death with respect or fight it with fear and regret. Dying with regret, I've learned, is the worst of all." She paused, than added, "for everyone."

As if swimming to the surface of a deep pool, Joe suddenly let out a gasp and opened his eyes. "Dad?" said Kim, leaning close. "It's Kimmie. I'm here." Monica rose and silently withdrew from the room. "I don't know when I'm going to get another chance to be alone with you," Kim continued. "I just want you to know . . . if you have to go, I understand. I don't want you to hurt." She took his hand and squeezing it, was surprised to feel her father's fingers tighten around her own.

"Important . . ." the dying man wheezed. "You need to know . . . have to tell you . . . the truth . . . not so bad . . ."

"What, Daddy?" Kim asked desperately. "What truth. What are you trying to say?"

From downstairs the harsh voice of her sister suddenly startled her. "Kim," Kate was shouting. "We need to talk. Now!"

"Can't it wait?" Kim called back.

"Now," came the answer and Kim sighed. "I'm back in the house ten minutes and she's already acting like my mother." She patted her father's hand. "I'll be right back, Daddy."

Joe's eyes followed his daughter as she left, then widened as, a moment later, a strange man in a white suit and surrounded by a golden glow entered and leaned over the bed.

"Hello, Mr. Carpenter," the apparition said. "My name is Andrew. I'm an angel and I'm here to help you make this passage."

"Death?" Joe murmured and when Andrew nodded, the dying man shuddered. "Afraid . . ." he whimpered.

"Do I look scary, Mr. Carpenter?" Andrew kindly asked. "Please don't be afraid. We're going to take this in steps. Some of them won't be easy, but there's nothing to fear. Believe me."

A sound behind him drew Andrew's attention to Joe's son Chris, standing in the doorway. Like his sister before, Chris quietly entered and sat on the edge of the bed, unaware of the presence of the Angel of Death in the room. A long moment passed as Chris tried to find words to express what he was feeling until, at last, Andrew stepped in to help. "You know, Chris," he said in a voice that his spirit could hear. "This is it . . . your last hours with your father. Better say it now."

Chris blinked, as if an idea had suddenly come to him. "I wanted to thank you, Dad," he said. "You taught me a lot. You're a good man and you lived a good life."

"Did you ever think of him as a strong man?" Andrew prompted.

Chris wrinkled his brow. "Maybe I never thought of you as a strong man," he confessed. "Patient, maybe. But how could a strong man live with a woman like Mom?"

"Maybe that's the only kind of man who could?" Andrew suggested.

Chris leaned closer. "But, all of a sudden I'm starting to think it takes more than strength to stick with it." Tears began to well in his eyes. "Was it worth it, Dad? Hanging in there all those years. What did you get for it?"

Joe could only stare at his son, his eyes longing to answer the question. At last, the dying man looked over to Andrew, who once more spoke to Chris in the silent language of angels. "He got you."

It was late that night when Tess appeared in the room to check on the progress her two apprentice angels were making. All three were now bathed in heavenly light, visible only to Joe as they stood by his bedside.

"Mr. Carpenter," Tess began with a gentle smile. "I believe your time is at hand. It's going to be a long night, but you've got the best angels in the business handling this. And I promise you, God has heard your prayers. We're going to get this thing settled up real good before you leave."

The old man could only blink to convey his gratitude to the elder angel.

The morning light found Kim and Chris sitting a bedside vigil with Monica. While Kim dozed fitfully in an armchair, Chris carefully polished a pair of old shoes he had found in his father's closet. The scene was somber, but somehow peaceful until Kate announced herself by bustling in and pulling back the curtains.

"Why is it all closed up in here, like death?" she demanded.

Kim woke and, sitting up, replied sarcastically, "It's a theme party, Kate."

Chris stifled a snicker as Kate glared at them. "I hope to God he didn't hear that," she sputtered and, noticing the shoes in Chris's hand for the first time, demanded, "What are you doing?"

"I'm getting his suit ready," her brother replied, pointing to pair of pants and a jacket hanging on the closet door. He glared back at Kate and added defiantly, "For his funeral." He turned to his father. "This is the one you wanted, right, Dad?" he asked loudly.

"This is outrageous!" Kate spat furiously. "It's cruel."

"Why?" countered Kim, jumping up and matching her sister's anger. "He's dying. He knows it and we know it. Why can't we talk about something real for once in this family? This is what he wants. To die with us. But he can't if we pretend it's not happening. You're in denial, Kate. Serious denial. You can't come in here and make every decision just because you're the oldest. Who do you think you are?"

"I'm his daughter!" was Kate's seething reply.

"Well," Kim retorted, "so am I."

"No you're not!" Kate said, and an instant later held her hand to her mouth as if she wanted to recall the words she had blurted out.

On the bed Joe groaned when, from behind them, a voice was heard querulously asking, "What the hell is going on here?"

All three children, along with the angel in attendance, turned as a stunned silence descended in the room. "Hi, Mom," Chris said, with an awkward smile.

The family stood frozen under the stern glare of Elizabeth Carpenter, standing in the doorway with her suitcases at her side. "Will someone please tell me why I can't take a few days for myself for the first time in six years without this whole family falling apart?" she demanded.

"Is it true, Mommy?" Kim asked in a barely audible voice. "He's not my father?"

For a long moment the children held their breath as their mother seemed to sway under the impact of Kim's question. She closed her eyes, but there was no way to block out the reckoning she had been expecting for forty years. "No," she said at last and the word hung in the air like a poisonous fume.

"Oh, my God," Kim moaned, burying her face in her hands. "My God." She looked up at the others standing like statues around her. "This explains everything," she continued reproachfully. "Now I know why I never felt like I was part of this family, because I wasn't."

Elizabeth looked at Monica, acknowledging her presence for the first time. "Tell me straight, nurse," she said. "What are we looking at?"

"A few hours," the angel replied. "He's had a series of small strokes. He can hear you, but he can't respond. Except with his eyes."

"He's got great eyes," Elizabeth said tearfully. "That's all we ever needed to communicate." She sat on the bed next to her husband. "We've got a mess here, Joe," she said softly. "I've got to clean this up and I'll get back to you." She looked up at her children. "I'm going to make myself a cup of tea," she continued with an eerie calm. "There will be a family conference in the kitchen in five minutes."

Kate and Chris rose to leave, but Kim lingered, moving to the bedside of the man she called Daddy, and leaning down close to his familiar, but now pale and wrinkled face. "Is this what you were trying to tell me, Daddy?" she asked, and in response the dying man's eyes filled with tears. "You know," Kim continued, as she, too, began to weep. "In some funny way, I think I always knew."

"Family secrets are like that," Monica ventured. "Nobody talks. But everybody knows."

Kim nodded. "All I ever wanted was to feel comfortable in this family," she explained. "Whenever I'd blow out the candles on my birthday cake, that was my wish. And whenever we'd pray at Thanksgiving, that's what I'd ask for."

"I'd put my money on the prayer over the candles," Monica replied with a smile as she sat down next to her. "Every prayer gets answered, Kim. Sometimes the answer is 'no.' But sometimes the answer may be 'not yet.' "

She watched as Kim kissed her father's forehead and, rising, followed the others downstairs.

"That was good," was Andrew's angelic appraisal, as he reappeared in the room and, turning to the dying man, added, "Wasn't she great, Joe?"

As Joe blinked in reply, Monica's expression grew thoughtful. "Andrew," she asked, "what do you think the chances are for a special dispensation?"

The Angel of Death shook his head. That was one tall order. "Oh, man," he said. "I don't know . . ."

"It's worth a try," Monica replied with a twinkle in her eye. "Because sometimes the answer is 'yes'!"

Elizabeth stood by the kitchen sink, her cup of tea growing cold on the counter. "Those Friday afternoons when I was supposed to be at my book club," she was saying in a low voice, then shook her head slowly. "I spent them with Tony."

Kim gasped. "Daddy's old partner?" she said, shocked and angered. "How could you do this to him?"

"I'm not proud of it, Kimberly," Elizabeth replied. "But I've forgiven myself. I hope one day you'll forgive me, too."

Kim only glared at her in reply. "How long did this last?" she wanted to know.

"A couple of years," Elizabeth replied. "After that your father took another job . . . more work for less pay. That's when I knew he had found out. And that's when it ended."

"But you didn't say anything," Chris interjected.

She shook her head. "We never discussed it. He could have thrown me out . . ." her voice cracked as she tried hard to suppress the sudden surge of emotion. "But he kept on loving me instead." She turned to Kate. "How did you know?"

Kate pursed her lips. "Remember when I dated Billy Warchowsky? His father owned the Riverview Motel. It wasn't much of a leap to figure out the rest."

"Me being 'the rest,' " was Kim's sarcastic rejoinder. "So I guess I'm not a Carpenter anymore."

"Of course you are," Kate snapped back.

Chris shook his head. "Man," he said, admiringly. "Dad is really something. If it were me, I would have walked out."

"You *did* walk out," Elizabeth reminded him. "On your own marriage. That's what happens these days. People just bail out when there's a bump in the road. In the old days we couldn't afford to break up just because things got tough."

"That's easy for you to say," Kim commented derisively. "The old days obviously weren't that tough for you."

It was Elizabeth's turn to glare. "You can't judge a marriage until you're in it," she snapped.

"And you can't judge a family until you're in it," Kim shot back.

Suddenly the bickering and recrimination stopped as, from the parlor door, an eerie sound filled the house. The familiar notes of an old family favorite were being played on the piano and the Carpenters listened, each overcome by a flood of memories as they listened to "Til We Meet Again."

Joe Carpenter, miraculously revived and dressed in a bathrobe, sat at the bench, his long pale finger flowing effortlessly over the ivory keys. A blissful look suffused his features as he glanced up at Monica and Tess, standing beside him and bathed in a soft golden light.

The family rushed in from the kitchen, led by Elizabeth who stopped dead in her tracks, the iron control she maintained beginning to crack at the strange and unearthly sight that greeted them from the parlor.

"Who are you?" she stammered, staring at Tess. "And will someone please explain what's going on here?"

Tess smiled. "Monica and I are angels," she stated, as if it were the most natural of occurrences to discover heavenly beings paying a visit. "God has sent us, along with another angel, to bring your father home. But we all have some business to do before that." She smiled at Elizabeth, adding, "You may want to sit down."

"I'm confused," Elizabeth admitted as she accepted the invitation.

"That's abundantly clear," Tess agreed. "But God is not the author of confusion. He likes to write happy endings. And they're so much better than the endings we try to write for ourselves. Like pretending that something never happened."

"What do you mean?" Elizabeth asked, but the anger in her voice was undercut with sorrow.

"You want to make this all go away," Tess continued and, turning, smiled at Kim. "But you had this girl running around every day reminding you of what you'd done. You couldn't let her get close. You couldn't let anyone get close. Loving them was too dangerous. You had to control them to protect your secret. And now your family has paid the price." She looked at Chris. "You've got a son who's mistaken his father's strength for weakness." Her gaze fell next on Kate. "You've got a daughter who can't tell where you end and she begins." Turning to Kim, she continued. "And you've got a little girl here, crying out to know that she belongs in this house."

"Not to mention this wonderful man who deserves to die in peace," added Monica, putting her arm on Joe's shoulder.

"It's too late for that," Elizabeth said with a tremor in her voice.

"No," Tess replied. "The peace is just beginning."

"Then Dad is okay and this is some sort of miracle?" Chris asked.

Tess smiled. "Technically speaking, this is what we call a 'special dispensation.' Your father is going to die, Chris. You may conclude from the presence of angels that this is not a bad thing."

"You know," said Monica, stepping forward, "as families go, you've got a pretty good one here. But it has nearly broken under the strain of this secret. Kate has missed the joy of being a sister because she was trying so hard to protect her mother. Chris' suspicions about his mother have now become terribly destructive suspicions about his wife." She turned to Kim. "And you knew something was different about you, but you could only guess what it was. And you always guessed wrong." The angel's smile was like a radiant blessing. "There's nothing wrong with you, Kim. In fact, you are a shining example of how God can take the saddest things and turn them into something beautiful."

"That's true," piped in a weak but clear voice next to her. The family turned as one to Joe, the same look of utter amazement on each of their faces. "I always knew, Elizabeth," he said, without rancor, to his wife. "I didn't like it, but I loved you so much. I just prayed you'd come back. And you did." He turned to Kim, with a sparkle of pure love in his eyes. "And look who you brought with you!"

"Oh, Daddy!" sobbed Kim.

"It hurt," Joe continued, realizing that his time of dispensation was short-lived. "I won't deny that. But I decided that being together—all of us—was more important than being right." He turned to his son. "If that makes me weak, than I'm guilty." He nodded encouragingly to Chris. "Go home, son," he urged him. "Give it your best. It will be enough." His large, moist eyes next fell to Kate. "You can't fool me, Katherine," he told her. "I know you're not such a tough bird. You were the first baby I ever loved and you always will be. Share it with the rest of them, will you?"

Joe looked at his family, over the top of the piano, with its collection of photos from the life they had shared. "I'm proud of you all," he said, his voice growing weaker. "All your instincts acted to preserve this family. But it will only survive in truth now. Don't be afraid of the truth, to speak it, to look at it, to live it. I've seen a little corner of it myself in the past few days . . ." he looked up trustingly to Monica and Tess, "and it's beautiful. Remember this," he told his family, "I had a choice. I chose to love. And it's been a privilege to be your father." His eyes fell on Elizabeth. "And to be your husband."

"Oh God!" his wife sobbed. "Please, God, don't let him go. I love you, Joe. Please forgive me."

With his strength quickly fading, Joe managed one last smile. "I did that a long time ago," he said.

Joe was back in his bed, his body motionless and his breath so shallow it hardly moved the sheets. His family had gathered around him.

"Can he hear us?" asked Elizabeth in an awed whisper.

Tess nodded. "He can, but he's too busy to answer."

"Busy?" echoed Chris.

"There is a moment at which a man removes himself from this place and gets down to the business of dying," Tess explained. "His spirit is straining to leave a body that doesn't want to release it."

"Is he in pain?" asked Kim.

"The pain is over," Tess assured her. "There is more death here now than life."

"Is he here?" Kate wanted to know. "The other angel?"

Monica nodded, looking over to Andrew who also stood, invisible to the humans, at Joe's bedside. "He's right here," she said. "He's in touch with the part of your father's spirit that can't communicate with you."

Chris leaned in close. "We'll see you again," he said to Joe, then turning to Monica, asked, "Won't we?"

Monica looked at Andrew who turned to the dying man as if in a deep conversation. "Your father says you can count on it," she told them, as the Angel of Death passed along the message to her. "And Andrew tells me that Joe has a special request." She smiled at them all. "Sing the song."

A long moment passed until Elizabeth drew a deep breath and turned to her children. "Chris you take the bass," she said. "Kate, you take the alto. I'll take the tenor." She looked lovingly at her youngest daughter. "And Kim, you take your daddy's part."

"Smile the while I kiss you sad adieu," they sang, their voices blending harmoniously. "When clouds roll by / I'll come to you / So wait and pray each night for me / Til we meet again . . ."

As a doorway opened into golden light, Joe Carpenter stopped for a moment before following Andrew through to the other side. Turning around he looked one last time at his family, his eyes full of love. Then he smiled, put his arm around Andrew and walked out into the light while his family sang in perfect harmony.

The Face on the Barroom Floor

Everett Clay, whose aristocratic bearing was enhanced by an elegant and expensive suit, sat in disbelieving silence in the office of his father, Benjamin, also well-dressed but, unlike his son, with the bearing and demeanor of a man who had worked hard to achieve success. He could hardly believe what the old man was saying. This couldn't be happening to him. Just a few hours earlier, before he'd been summoned to this morning meeting at the office of Clay International, the most pressing decision he had to make was whether to spend his next holiday on his yacht or skiing in Aspen.

It wasn't as if Everett didn't have problems in his privileged and lavish life. There was his son, Carson, for example, who had somehow managed to burn through five million dollars of his grandfather's fortune on some harebrained Internet start-up. Yes, it was true that Carson had difficulty understanding the value of money. He was like his father in that respect. But as long as the multinational enterprise founded by his great-grandfather, Jack, continued to be one of the most successful manufacturing firms in the world, neither Everett nor his profligate son really had much to worry about.

That is until this morning. As he looked around the office, decorated with displays of the various buttons upon which the Clay empire was built, he tried to make sense of what his father was telling him. He had never been close to Benjamin Clay, and while he had respect for his old man, he was also of the opinion that his father worked entirely too hard. With all the wealth accumulated by the Clay family over the past hundred years, wasn't it well past time for them all to enjoy it a little? Or, as in Everett's case, a lot?

"Life has been just one long party for you, Everett," his father had said, after Everett had been ushered in. "You have played and spent and drunk your way through the last sixty years and, if you don't die of a heart attack, you'll die from sheer overexposure to unlimited wealth. And when that happens, it won't be your fault. It will be mine."

Everett had heard it all before and had learned it was best to just let the old guy blow off some steam. He listened with half an ear as he returned to the vexing problem of his summer vacation plans.

"There's a story in the Bible," Benjamin Clay continued, "about the prodigal son. Perhaps you've heard it. He takes his share of his inheritance, leaves home and piddles it away until he ends up penniless and miserable, sleeping in a barn and slopping pigs. At last he returns home, having learned that money is no substitute for the things that really matter in life, like hard work and family. And his father welcomes him home with open arms and tears of joy." Everett thought he could even see tears in his own father's eyes as he told the story. The old man was definitely losing his grip. "Well, son," Benjamin had continued after a moment. "I've been waiting to welcome you home for years. But you never came. I guess you were never miserable enough. And so, I'm going to help you out."

"How?" Everett had asked, still only half-interested in this sentimental display.

"You are cut off, son," Benjamin replied bluntly. "Your credit cards, your limousines, your penthouse, your monthly allowance, everything this company has provided you. It's all being taken back. You are disinherited."

Everett jumped to his feet feeling a sudden tightening in his chest as he did so. "You've got to be kidding!" he shouted breathlessly. "I'm almost sixty years old! How will I live?"

"By your wits and your ability and the grace of the good Lord," Benjamin replied. "This is something I should have done long ago." Rising from his desk, he walked to a wall where a well-worn fringed buckskin jacket was lovingly displayed in a gilt-edged frame. Hand-carved buttons ran down its front, except for a gap halfway along where one of the antler-tipped fasteners was missing. "Your great-grandfather Jack started this company carving buttons," he explained to the still-reeling Everett. "He sold them, two for a penny, and did an honest day's work for an honest day's pay." He turned back to face his son. "I'm proud of that," he said. "And someday, I want to be proud of you." Taking the framed antique jacket down from the wall, he handed it to Everett.

Everett Clay emerged onto the streets of New York carrying the framed jacket just in time to see his limousine pulling away. Frantically he punched up a number on his cell phone only to hear a recorded message informing him that his service had been disconnected. Enraged, he hurled the useless phone into a trashcan and then directed his anger and frustration at the framed jacket that had been his father's parting gift. Smashing it with his designer loafers, he yanked the jacket off its mounts and stuffed it into the trashcan as well, then looked around for something else on which to vent his rage.

"Need a lift?" said a voice from behind him. When Everett spun around, he saw a large woman with a full mane of curly hair and a broad smile standing next to a vintage red Cadillac.

"Who are you?" he demanded.

"My name is Tess," the woman said, "and I can just imagine how you must feel, poor baby." She shook her head. "A man gets disinherited and loses millions of dollars. No wonder he wants to break things up."

"My God," Everett gasped. "It must be all over town. I'll never be able to show my face around here again."

"Well," Tess suggested helpfully. "They say Aspen is very nice this time of year."

Everett's face brightened. "That's right!" he exclaimed. "My friend said I could use his chalet anytime." His expression sagged. "But how am I going to get to Colorado? I can't even afford a taxi back home. That is, if I still have a home."

"Well, this is sure funny," Tess said, "but I just happened to be on my way to Colorado this morning." She pointed to the red Cadillac. "You're welcome to come along."

Everett stirred uncomfortably on the front seat of the car, his expensive blazer rolled up for a pillow against the window. Blearily he opened his eyes and was surprised to see pristine mountain scenery already.

"Good morning!" chimed Tess from behind the wheel. "And welcome to Colorado." She drove cheerfully past a sign that read WELCOME TO CENTRAL CITY—THE RICHEST SQUARE MILE ON EARTH.

"We're here?" asked the puzzled Everett. "Last thing I remember we were in Indiana. That's two days from here."

"Not the way I drive," chirped Tess. "How about some breakfast?" Even as she spoke they passed the town limits of Central City, a one-time mining town in the Colorado mother lode that had still managed to retain some of its Old West charm. She berthed the big red car outside an old wooden hotel and restaurant that, from the bustle in its lobby, was obviously the town's primary tourist attraction. The carefully restored building sported a staff in period costumes and, in the middle of the lobby floor, visitors had gathered around a well-lit display cordoned off with velvet ropes.

"Ever heard of the Face on the Barroom Floor?" asked Tess as they made their way to the attraction.

Everett shook his head as he stared at the strange and hauntingly familiar face painted on the wooden planks of the floor. "She's beautiful," he said. "But who is she?"

Tess grinned. "She was a friend of your great-grandfather. Her name was Monica."

"Now how would you know that?" Everett asked skeptically.

Tess snorted impatiently. "I'm a history buff," she insisted. "For instance, I know that deerskin jacket you almost threw away belonged to your grandfather Jack, right?" Everett, mystified, nodded. "And I know it's got a missing button, right?" She leaned forward. "Want to know why?" she whispered.

"I admit it's somewhat intriguing," Everett grudgingly replied. "But frankly, I'd rather be on the road to Aspen. I'm not much interested in my family tree."

"Excuse me for saying so," Tess asserted, "but your not being interested in your family tree is what got you on the road to Aspen in the first place." Taking him by the arm, she led him forcefully to a table, calling as she went for the bartender to send over a cup of coffee and some tea. "Right away, ma'am," came the familiar voice of the angel Andrew from behind the bar.

Everett had to admit—Tess was one good storyteller. As she described his great-grandfather Jack Clay, Everett could almost see him. With handsome, distinguished features, much like his own, Everett could imagine Jack coming through the swinging doors, still hot and dusty from the trail and looking for a chance to sell some of his famed Snakebite Jack's Miracle Elixir.

Jack's sales techniques were tried and true: a few verses of the Gilbert & Sullivan crowd pleaser, "H.M.S. Pinafore" to get the boys in a good mood and then a bit of his patented silver-tongued persuasion to seal the deal. He'd even considered peddling his potion to Andrew the barkeep and a charming Irish girl named Monica who served as help, but there was something about the look in their eyes that made him feel a little strange about passing off to them his mix of maple syrup and water as a cure-all.

But everyone else in the saloon was fair game and once he'd collected a respectable pile of coins, he settled down for a friendly game of cards with one of the locals who went by the name of Barkley Stubbs. The game had gone on late into the evening until it was down to one last hand. Holding three kings, Jack was sure of walking away with rich winnings, but with nothing to raise the ante he could only offer his gun and his horse as collateral.

Stubbs seemed willing enough to take the wager, and Jack Clay was soon to find out why: He watched in dismay as his opponent fanned out a full house, queens over nines. It wasn't until the next morning that the snake oil salesman found out he had been cheated out of everything he owned by the card shark Stubbs, whose signature hand was that telltale trio of queens over a pair of nines.

Jack swore he would get his property back, even after an old miner told him that Barkley Stubbs had hightailed it into the mountains for parts unknown. It was then that the barmaid Monica spoke up, volunteering to come along on the hunt.

"You're a woman," was Jack's dismissive answer.

"I'm also an excellent tracker," Monica retorted and to prove it, she started to sniff one of the patrons at the bar. "You're from Tucson originally," she announced after a moment. "You haven't handled any gold for over three weeks and—" sniffing again "—you had eggs with sourdough toast and lingonberry jam for breakfast."

"She's right," said the miner. Baffled yet intrigued by the charming waitress, he quickly agreed to take her along, even allowing her to bring Andrew the bartender in the bargain.

Tess stopped in the midst of her tall tale of the Wild West, watching with alarm as Everett clutched suddenly at his chest, his face twisting with pain.

"Just a little short of breath," Everett said between sharp breaths. "Must be the altitude."

"Let me get you some water," Tess volunteered and, crossing to the bar, leaned in close to talk with Andrew. "I thought we'd have more time," she said.

Andrew shrugged. "It happens when it happens," the Angel of Death replied.

When Tess returned with the water, she could still see a stricken look on Everett's face, but this time, she knew, it was from something more than the tightening sensation in his chest. "You've been through a lot," she said sympathetically. "I know it must be hard to lose so much, so suddenly."

Everett shook his head. "I was just wondering if I really had anything of my own to begin with."

"You have a son," Tess reminded him.

Everett smiled at the mention of Carson. "Yes," he agreed. "He's the only thing I ever did right. But he's no good with money and I can't even be there to help him out."

"The boy doesn't need more money, Everett," Tess countered. "What he needs is the same thing you could do with, and that's character. Problem is, you can't buy character. You have to get it, the old-fashioned way."

Everett shook his head angrily. "Don't tell me you think old Jack Clay was the model of moral rectitude, Tess."

The angel considered for a moment. "Jack Clay was just a man who was willing to change," she said at last. She sat and motioned for Everett to join her. "Now," she said, "where was I?"

Monica and Andrew sat around a crackling campfire under a vast western sky, watching Jack Clay carefully carving a small piece of wood. "It's going to be a button," he announced with a hint of pride when Monica asked what he was making. "An odd thing for a man to make, don't you think?"

"Not at all," replied Monica. "Buttons are very important."

"Yes, indeed," Jack agreed. "Buttons hold the whole world together. That's what Helen says." He reached into a hidden pocket of his deerskin jacket and produced a tintype photo of a woman posed with a small girl. "Helen's my wife. She's the best thing that ever happened to me. Her and my little Jenny."

"And you're making the button for her?" Andrew inquired.

Jack nodded. "You'd think they were diamonds, the way she goes on about buttons," he told them with a smile. "Pearl buttons, mahogany buttons, ivory buttons. Buttons I can't afford to buy her." He held up his handiwork. "So I make them from stone and wood, anything I can find." He gestured to the hand-carved buttons on his jacket. "I made these from antelope horn," he continued. "In fact, I've made a button for every day I've been away. Had a saddlebag full of them." He scowled. "That is, before that cheating Barkley Stubbs rode off with my horse." He settled back onto his blanket. "Better get some rest, if we're going to catch up with him," he told them. "Every day we spend looking for that skunk is another day that he keeps me from making my own fortune."

It was early the next morning, Tess told Everett, that the trio, with Monica in the lead, picked up the trail of the card shark, finally spotting him digging a hole near a ramshackle cabin in a box canyon. Hiding behind an outcropping, they watched as Barkley pulled an iron strongbox from the ground and, opening it, deposited his winnings from the crooked poker game along with a substantial horde of ill-gotten gold and jewels already in the box.

"Looks like you've been a busy man, Barkley," Jack said as he stepped out into the clearing, his gun drawn. "How many other people have you swindled out of everything they owned?" He raised the gun and took aim.

"Jack," Monica pleaded, "I didn't bring you here to kill this man. I only want you to get back what's yours."

"Too late," sneered Barkley as he stood, regarding the others warily. "I already sold the horse. Tell you the truth, though, I got more for that saddlebag full of buttons than that old nag."

"I ought to shoot you in the back right now," cried Jack angrily as he pulled back the trigger.

"How could you go back to Helen with a man's blood on your hands?" Monica asked in desperation, and watched as the words took effect in Jack's heart. Slowly he lowered the gun and, at that moment, Barkley sprang into action, grabbing Jack's pistol as he tried to wrench it away. In the desperate struggle that ensued, Barkley ripped one of the buttons from Jack's jacket. A moment later, a shot echoed across the canyon and then the card shark slumped to the ground, clutching his chest.

"It was an accident," exclaimed Jack, his eyes wide with horror as Andrew rushed over to the fallen man.

"Nearest hospital is clear up to Denver," the Angel of Death said grimly. "He's not going to make it off this mountain."

As Monica knelt down and tried to make the dying man more comfortable, Barkley saw an angelic glow around her. As he gazed up at her in awe, a light of recognition began to dawn in his eyes. "All that gold sitting there," he wheezed. "I'd trade every ounce for a hospital." Wincing, he turned to Jack. "What about that miracle elixir of yours?"

"It's not worth the bottle I put it in," was the shamefaced reply.

Barkley nodded. "What happens to men like us, Jack," he said between gritted teeth. "How'd we get so low? I was a decent man when I left Wichita." He coughed as the life leaked out of his body. "Those buttons you made," he said in a hoarse whisper. "The lady I sold them to said they were first quality." He gestured for Jack to come closer and, holding onto his lapel, drew him down. "You got a real talent, Jack. I hope you're smart enough to use it. Not like me. I'm going to die on this mountain . . . never see my wife and kids again." Reaching into his vest, he pulled out a crude map drawn on a scrap of leather. "This map will get you back here from Central City," he gasped. "Don't take that gold now, or someone will kill you for it, sure as I'm dying." As Jack took the map and slipped it into the secret pocket of his deerskin jacket, Barkley turned to Monica and Andrew. "Now," he said, between heavy breaths, "if you don't mind I've got to talk with these angels. There's something I need to get straight with God."

Jack looked up at Monica and Andrew. "He's hallucinating."

"No," Andrew said, as a golden light enveloped the pair. "No, he's not, Jack."

Tess leaned back in her chair, noting with satisfaction the enthralled look on Everett Clay's face. "He only took what belonged to him out of that box," she concluded, "and left the rest right where he found it. He came back to New York, to his wife and little girl, and started that button company with nothing but hard work. Well, you see what it is today."

Everett shook his head in grudging respect. "I guess that old guy had some character after all," he admitted. "I don't know if I could have just walked away and left all that gold there to rot—" It was then that it hit him. Leaping to his feet he tore past the Face on the Barroom Floor and out onto the street. By the time Tess emerged, Everett had already retrieved the tattered deerskin jacket from the trashcan and had discovered the secret pocket. With a triumphant cry he pulled out the map. "Happy days are here again!" he crowed at the top of his lungs.

It was late afternoon by the time Tess and an impatient Everett navigated the old Cadillac up a dirt road to a dead end in a dusty box canyon. Everett paced across the parched ground, counting out the steps past the stump of an old oak tree, until he saw the weathered remains of a miner's cabin half hidden in the trees. He turned expectantly to Tess, who handed him a rusty shovel she had picked up from the miner's camp. "Knock yourself out," was her dubious invitation.

"The gold is still here, Tess," he exclaimed as he began to dig. "I can feel it." Dirt flew as the hole widened. "Do you know what this means? I don't need my dad's money anymore. I don't have to crawl back and beg for anything. Finally, after all these years, I'm a free—" He stopped as the shovel hit something solid and metallic. Lifting out the box and brushing off the dirt, he took a deep breath. "Okay," he breathed. "Here we go." Opening the rusty, creaking top and expecting to be dazzled by Barkley's hoard of stolen gold, Everett was shocked and dismayed to find nothing but an old carved antler button at the bottom of the box. "It's . . . a . . . button," he said in a barely controlled fury.

"Yes," replied Tess, incongruously pleased by the discovery. "It's *the* button. Remember you wanted to hear the story about what happened to the missing button on the jacket? Well, it's been in that box the whole time."

An apoplectic rage coursed through Everett's body and his heart began pounding wildly against his rib cage. "No!" he shouted. "I want to know where the money is! You told me he didn't want it!"

"Well," said Tess, pursing her lips. "He changed his mind."

"That's it?" screamed Everett, his face turning red and sweat breaking out on his brow. "You wasted my time telling me a story about a button?" He was trembling now and could feel a sharp pain begin to shoot up his left arm. "I need money! What good is a button in an empty box going to do me now!?"

"Well, baby," Tess replied matter-of-factly, "I'm afraid you're just about to find that out."

Sensing a presence behind him, Everett spun around to see Andrew, clothed in light. He began to demand an explanation when he was gripped by a sudden searing agony in his chest. Dropping to his knees, Everett saw the Angel of Death come closer and kneel beside him. "You're having a heart attack, Everett," Andrew said. "It's been coming for a long time, hasn't it?"

Everett managed to nod. "I'm going to . . . die . . . out here," he groaned. "Just . . . like . . ." He keeled over, falling face-first into the dirt.

The paramedics rushed down the hospital corridor wheeling a gurney on which the unconscious form of a man was laid out. As the doctors began a desperate attempt to save his life, Everett found himself standing, with a curious sense of detachment, as he watched his own body struggle for every breath. Was he dead or was he in some strange twilight realm between life and death? He wasn't sure and didn't know whom to ask, since no one in the emergency room seemed to even know he was there.

Except, that is, for a haunting familiar figure in a vintage high-collared dress standing nearby and illuminated by a golden light.

"I know you," Everett said after a moment. "You're the face on the barroom floor."

"Yes," replied Monica. "That's why He put it there. So that when this day came, you would recognize me."

"Who?" asked Everett. "Who put it there?"

"God," was Monica's simple reply. "You see, I'm an angel."

"An angel," Everett echoed. "I understand," but from the expression on his face Monica could tell that his thoughts were far away.

"What are you thinking about, Everett?" the angel prompted.

"I'm thinking about my son," he replied. "I'm thinking about how I wasted sixty years on high living and friends who won't even come to my funeral." His eyes filled with tears. I'm thinking about my father and how I let him down." He lowered his eyes, ashamed to look directly at the being of light. "My father told me the story of the prodigal son. I'd give anything now to be in his place, sleeping in a barn and slopping pigs. But I don't even deserve that." He looked up. "And, if you're an angel, then that means there's a God and I'm about to find out what I *do* deserve. Some special sort of hell for lavish spendthrifts, I suppose."

Monica shook her head and smiled compassionately. "That's not how it works," she told him. "You see, Everett, God is a Father, too. He gave you this life you had and, yes, He is disappointed that you used it to spend money instead of love. But children disappoint their parents every day. That doesn't stop fathers from loving sons, and it doesn't stop God from loving you so much that He will wait a lifetime, in that's what it takes to help you become the man He created you to be."

"I don't know how to do that," Everett whispered.

"Yes, you do," Monica insisted. "Remember the button? I think your great-grandfather left that button behind as a way to say to whomever found it someday: 'I started all over again with nothing but a decision to try and live simply and honestly. I'm going to do that. And you can, too.' " She took a step closer. "You're going to get a second chance, Everett," she told him. "And no matter how much life is left to you, just remember, you'll always be your father's little boy." She pointed to his inert body on the gurney and as Everett watched, his breathing became steadier and the color returned to his pale face.

"We got him back," said the doctor. "Good job, people."

The phone rang on the desk of Benjamin Clay and the voice of his secretary announced that his son Everett was on the line. "The answer is no," were the first gruff words spoken by the old man, anticipating his son's request for money, a request made so many times before.

"You're right," replied the calm and contrite voice on the other end of the line. "If the question is, did I ever appreciate everything I had, the answer is no. If the question is, am I a good son or a good father, the answer is no. And if the question is, do I deserve another chance, the answer is no." There was a long pause as Benjamin Clay listened with baited breath. "But I'm not the same person who left New York," Everett continued at last. "I know it's hard to believe because I haven't been gone very long, but I just want a chance to prove it to you, if you still want me." Another pregnant pause was follow by a simple word. "Dad?"

"Come home, son," Benjamin said with tears in his eyes. "Just come home."

The day dawned bright and sunny as Everett left the hospital and walked with a new spring in his step to the red Cadillac idling at the curb. Tess was waiting behind the wheel and, as Everett climbed in, she presented him with his great-grandfather's deerskin jacket. "Might get windy on the road," she advised, adding, "especially the way I drive."

It wasn't until Everett put on the old garment that he noticed the missing button had been replaced. He smiled at Tess. "You know," he said, as they pulled out of the parking lot and headed for the open road. "You never did tell me what old Grandpa Jack did with all that gold."

Tess smiled. "You're right," she said. "I never did."

She turned the car east and as they pulled away, a sign came into view. HOSPITAL OF THE ROCKIES, it read, and underneath, FOUNDED IN 1893 BY JACK CLAY. It was the hospital that would have saved Barkley Stubbs's life. And it had just saved the life of Jack's great-grandson.

The Wind Beneath My Wings

Judge Dorrie Chapin, an attractive woman in her early forties with lustrous black hair and a no-nonsense demeanor, turned up her driveway, unsettled to see find her mother's home empty and dark. They had arranged to meet with Jenny—the judge's ten-year-old daughter—for dinner that evening and had even invited two guests, her new law clerk, a charming young woman named Monica, and a genial gregarious lady named Tess who'd been befriended by Emma—Dorrie's mother—during one of her almost-daily visits to the courtroom.

The rendezvous had been set for six o'clock and it wasn't like Emma to forget or, for that matter, leave any detail unattended to in the daily life of her daughter. Dorrie was grateful for her mother's constant and consistent help, everything from paying her bills to picking up Jenny from school to offering her advice on difficult court cases—the same sort of advice Dorrie remembered hearing from her father, a respected judge in whose footsteps she was, somewhat tentatively, trying to walk. Thank God her mother was there. Without her support and encouragement, Judge Dorrie Chapin wasn't at all sure she could handle the pressure of her job and the responsibility of being a single mother.

Take today, for instance. The Miller case was proving to be a difficult one to rule on. Two siblings were battling over how best to take care of their aging, wheelchair-bound father. The son wanted to move him into an old age home. The daughter insisted that taking care of him was the only way she could pay him back for all the years he had spent providing for her. While Dorrie was inclined to side with the daughter, she had decided to postpone her ruling until she could hear from old Mr. Miller himself. It was the kind of judgment she really needed to talk over with her mother.

As she closed the car door and moved up the walkway to the front door, she tried to quiet a quick flurry of concern. Wherever her mother and Jenny might be, she knew everything was all right. Except that, recently, things hadn't exactly been "all right." Her mother seemed to be walking and talking a little more slowly these days, and sometimes Dorrie caught a glint of confusion in her eyes as she tried to keep everything tidy, in order and on time, the way she had seemed to do, so effortlessly, for so many years. Honestly, she thought, as she fished for the door key and walked into a darkened hallway, she didn't know what she'd do with her beloved mother.

Entering the kitchen, she saw immediately that no food had been prepared. "They're fine," she murmured to herself, then added. "Of course they're fine. The question is, *where* are they fine?"

The doorbell was heard, bringing with it a flood of relief. Dorrie hurried back down the hall, only to find Monica and her mother's friend Tess standing expectantly on the porch. "I hope we're not too early," Tess said. "We wanted to give your mother a hand in the kitchen."

"My mother's not here," Dorrie replied, unable to hide her concern any longer. "She should have been here with my daughter hours ago."

"I'll go check with the neighbors," Monica volunteered helpfully.

"And I'll just get dinner started," said Tess, patting Dorrie on the arm as she moved toward the kitchen. "Those two will be home before you know it, and they'll be hungry."

It was then that the welcome cry of "Mommy!" was heard at the front door, as Jenny rushed in to embrace her mother.

"Jenny!" Dorrie exclaimed as she knelt to hug her daughter. "You scared me to death. Where were you?"

"We got lost," the child explained.

"Nonsense," said a voice from outside and a moment later a small woman with a bright light in her eyes and a determined stride to her step marched into the house. "We didn't get lost. We just . . . lost track of time."

"How can you lose track of five hours, Mother?" Dorrie asked. "You really had me worried."

"Oh, come on," Emma said, with a dismissive wave of her hand. "I can take care of myself . . . and you." She held out her arms. "Now come give me a hug, Judge Chapin. I want to hear all about your day. And don't leave out any details."

Emma and Tess bustled around the tidy kitchen as if they were the oldest of friends, despite having only met a few days before. Tess knew only too well what her and Monica's mission was, and just how difficult it would be. Apron strings had twisted this mother and daughter so tightly together, it was impossible to tell who was holding on to whom. Their job—cut those strings. But it was a very complicated operation and God wanted both the patients to survive.

"Did I salt these potatoes, Tess?" Emma asked, holding a shaker in her hand and interrupting Tess's train of thought.

"Do you want me to taste test them for you?" Tess replied.

Emma shook her head adamantly. "Everything is a test these days," she said irritably. Then, after a moment of somber reflection, continued, "Please don't say anything about this, but after I picked up Jenny from school today, I . . . just couldn't find my way home." Her face betrayed the fear behind her words. "A home I've lived in for forty years . . ."

"Why don't you tell Dorrie?" Tess prompted. "There's nothing wrong with needing a little extra help now and then."

"Oh, no," Emma responded, the fiery light returning to her eyes. "I don't want to be a burden to her. She counts on me for everything."

"Baby," Tess said with characteristic candor. "She is a grown woman. It's time for her to take care of herself."

In the spacious study of the house, Dorrie and Monica conversed quietly as they waited for dinner while, at a small table in one corner, Jenny sat engrossed in her homework. "I grew up in this house, Monica," the judge was saying and, pointing to a comfortable armchair, continued, "My father used to sit right there, every night, and tell us about the cases he heard that day and the judgments he'd rendered. I always thought he must be the smartest man in the world."

The angel smiled. "He was the one who inspired you to be a judge, then," she ventured.

"He inspired me," Dorrie replied. "But my mother convinced me." A pensive look passed over her sculpted features. "She's always made everything seem possible." Crossing the room she sat down at an old-fashioned roll top desk. "When I was a kid, this desk was strictly off limits," she explained. "Mom's territory. One day, I jimmied the lock and discovered nothing but bankbooks and bills inside. It was then that I realized how hard it was to make ends meet." She smiled. "But every month she managed to keep everything in balance. I realized then that she's the reason I've always felt so safe. There's nothing she can't handle." From the top of the desk she picked up a framed photograph showing Emma as a young woman, smartly dressed in a military uniform. "Did you know that my mother was a member of the WASPs in World War II?" she asked proudly.

"WASPs?" a puzzled Monica repeated.

"Women's Airforce Service Pilots," Dorrie explained. "The army needed to free up men to fight, and Mother flew planes from the factories where they were made to the bases near the front-lines." She smiled. "Their motto was 'We live in the wind and the sand, but our eyes are always on the stars.' " She looked up at Monica. "I know my relationship with my mother might seem a bit unusual to some people," she admitted, "but she's not just my mom. She's my best friend. I don't know what I'd do without her."

"Have you ever tried to find out?" Monica gently asked.

"That's kind of a scary thought," Dorrie admitted after a moment. "She's always been there for me. I mean, every time I get up on that bench, I have people's lives in my hands. And there are days when I honestly feel like I can't do it. Then, I look out and see her, the one person who's always believed I *could* do it, and that keeps me going."

"Dinner!" came the cry from the kitchen as Jenny jumped up and urged her mother and Monica to hurry. Grandma was making her famous meatloaf.

The next morning, Dorrie and Emma hurried down across the lobby of the domed courthouse to the early session. The judge, pre-occupied with the decision she knew she would have to reach in the Miller case, didn't seem to notice how her mother struggled to keep up the pace, and Emma, for her part, was relieved when a young man hurried over to Dorrie and she stopped to find out what he wanted.

"Judge Chapin," he began, "my name is Andrew and I'm from the Governor's office. As you know, he's been considering candidates for the open position on the State Supreme Court." He smiled. "And he narrowed down his list . . . to you."

Emma and Dorrie shared a stunned look. "Me?" the judge stammered. "On the State Supreme Court?"

"We'll take it," interjected Emma, barely able to contain her elation.

Her daughter gave her a sharp look. "We'll think about it," was her reply. "My mother, in her more rational moments, taught me to always consider every aspect of any decision."

"Actually," Emma said with a shrug, "that was her father's approach. I'm more of a 'fly by the seat of your pants' girl."

"Well," said Andrew, "you're the Governor's first choice, Judge. But he needs an answer soon."

"I'll get you one," Dorrie promised. "And thank you."

She and Emma waited in dignified silence until the angelic emissary was out of sight, then they let out a triumphant howl that echoed through the marble expanse of the busy courthouse.

Judge Chapin's court was in session. At the defense sat an anxious, but determined looking young woman, while next to the prosecutor was a man with angry and equally determined mien. This was the Miller case and, though it distressed Dorrie to see a family torn apart like this, she was resolved to see justice done— whatever that might be.

Called to the stand, Ms. Miller spoke through tight lips. "I don't mean to get so upset, Your Honor," she insisted, "but he's my *father* and naturally I want to help him, now that he can't tie his shoes or take a bath or make his own meals. I want the chance to do for him what he did for me." She glanced over to the prosecution table. "I love my brother," she continued, "but I will never let anyone, not even him, put my father in a home as long as I can take care of him."

It was Mr. Miller's turn next. "Look," he began, equally resolute, "my sister talks a good game, but when push comes to shove, she never follows through. She'd like to be the devoted daughter, but she doesn't have a clue what it takes. She can't think that far ahead."

"Oh yeah?" shouted his sister, jumping up and pointing an accusing finger. "Well, I can think circles around you, you moron!"

Judge Chapin banged her gavel. "That's enough," she warned, sternly. "You will both show respect for this court. Now—" She stopped suddenly, as, from the back of the courtroom, the sound of loud snoring could be heard. Glancing up, she saw Tess gently shaking Emma as she tried to wake the sleeping woman from her noisy slumber. "We'll take a recess now," she murmured and, a moment later, rushed down the aisle, along with Monica, to be at her mother's side.

Bending down, she gently called out Emma's name until the old woman began to stir, and opening her eyes she looked with confusion around her.

"You fell asleep, Mom," Dorrie said with a mixture of relief and concern.

"Mom?" replied Emma with a puzzled expression, then asked, "Who are you?"

Tess and Monica exchanged a look. "Why don't I take her over to see the doctor?" Tess suggested, as the litigants and their lawyers began filing back. "It looks like you've got your hands full sorting out these folks' lives."

Later that afternoon, Dorrie held a hushed conversation with the family doctor over the phone while, at the far end of the office, Monica filed papers. Hanging up the phone slowly, the judge sat in troubled silence until the angel approached and gently asked, "Is everything all right?"

"That was our doctor," Dorrie replied. "He just told me he prescribed pills for my mom's heart over a year ago. She never told me. And now, he says that she's forgetting to take them." She shook her head angrily. "I hate these doctors who look at a calendar and de-cide it's time for you to start falling apart."

"But," the angel quietly added, "people do get old."

"People do," Dorrie said, a sudden flash of fear in her eyes, "but not my mother." She smiled, putting on a brave front. "It was so te-dious out there today, I almost fell asleep myself."

Monica shook her head. "Your mother didn't fall asleep because she was bored. She was just tired, Dorrie. She's getting older and she's slowing down."

"My mother doesn't know *how* to slow down," Dorrie insisted adamantly.

"Your mother is doing her best to make you believe that noth-ing has changed," the angel continued, taking a step forward. "But it has. Her body is changing and her mind is changing. She hides it from you very well. She is saving the best hours of the day for you and Jenny. But she's not as good at hiding it as she used to be."

"The truth is she has something important to do," came a voice from the doorway, and Monica and Dorrie turned to see the formi-dable figure of Tess. Stepping into the room, the senior angel contin-ued. "It's more important than keeping your checkbook balanced and being your cheerleader, Judge," she added, with a piercing look at Dorrie. "You've got to start recognizing that good woman's limi-tations and then you've got to start recognizing her potential."

"She's seventy-eight," Dorrie shot back. "What 'potential'?"

"You see potential in your little girl, don't you?" Tess asked.

Dorrie stiffened. "Jenny has great possibility."

"Well," Tess replied intently. "Emma is somebody's little girl, too—God's little girl. She may be seventy-eight, but to the Father, she's still His baby and He's got plans for her. When He looks at your mother, He sees lots of possibility."

Dorrie shifted uncomfortably on her feet. "God," she repeated with a slight touch of scorn. "That's very sweet, Tess. But I live in the real world and, if you don't mind, I'd like my mother to keep living here, too. Now," she continued, turning away, "if you don't mind—"

"It scares you, doesn't it?" Tess interjected boldly. "Having to imagine life without your mother."

It was late when Dorrie drove up to her mother's house, and once again the old familiar windows were darkened. With Tess's words still echoing in her mind, she slipped in the front door and headed directly for the kitchen. Checking to see that all the gas knobs on the stove were off, she next opened the refrigerator and, taking out a carton of milk, sniffed it, recoiling at the sour odor. Emptying it into the sink, Dorrie moved to the study and there, as she had done so long ago, she used a letter opener to pry loose the lock from the old roll top desk. She drew a sharp, shocked breath at what she found inside: piles of overdue bills, late notices and bank notices for an overdrawn and under-funded account. One envelope especially caught her attention and, picking it up, she next moved to the bathroom where she found bottle after bottle of prescription medication, some half empty, others never opened.

"What are you doing here at this hour?" came a sharp voice behind her, and a startled Dorrie spun around to see her mother angrily confronting her. Wrapped in an old housecoat, her hair thin and gray in the harsh light of the bathroom, Dorrie's mother looked older and more frail than she had ever seen her. But there was no mistaking her irate tone of voice. "This is my house! How dare you go through my things. You have no right to invade my privacy!"

"It's a good thing I did," Dorrie replied defensively. "They're going to turn off your electricity next Thursday. The phone bill is five weeks late. And you've paid the magazine subscription three times." She stepped forward. "It's a mess, Mom."

"Well, it's *my* mess!" Emma insisted petulantly.

"It's mine, too," was Dorrie's grim reply and she held up the envelope from the desk. "You didn't mail my insurance, Mom. I've been driving around with no coverage."

A horrified look came over Emma at the news. "Oh, no . . ." she murmured. "I must have forgotten. I'm so sorry . . ." She stopped, straightened her shoulders and looked her daughter square in the eye. "Dorrie," she said, "there's something you have to face . . . something we both have to face. I'm getting old. I want to help you as much as I can, but I can't keep up like I used to."

It was Dorrie whose face now had a look of horror . . . and fear. "That's ridiculous," she said, her voice trembling. "You're not getting old. You're just—"

"Dorrie, please," Emma snapped, cutting her off. "I'm slowing down. I'm not senile and I don't have Alzheimer's but it takes twice as much energy for me to do half as much."

"We've got to fight this, Mother," Dorrie responded in a pleading tone.

"Now, sweetheart," her mother answered firmly. "We've got to accept this."

Her daughter glared at her. "You're not getting old," she told her. "You're just giving up." She turned to leave. "And I'm ashamed of you."

Mr. Miller, his eyes rheumy with age, sat in a wheelchair in the witness stand, facing his son and daughter on opposite sides of the courtroom aisle. He spoke in a voice so low there was utter silence as those gathered strained to hear what he was saying.

"I know we're here today to decide who's going to feed me and change my diapers and take me for walks," the old man said. "And I know it's hard." He turned to Judge Chapin. "Funny thing is, I raised my kids to do the right thing, but I guess they've got different ideas about what that is." He squinted in the direction of his children. "I love my boy and I know he only wants to do what's best for me. And I love my little girl and appreciate that she's willing to take care of me. But I can't let her do that." He smiled at his daughter. "I know you love me, honey," he said. "But you don't have to prove it this way. Just make sure you and the kids come and visit when you can." He smiled. "Truth is, I'm going to a nice, clean place where nobody's heard my stories yet. I can't ask for much more." His voice suddenly became firm and he spoke with authority. "Now I don't want to hear another word about it."

Andrew was waiting in her chambers when Dorrie recessed for the day. "I'm sorry to disturb you, Your Honor," he said, "but the Governor needs your answer today."

She nodded. "Tell him I appreciate the offer very much," she said taking a deep breath, "but I'll have to decline."

Andrew shook his head sadly, and as he left he exchanged a quick, meaningful look with Monica who stood outside the door. The angel stepped into the room and saw the judge, so stern and confident on the bench, weeping inconsolably. "You can't make this decision when you're upset," Monica pleaded. "You're only react-ing to your fear."

"You're damned right I'm afraid," Dorrie lashed out. "I'm losing my mother, Monica, and now that she needs me, this is no time to take on a new job."

"It would kill your mother to think you gave up this chance be-cause of her," Monica responded.

"I'd give up anything for her," Dorrie insisted through tears. "When I listened to that poor, dear man out there today, I knew I'd rather die than let someone I love waste away in a wheelchair among strangers. I can't let that happen to Mom . . . and I can't let it happen to me. I need her and if that's selfish and childish, then I'm guilty. The thought of losing her scares me to death. Because when that day comes, I will finally, truly be alone in this world."

"I know you're afraid, Dorrie," Monica replied. "But you haven't lost your mother yet. You just found out she's human."

Dorrie sat alone in the empty courtroom, looking up at the bench from which she dispensed justice day after day. She had felt so unprepared and insecure at first, and it was her mother who had urged her on, given her the confidence to excel. How could she continue now, without that constant encouragement? In that moment, it was as if her entire life were on trial and all she wanted to do was throw herself on the mercy of the court.

As if in answer to her unspoken plea, the courtroom door swung open as Tess, with Emma in tow, marched down the aisle. "What's going on here?" Dorrie demanded. "This is between my mother and me."

"Well, Your Honor, that's not exactly true," said a voice from behind her, and she turned to see Monica entering from the back of the courtroom. She crossed and stood beside the other two women. "You told me how afraid you were to be alone," she continued. "But no one is ever alone. You've had angels watching over you your whole life." As she spoke a soft golden glow began to appear around her and Tess.

"What are you saying?" Dorrie asked, frightened by the light.

"I think they're saying that they're angels," her mother answered. "Sent from God."

"The Father wants you to let go of the fear of being alone," said Tess. "The fear of growing old and losing each other. The fear of death itself."

"Fear is a thief," Monica added. "It will steal all your todays by making you dread tomorrow. But there is no reason to worry about tomorrow. God is already there."

"I get so scared," Dorrie said, turning to her mother with tears in her eyes. "How am I ever going to go on without you?" she sobbed. "I won't be anybody's baby anymore."

"You'll always be my baby," Emma reassured her with a warm embrace.

"There's one more item on the docket," Tess informed them with a smile. "God has a mission for you, Emma. You may think you're nothing but a little old lady. But what you have, baby, is knowledge and experience that other generations need to hear."

"There's a new millennium coming, Emma," Monica interjected. "The next thousand years could be peaceful ones, if the next generation could only learn the lessons of peace that you and others have learned from the wars of the last century. But there are only a few voices left to tell the story. Yours is one of them and God has called you to lift up that voice."

"Are you still in touch with any of the women from your old squadron?" asked Tess.

"The Flying Tigerettes?" replied Emma. "Well, I know Esther's still around. I get a card from her every Christmas. But what does that have . . . ?" she stopped as, suddenly, a bright light returned to her eyes. "Of course," she said after a moment, then turned to her daughter. "There's life in the old girl yet!" she exclaimed.

A minivan sat idling at the curb in front of Emma's house. A banner tied to its side read THE FLYING TIGERETTES and it was full of woman happily chatting together about old times.

Emma stood with her daughter and granddaughter at the door to the bus, along with the angels. "Grandma and her friends are coming to my school first," the child was telling Tess. "There's going to be a big assembly and everything."

Monica looked at her watch. "You're going to be late, Your Honor," she reminded Dorrie.

"Right," the judge responded. "I guess that wouldn't be a good idea for my first day at a new job." She turned to her mother, tears in her eyes. "I'm going to miss you," she said, "but I want you to know just how proud I am of you. And I think Daddy would be proud, too."

"Oh, he is," Emma replied with a grin and, turning to the angel, winked. "I have it on very high authority."

Pandora's Box

Charlie Radcliffe sat at his office computer, mesmerized by the pictures flashing across the glowing screen. His finger clicked the mouse button again and again, as if it had a life of its own. His heart beating faster, Charlie absorbed the alluring and enticing images that seemed to scroll endlessly from the Internet directly into his brain. Charlie had lost all volition, all choice, and, along with them, the will to resist, as the pornographic website erased his conscience bit by bit, replacing it with an insatiable urge to click the mouse again and again.

Suddenly, his office door opened and, as if coming out of a dream, Charlie quickly signed off with a few keystrokes. He looked up to see his boss, Harold, staring at him with a look that mingled anger with disgust. "I'm not a guy who pries into his employees' lives," Harold said brusquely. "I'm too busy for that. But we've been monitoring your Internet log, Charlie, and as you know, we've got a zero tolerance policy around here."

"It's not what you think," Charlie stammered, but his boss silenced him with a wave of his hand.

"It doesn't matter what I think," Harold snapped back. "We're on a network here, remember? We're all connected." He shook his head, his mouth drawn tight. "We're going to have to let you go,

Charlie. Unless you want to resign. That way, no one will know. It's your choice."

"Oh, no," a stunned Charlie replied, "You can't—" But it was too late. Harold was gone, and Charlie was left alone with only the slight hum of the computer to fill the sudden silence of the office.

He sat for a long moment, trying to make sense of what had just happened. It had all begun so innocently, only a few days before. He had been in the kitchen, helping his wife, Kate, clean up after dinner, when he suddenly heard a stifled cry coming from the other room where his thirteen-year-old daughter, Sarah, was at the family computer, researching a school report on Hawaii. With a strange premonition that something was wrong, he crossed into the living room in time to see a series of lewd and suggestive pictures appearing on the screen in front of his little girl's wide eyes.

"Sarah," he said in a shocked tone. "What are you doing?"

"I don't know," his daughter replied. "I just typed in 'Hawaii' and this came up. I tried to exit but it won't let me."

"I'll take care of it," Charlie said. "Finish your homework in your room." He sat down in front of the screen and reached for the power button as the images continued to flash and a suggestive woman's voice could be heard. A long moment passed, as Charlie stared, before, with a sudden shake of his head, he switched the machine off.

What Charlie didn't know was that, watching unseen over his shoulder, were three angels about to begin their latest assignment. "It used to be that families gathered around the hearth," Tess said with a sigh. "Now they gather around the hard drive."

"But computers are so useful," Monica countered. "They're a bridge across the entire world. And they seem to bring out the human urge to chat."

"That and play solitaire," remarked Andrew wryly.

"Computers are toys," Tess replied sternly. "They define a personality. Look at the Radcliffes here." She pointed to Kate, who was carefully sorting through a box of old photographs for display in her downtown antique store. "She lives in the nineteenth century with her antiques and her old-fashioned ideas." Her eyes fell next on Charlie. "Her husband is living in the twentieth century, all wide-screen TVs and microwaves." She turned to Sarah. "But their daughter lives in the twenty-first century—the Computer Age." She shook her head and sighed. "Technology can do a lot of wonderful things. But it's the same as any other tool. Like a hammer, it can build a house . . . or it can tear one down."

Sarah, the Radcliffe's bright-eyed and blond thirteen-year-old daughter, giggled conspiratorially through a mouth full of braces with her best friend, Kiki, as the two sat in Kiki's bedroom doing their homework. While both girls were the same age, Sarah's aura of innocence contrasted sharply with Kiki's precocious attitude, as evidenced by the direction their girlish conversation was taking.

"How far have you ever gone with a boy?" Kiki asked with a mischievous smile.

Sarah shrugged. "I kissed Jimmy at camp once. How about you?"

"Further," Kiki replied with a toss of her hair.

"It's weird to think about going further," Sarah said pensively. "Kind of like how I felt when I saw that website the other day."

Kiki's playful grin grew wider. "Let's look at it again," she urged.

A troubled look passed over Sarah's face, a look she did her best to hide as Kiki jumped up and ran to her computer. A few mouse clicks later, both girls were staring wide eyed at the scantily clad women, posing on a tropical setting. "It's not very romantic," said Sarah, wrinkling her nose.

"You want romantic?" Kiki replied and, sending the point to a desktop icon, called up a chatroom screen.

"What's this?" asked Sarah, as she peered at the dialogue scroll on the screen.

"You are so out of it!" was Kiki's derisive reply. "It's a chatroom. You can talk back and forth to boys online about anything you want." A pop-up message suddenly appeared reading DEAN 16, followed by the one-word greeting, "Hey."

"Say something back," Kiki urged Sarah, who paused a moment before typing her password.

"I'M DEAN," came the reply. "I'M SIXTEEN. HOW ABOUT YOU?"

"What do I say?" Sarah asked excitedly. With an exasperated sigh, Kiki leaned over and typed, "ME TOO."

"But I'm only thirteen," protested Sarah.

Kiki nudged her. "He doesn't have to know that," was her sly answer.

Kate Radcliffe looked up from sorting a new consignment of antiques as Charlie walked in the front door, a cardboard box of office supplies in his arms. "Charlie," she said with surprise. "What are you doing home? It's four o'clock in the afternoon."

One look in her husband's eyes immediately told Kate that something was very wrong and, in the next few minutes she listened with growing anger and disbelief as he told her what had happened. It all seemed so incredible, and so unfair. Charlie had simply shown a fellow worker the website that Sarah had stumbled into and the next thing he'd gotten an e-mail from the same site. He'd opened it and, at that very moment, his boss had appeared in the doorway. It was a simple misunderstanding, but nobody seemed to care. It could have happened to anybody, and Charlie had assured her that he'd done the right thing by shutting off the computer immediately. She didn't know what made her angrier; that pornographic filth had gotten Charlie fired or that it had all started right here in their own home.

"Well," she said, still fuming. "I know one thing for sure. We're going to get rid of that computer."

"Wait a minute, Kate," Charlie protested. "I've got to take some responsibility here. I can't blame it on the computer."

"Charlie," Kate replied. "We have been totally involved with Sarah since she was born. We always knew where she was and that she was safe. But now there's another world inside that computer that we can't protect her from. You would never bring pornographic pictures into our home, would you?"

"Of course not," Charlie insisted.

"Well," said Kate, "that computer did."

The terminals of the Global Village Cyber Café, a coffeehouse and computer center that had just opened in the neighborhood, were busy with Internet surfers when Charlie wheeled in a wagon full of components and looked for the café's proprietor. "Interested in buying a computer?" he asked the helpful young man by the name of Andrew.

"That's a nice one," remarked the angel. "Why are you getting rid of it?"

Charlie sighed. Even though it was a long story, there was something about Andrew's open and honest manner that encouraged him to unburden himself. "Money's tight," he said. "I lost my job." He sighed. "I accidentally hooked into a porn site and I got popped for it."

"Accidentally," repeated Andrew as he pulled up two chairs and poured out coffee for them both.

"You know what I mean," countered a defensive Charlie. "It was weird and twisted and fascinating, all at the same time." He shook his head angrily. "You try to be a decent human being, you keep

your nose clean and stay out of trouble and suddenly—Wham!—
you plug into a computer and trouble finds you. Now I've got that
stuff in my head and I can't get it out."

"Your brain's kind of like a computer, you know," observed Andrew. "You're the one who decides what to input, but the trouble is,
some of those files never get deleted." He paused, taking a deep
breath. "But I wonder," he said at last, "if I'm really the one you
should be having this conversation with."

Kiki sat on her bed amidst a menagerie of studded animals,
blowing on her freshly painted fingernails, as Sarah, stretched out
on the floor, did her homework. She looked up excitedly as an instant message chime sounded at the computer.

"It's him!" Kiki squealed. "It's your boyfriend!"

"He's not my boyfriend," admonished Sarah as she jumped up
and ran to the terminal where a message was waiting: "DEAN 16: I
LOVE TALKING TO U. OK TO SEND U MY PIC?"

"He's so polite," swooned Sarah as she quickly typed back
"YESSSSS." Both girls watched breathlessly as a photo of a hand-
some teen formed on the screen, along with the message: "YOUR
TURN."

"What do I do?" Sarah cried in a giddy panic. "He's sixteen and
I look like I'm eleven."

"Don't worry," Kiki replied with a smirk. "You'll look like a
movie star when I get done with you."

Two hours later, Sarah, her young face still heavily made up with
the lipstick and eye shadow Kiki had applied before snapping a dig-
ital photo, sat glued to the screen typing furiously at regular inter-
vals. "You're been chatting with Dean all afternoon," Kiki said as
she flipped through a fashion magazine. "In chat years, that's like a
relationship."

"He likes my eyes," Sarah said, with a dreamy sigh, then read out loud, "THEY SAY EYES ARE THE WINDOW TO YOUR SOUL AND YOU MUST HAVE A BEAUTIFUL SOUL." She turned to her friend. "And guess what. He lives right here in town. And he wants to meet me. Tomorrow."

The next afternoon, the bell above the door to the antique shop chimed to announce the arrival of a customer, and Kate emerged from her back office in time to greet an engaging young woman with a warm Irish accent who had a vintage telephone for sale. "I was hoping to put it on consignment," said the woman, who introduced herself as Monica.

"Absolutely not," insisted Kate. "I'll buy it myself." She smiled. "That's the trouble with running this place. I can't bear to sell a thing."

Ah," remarked Monica. "You like to give history a home."

Kate nodded. "I think I was born in the wrong century," she sighed. "I read *Pride and Prejudice* and mourn the demise of manner and civility."

At that moment Sarah burst into the store and rushed up to her mother. "I'm going to Kiki's to do my homework," she explained breathlessly. "And I'm already late."

"Why this sudden need to go to Kiki's all the time?" asked Kate. "What about the library?"

Sarah looked away. "She's my best friend," she replied with a nervous flutter in her voice.

"Fine," Kate conceded, throwing up her hands, and a moment later her daughter was gone.

"Thirteen is such a lovely age," she remarked ironically to Monica, who had turned to look at a vintage coffee pot. Kate sighed. "She's still upset with us for getting rid of our computer."

"And why did you do that, if you don't mind my asking?" inquired Monica.

"I have a duty to protect my child," was Kate's prompt reply. "Have you seen what's on the Internet, available for anyone to access?"

"But you can't keep a child locked away forever," was Monica's gentle response. "That's why parents teach them to look both ways before they cross the street. Because sooner or later, they're going to have to do it for themselves."

"So you think I'm wrong?" asked Kate frankly.

Monica shook her head. "I'd never tell you how to raise your daughter," she replied. "I just think that computers are here to stay." She pointed to a silver coffee urn. "Just like fine antiques."

It was that evening when Charlie, a somber and determined look on his face, walked into the bedroom to confront his wife. "We have to talk, Kate," he said.

"What is it?" a concerned Kate asked her husband. "What's wrong?"

Charlie heaved a heavy-hearted sigh. "There's something I need to tell you. That website I saw at the office?" A long moment passed. "I didn't click off as fast as I said I did."

"You lied to me?" was Kate's aghast response.

Chagrined, Charlie nodded. "I'm sorry," he replied. "I was so embarrassed. I felt awful. I just got caught up and I never thought of myself like that before. But . . . they were more than pictures, Kate. They were . . . fantasies. At first, it felt uncomfortable. But after a while, it was like I was there and they wanted me to be there." He tapped his forehead. "And now that stuff is in here and I can't get rid of it."

Kate just looked at him, trying to sort out her feelings. "I haven't been able to explain it," she said at last, "but things don't seem as . . . close between us as they usually are. Has this got something to do with it? Tell me, Charlie."

Charlie struggled to find the right words. "When I'm with you," he said at last. "It's like there's you and me . . . and those pictures."

"Charlie," Kate asked in a quiet voice, "are you telling me that you're hooked on that stuff?"

"No," her husband replied. "I just need to be honest with you. I want you to understand what I'm dealing with. So that it won't get between us . . . anymore than it already has."

Kate just looked at him for a long moment as she tried to sort out her conflicted emotions. She wanted to believe her husband and to trust what he was telling her. But she couldn't help but feel that something, dark and evil, had come between them. Turning away to hide her tears, she shut off the light and lay in darkness, feeling isolated and alone.

Sarah waited nervously in a small park where she had made an afternoon appointment with the charming DEAN 16. She sat on the bench, where only an occasional passerby hurried along through the shadows of trees. A good-looking man in his early twenties approached her from behind. "You look different from your picture," he said in an affable voice.

Sarah, startled, spun around. "Dean?" she asked and when he smiled and extended his hand, she gingerly shook it. "You're not sixteen," she said dubiously.

The man who called himself Dean looked chagrined. "I was afraid if you knew I was older you wouldn't want to meet me. Is it a problem?"

Sarah hesitated. "I guess not," she finally said. "I guess everyone exaggerates online, right?"

"Right," replied Dean with a charming smile, then stared unabashedly at her for a long moment. "Your eyes are even more amazing in person," he said at last.

"Really?" Sarah replied, blushing and looking away. "So . . . how old are you, really?"

"Nineteen," Dean said without blinking an eye, depending on the fact that, like most young girls, Sarah wouldn't know nineteen from twenty-nine.

He was right. "I don't know any nineteen-year-old guys," she said.

Dean grinned. "Sure you do," he replied. "You know me." He took a step closer. "Online you find out who people really are. On the inside. How they feel about things. Without all the regular junk getting in the way."

"That's true, I guess," was Sarah's reply. She wanted to trust this handsome stranger, to believe that she really did know him even though the small voice in the back of her mind kept repeating every warning her parents had ever told her. She nodded when he asked her if she was hungry. She really wasn't, but her parents had also taught her to be polite.

"I know a good place right around the corner," Dean said, luring her along. "Except, I forgot my wallet back at my place. Maybe we can stop by and pick it up."

"You have your own place?" asked Sarah, her warning radar sounding once again.

Dean hesitated a moment. "I just moved out of my mom and dad's," he replied, covering quickly, then added, nonchalantly, "You can wait here if you want."

"No," Sarah said, thinking to herself that that's how a thirteen-year-old would act. "It's cool." She followed him as he led the way through the park toward a seedy apartment building down the block. As they headed down the path together, they passed an unseen pair standing by and watching harshly.

"One little girl typed a simple word in a computer," Andrew said. "Nobody was watching, nobody knew enough about how it works to prevent it."

Tess nodded in angry agreement. "One little unprotected moment and now a man has lost his job. His marriage has lost its joy. And his daughter could lose her life." She turned to the Angel of Death. "You better get going, Andrew."

Charlie sat at a terminal in the Cyber Café, carefully working to format his new resume, when suddenly the door flew open and Kate rushed in. "Is Sarah with you?" she asked urgently.

"No," replied a mystified Charlie. "I thought she was at the library."

Kate shook her head. "She's not at the library and she's not at Kiki's." Her voice trembled. "I've been looking for her all afternoon."

"Calm down," urged Charlie. "Let's take this one step at a time." At that moment, Andrew, with Monica in tow, burst into the café.

"Monica," Kate exclaimed. "Have you seen my daughter, Sarah? She came into the store when—"

"We don't have a lot of time to explain," Monica interjected, then turned to Charlie. "You don't know me," she continued, "but Andrew and I have been sent by God to fight an evil that has been attacking your family. It's not the Internet, but something else that uses any open door to walk in and destroy what is good."

A golden glow began to emanate from both angels, as Kate and Charlie stepped back in amazement. "What's going on?" Charlie asked in a hoarse whisper.

"Andrew and I are angels," Monica continued. "I know it's hard to believe, but you must try."

"Sarah has been going online and talking to someone she met in a chatroom," Andrew explained.

"That's impossible," protested Kate. "We got rid of the computer."

In reply, Andrew sat down and quickly typed commands at the

computer terminal. "You can log on from any computer," he explained as the complete record of Dean and Sarah's chat scrolled into view.

Charlie scanned it quickly. "Who is DEAN 16?" he asked.

"He's a very dangerous man," Monica answered. "And Sarah's with him right now."

The color drained from Kate's face. "God help us!" she sobbed.

"That's why we're here," Monica replied, as Andrew gestured to Charlie and the two men rushed out the door.

Dean opened the door to his apartment, a single room littered with videos, magazines and empty beer bottles. An ashtray overflowing with cigarette butts sat next to a computer terminal. "Sorry it's a mess," he said with a shrug, "but the rent's cheap and nobody bothers me." Crossing to a stereo unit he pulled a CD off a stack. "Hey," he said, "you want a soda?"

"No thanks," Sarah replied, lingering at the front door. "We're just getting your wallet, right?"

"Right," replied Dean. "Why don't you listen to this cool CD while I look for it?"

Reluctantly Sarah stepped into the room while Dean slipped a pair of headphones over her ears and closed the door behind her. Walking to the refrigerator, he took out a can of soda, pulled a dirty glass from the sink and filled it. While Sarah swayed to the rhythm of the song, Dean surreptitiously reached into his pocket and pulled out a small vial of darkly tinted liquid. Opening the top he filled a dropper and, squirting it into the glass, stirred it with his finger and carried it out to Sarah.

"Thanks," said Sarah, slipping off the headphones. "Good song." She took the drink as he held it out to her and was about to sip it when, from the corner of her eye, she spotted the clogged ashtray and beer bottles for the first time.

"What's that?" she asked, moving the glass away from her lips. "I thought you said you didn't drink or smoke."

"Why don't you drink up," Dean said, nervously trying to change the subject. "And let's get out of here."

"I think I'd better go," Sarah replied and tried to hand him back the glass.

"No," Dean insisted, with sudden intensity. "You need to drink your soda."

Sarah took a step backward. "Stop it, Dean," she said. "You're scaring me." He grabbed her by the hand and pulled her toward him. "What are you doing?" she whimpered.

At that moment, the front door splintered off its hinges as Charlie and Andrew rushed in. "Don't drink that!" shouted the angel as he knocked the glass from the girl's hand, and Sarah rushed into her father's arms with a cry of relief.

"Hey!" snarled Dean. "You can't just break in here! I'm not doing nothing."

The angel nodded. "You got that right," he said. Then, in a blurred rush of motion, Dean grabbed a baseball bat and took a swing at Andrew. Sidestepping the attack, Andrew watched as the bat crashed into a lamp and sent shattered glass across the room. Sarah screamed as Dean took another swing. Incredibly, Andrew stopped it cold with one hand and, yanking it away, swung it himself, sending it crashing down onto the computer, which exploded in a shower of sparks. The predator slunk down to the floor and covered his head. Andrew reached for the phone to call the police, while Sarah sobbed uncontrollably in her father's arms.

Monica was waiting in the house, trying her best to soothe the distraught Kate, when the men arrived back, Charlie holding Sarah in his arms. "Sarah!" her mother cried, as she rushed to hold her baby. The next few minutes were a time of joyous relief and happy confusion as the family was reunited.

An hour later, after the family had returned to the safety of their own home, their eyes were drawn to Monica, who began to emanate a miraculous light. "God wants this family to know that He loves them very, very much," Monica said. "He knows that these last few weeks, you have been attacked by an enemy as old as the world itself. Some call it the devil or Satan, but whatever you call it, it's evil and it roams the world looking to destroy everything that is good and beautiful: happy families, loving relationships, young innocence, all the things we hold sacred. When good people use the Internet to communicate, the enemy will use it to lie. When good people use photographs to recall beauty, the enemy will use pornography to cheapen it. When a husband and wife share one life and one heart, the enemy will attack their minds to divide them. That is why evil is our enemy and that is why God sent Andrew and me."

Kate shook her head. "It's just too frightening," she said, in a still-fragile voice. "In the blink of an eye, we almost lost our daughter. I don't want this Internet in our life."

"The Internet itself is not evil," Monica explained. "In can be amazing. Just imagine all that information, all the opportunity to learn and to share. These are very exciting times. They don't have to be frightening when you remember that time and progress are in God's hands, not in technology's. Yes, we are at the beginning of a new century, but God was the same yesterday, as he is today and will be forever. It's His will, not for you to stumble into this new world, but to embrace it without fear. Remember when you sit down at the computer, that good and evil are both competing for your mind. Ask God to sit with you. Ask Him to protect you and teach you how to protect your family. This world has great potential for good. But it takes good people to accomplish that."

Andrew, who was also suffused in a golden glow, turned to Charlie. "Speaking of potential," he said, "that Cyber Café is growing all the time. I'm going to have to be moving on. Maybe you'd like to run it for a while."

"A family antique and computer café," said Charlie and he turned to Kate. "Imagine that."

The couple smiled at each other as Sarah moved into the shelter of their arms. The danger and trials they had undergone had brought them closer to one another and to the love of God who had sent His angels to protect and preserve their family.

Life Before Death

The bus full of Irish teenagers, gawking at the sights of America on the morning of their arrival, pulled up in front of a ramshackle row house in a blighted New York City neighborhood on a cold winter's day. The doors hissed open and, in single file, the teens exited onto the sidewalk carrying duffel bags and suitcases. As they gathered outside the house, they stayed carefully on either side of an invisible but very real line of separation—six on one side, six on the other. Across that line, the young adults eyed one another warily as they spoke in low tones, one to another, but never across the boundary that divided them. Both groups seemed to gravitate around their respective leaders: on one side a tall, dark haired boy with an open and honest face named Tommy; on the other, a striking redheaded girl with a ready smile named Rose.

Two angels stood on the front stoop of a rundown brick tenement, its masonry crumbling and covered with graffiti. Tess did her best to hide her doubts from Monica, whose green eyes were alight with excitement. "You know, Tess," she bubbled, "I think this is going to work."

Tess pursed her lips. "Getting them here was the easy part, baby," she replied. "Getting them to live with one another, that's going to be a lot harder."

Deep in her heart, Monica knew that Tess was right. There was so much to overcome—so many years of hatred, so many generations of violence. But peace and love had to begin somewhere and, for the angel, that somewhere was here, in an American ghetto where Irish boys and girls—Catholic and Protestant—would have a chance to live and work and learn together. All for the sake of her beloved homeland.

It was the Good Friday peace accords, the agreement between the warring faction in Northern Ireland, that had prompted this bold experiment. Under the auspices of an organization called Project Children, Monica had traveled to Belfast to meet with clergy on both sides of the conflict in an effort to recruit young people for a very special purpose. Using the lure of a free trip to America, the project would bring together the sons and daughters of Protestant and Catholic families to help with the renovation of a condemned tenement building that had been selected to house a new community center. There was certainly plenty to do to bring the derelict structure back to life, but, for Monica, the real purpose was even more important—to inspire these bitter enemies, victims of a long and bloody civil war, to become a generation that would begin to fight for peace.

Working through Father O'Malley and Reverend Thompson, Monica had interviewed and selected a dozen promising candidates for the project, overcoming their reluctance to cross secretarian lines with the promise of an adventure in America. It had truly been a challenge to convince them to take this journey together. Not one among them had not lost a relative to the "Troubles," and it was only too easy to blame the "Prods" or the "Taigs" for the misery they experienced all of their young lives. Yet, slowly, one by one, the hearts of those called by God were softened, breaching the walls of their prejudice, just enough for a single ray of hope to shine through.

There were the brothers, Angus and Ian Wexley, proud members of the Protestant Oranges; the good-natured Kieran and the bitter Maggie, both Catholics who had suffered more than their share of tragedy and turmoil.

Among the others were Anne and Fiona and Bridie, who all had their own stories of despair and rage and murderous enmity to tell. If it had not been for two among the group named Rose and Tommy, Monica might well have failed in her mission. But the others seemed to respect and trust these two natural leaders and it was around them that Monica was able to gather this small core of volunteers, willing to try and live with their sworn enemies, at least long enough to see the sights of that fabled land called America.

Tommy's father, an IRA activist, had been killed in a bloody showdown with British police and Protestant defense forces, and Tommy had nurtured the seeds of hatred ever since. It was his brother Gavin, however, who had at last convinced him to take up Monica's offer. The two shared not only their Catholic roots and Irish patriotism, but a love of poetry that bound them together with ties stronger than any political or religious cause. It had been in a small neighborhood pub where Gavin had told his brother that, because of the new beginning held out by the peace accords, he had quit his role in the militant IRA and taken a job at the local gasworks.

"Listen, Tommy," he had said intently, "a couple of beggars in suits signed a scrap of paper that says things will get better. And I want them to. I'm tired of the blood and you should be, too. Now, go see America. See how they live, the Prods and the Taigs together. And write me some beautiful letters. You've got a touch of the poet, so there's no excuse."

Rose's own father had been paralyzed while doing his duty as a policeman during a disturbance in the no-man's land between Catholic and Protestant Belfast. Wheelchair bound, he was dependant on his daughter for daily care and, as a result, she had missed her opportunity to attend college.

"He wants me to go to America," she had told Monica and Reverend Thompson when they had met to discuss Project Children. "He says he won't eat if I don't, the stubborn old thing." She turned to the angel. "Is your father stubborn?" she asked.

Monica smiled with secret knowledge. "I wouldn't say stubborn," she replied, "but He's always right. And, in this case, I believe yours is, too."

And so they had come from across the ocean, carrying with them not just a toothbrush and a few changes of clothing, but the memory of the horror and the tremendous courage that was a part of their Irish heritage.

As they sorted themselves out on the sidewalk, Monica turned to Tess, her face lit with expectation. "It will be hard," she admitted, her own Irish accent grown more distinct during her time away. "They're young and smart and they have so much in common."

As the old bus pulled away, the engine coughed and a loud backfire echoed down the street. Frightened by what seemed to be the familiar sound of gunfire, all twelve of the new arrivals hit the pavement, ducking for cover out of habit.

Tess turned sadly to Monica. "Yes," she said, shaking her head. "They certainly do."

Later that evening, the group gathered in the community center dining room for their first meal in America. They sat, rigidly divided, on opposite sides of the table, as an awkward silence descended over the room. "Well," said Monica at last, displaying an indomitable optimism. "Here we are, our first meal together. I thought it would be nice to start every meal with a prayer. Each of you can take a turn."

"I'll start," volunteered the one named Bridie.

"I won't be sitting here quietly for a prayer from a Prod," protested the fiery-eyed lass named Fiona.

"Not likely we'll be listening to a bunch of Catholic rantings, either," piped in Ian.

Everyone began talking at once, only to be silenced when Rose stood up. "Can't we just keep it simple?" she asked above the tumult. "Can't we just say something grateful without getting all religious on one another?"

The group eyed one another suspiciously across the table, until Tommy chimed in, "Aye, that's it. We'll keep it simple. Just the basics." He looked to Rose expectantly.

She smiled, than looked toward the ceiling. "Thank you for the food," she said.

"He says you're welcome," Tess announced. "Now let's eat."

Later that evening, while the others slept, Tommy made his way quietly back down to the dining room, a paper and pen in his hand. He was surprised, pleasantly so, to find Rose, sitting alone, her hands wrapped around a cup of tea.

"I promised my brother I'd write him every day," Tommy explained, holding up his writing implements after an uncomfortable silence.

"I made some tea," Rose replied, stating the obvious and pointing to the simmering kettle on the stove.

"Are you going to throw it at me or offer me a cup?" Tommy asked wryly.

"Depends on your attitude," was Rose's cheeky reply.

"My attitude?" responded Tommy. "If a woman like you can get a bunch of Catholics to pray with a roomful of Prods, then you're not one to be messing with."

She smiled and, rising, poured out a cup for him, her hand trembling as she held the kettle. "Are you all right?" asked Tommy.

"I had a bad dream," Rose answered.

"Is there any other kind?" Tommy replied and for a moment

they both sat in silence, recalling the recurring images of death and destruction that had shattered both their sleeps.

"So where do you live, Tommy?" Rose asked at last.

"Townsend Road," he replied.

"No joke?" she continued with a short laugh. "I live right across the way at the bottom of Shankhill. We're neighbors. Imagine that."

Tommy was looking intently at her. "I imagine all kinds of things," he said softly. "And right now I'm imagining the prettiest girl I've ever laid eyes on." He reached over and took her hand. "Do you believe in love at first sight, Rose?"

Rose withdrew her hand. "A good Irish girl doesn't fall in love in a day," she replied.

Tommy leaned forward and winked. "Ah, but haven't you heard?" he said. "This is America. Anything can happen." He reached again and, taking her hand, kissed it in a gentlemanly gesture. "Top of the evening to you," he said as he stood and left Rose alone with her thoughts and emotions.

Over the next several days, the volunteers had little time to nurture their prejudices and preconceptions. Their days were filled with sounds of saws and hammers as, slowly but surely, the old house began its transformation. The graffiti-covered walls were repainted, new additions added and windows installed to let in the bright sunshine. The tensions that had been so evident upon their arrival slowly began to melt away as the hard work required a spirit of cooperation and mutual support that allowed no time for old quarrels and sectarian divisions. From hostility came tolerance, and from tolerance, a kind of grudging respect, one for the other. But, as the angels watched and supervised, it was only too clear that the atmosphere of teamwork that had begun to emerge was like a layer of thin ice over a deep, dark chasm. It would take more than a little carpentry and a coat of paint to repair the breach in the hearts of these young people.

Throughout the long days of hard work, the attraction that had begun to grow between Tommy and Rose continued to take root. Often, she would look up from some chore to see him staring at her from across the room. At the dinner table, he would sometimes finish crossing himself, like a good Catholic, by throwing her a kiss. The others noticed and, at first disapproving, slowly began to accept the idea that it was somehow true—in America anything could happen. Even a budding romance between the son and the daughter from opposite sides of a divided nation.

Evening had fallen and, while the others had gone out for a night on the town, Tommy sat alone in one of the half-finished rooms, waiting by the light of a candle. The door opened and Rose entered, a little unsure of herself but true to her heart.

"I'm glad you came," Tommy said, rising to meet her.

"It can't work, you know," came Rose's blunt rejoinder. "We think we're in love, but we're really just in America. Everything seems different here, but when we go back . . ." she sighed. "There's no hope for two like us. We're like Romeo and Juliet. They tried to love each other, but they only ended up dying."

"That's because Shakespeare was a Brit," Tommy replied with a twinkle in his eyes. "Haven't you heard the Irish version?" He took a step closer. "It all ends very happily. Ah, but the beginning . . . the beginning is quite special. It begins with a kiss . . . like this." Rose allowed him to bestow a small, simple, almost innocent kiss. "I think you're something grand, Rose," he whispered as he took her in his arms. For a long moment they embraced by the flickering light of the candle, until Tommy felt Rose shuddering against him. "What is it?" he asked.

Rose stepped back, wiping tears from her eyes. "It's just my father," she replied. "He was paralyzed when I was little. He's in a wheelchair and . . . it's been so long since anyone held me." She began to weep again as Tommy put his arms around her once more, holding tight.

"Tell me about your da," he whispered.

"It was ten years ago at Easter," Rose recounted. "There was a riot down at Unity Flats." She felt Tommy stiffen and moved back to look into his eyes.

"I remember," he said, an edge in his voice. "But it wasn't a riot. It was a peaceful demonstration."

Color came to Rose's cheeks. "My father was a policeman," she countered. "He tried to keep order, but somebody threw a bomb and the police were attacked . . ."

"That's a lie," Tommy shot back, angrily. "My father was there. He led that demonstration."

Rose pulled herself away. "Your father . . . Tommy Doyle . . ." she gasped. "Dear God in heaven, you're *that* Doyle? Your dad was in the IRA? He probably threw the bomb that paralyzed my father!"

"More likely it was the police themselves," Tommy snarled. "They arrested my da on bogus charges and I never saw him again. He died in prison, Rose. My brother tried to find him, but we never did."

"You're brother . . . he's IRA, too, isn't he?" Rose asked accusingly. "And your father was a terrorist."

"My father was defending his country," Tommy countered. "At least you still have a father."

Blowing out the candle, he left Rose in the dark where she waited, her thoughts in turmoil, until she, too, sighed dejectedly and exited, leaving two invisible angels in dismay.

"I didn't expect them to fall in love," Monica said. "I wanted leaders. Not lovers."

Tess shook her head sadly. "Baby," she replied, "the best leaders in the world will never keep the peace unless it starts with love. I know how much you care about all this and that you've got a plan to stop the hate. But God's plan is about starting the love. Now, whose plan do you think is going to work? You can't do everything. So just do one thing." Monica's eyes filled with tears as Tess put a comforting arm around her. You've just got to trust Him, baby," she whispered softly.

The estrangement between Tommy and Rose affected all the other volunteers, and as the days drew on and the house began to take on the look of a clean, bright and welcoming place, the tension between the two factions became very more palpable.

It was a cold and cloudy winter morning when the entire crew had gathered in a large upstairs room to install and paint drywall, that a haunting and familiar sound drifted up from downstairs. In mute amazement, the group heard the distinctive sound of a Uilleann pipe, a high whistle and an authentic Irish fiddle and, rushing into the main room, they found a genuine ceiliband playing a sprightly Irish jig.

"I thought you might be a little homesick right about now," explained a beaming Monica, and looking at Tommy, added, "Perhaps dancing with a beautiful Irish lass might cheer you up a bit."

"I'm not much of a dancer," Tommy demurred.

Monica stepped closer. "I'm not asking you to let them see you dance," she said softly. "I'm asking you to let them see you change." Taking a deep breath, Tommy crossed to the other side of the room and put out his hand to Rose. With a broad smile she accepted and, within minutes, the entire room was vibrating with the sound of pounding feet as Protestants and Catholics joined in a large, reeling circle.

Joining in, Monica felt the exhilaration of the music to her core, until she saw Tess standing in the doorway, a grim look on her face. Signaling the musicians to stop, she asked with a sinking heart what was the matter.

"I have some very difficult news," the angel revealed and, turning to Tommy, said, "It's your brother, baby. He's been killed. A gas main exploded in the factory where he worked."

A stunned Tommy was speechless, but his Catholic mates were only too quick to jump to conclusions. "An explosion, eh?" spat Kieran. "You mean a bomb."

"Of course it's a bomb," cried Fiona. "It's Ireland!"

Tess shook her head vehemently. "No," she insisted. "It was an accident."

"That's what the Prods always say when they murder a Catholic," Tommy replied bitterly.

"And how many did your brother kill?" Angus shouted.

"Not enough," was Tommy's seething reply.

"Go to hell where you belong," cursed Maggie. "And give my regards to your brother."

"Stop it!" Monica shouted, her voice overflowing with sorrow and anger. "Filthy Taig! Dirty Prod! For the love of God, I beg you to stop! Every one of you has lost someone you love. A father, a mother, a cousin, a brother. But the score will never be even. You'll kill him because he killed her, and then they'll kill you, and on and on. As long as you're keeping score, as long as you both have to have the last word, the last word will never be spoken and there will be no peace!"

Her words fell on deaf ears as the two sides glared at each other, silent but simmering with rage and hatred. At last Angus picked up a spray can and scrawled the words GOD SAVE THE QUEEN across a newly painted wall, then turned and walked away.

Tommy stood staring at the words written on the wall, his packed bag beside him. His plane was leaving in a few hours to take him back home for Gavin's funeral. As he stood in mute grief and anger, he picked up the discarded spray can and, crossing out the word QUEEN wrote THE IRISH PEPUBLIC in its place.

"God save us all," came a voice from behind him and he turned to see Rose standing in the doorway.

"It's over Rose," Tommy said between clenched teeth. "The peace is over and so are we."

Footsteps approached and Monica entered the room. "Are you ready to go?" she asked Tommy, then turned to look at Rose.

"I was just saying . . . good-bye," she explained.

"It's very hard saying good-bye to someone you love," Monica observed.

"Sometimes you don't even get to say good-bye at all," was Tommy's bitter comment.

"That's true," the angel admitted. "You never know when death will come. Aren't you glad then, Tommy, that the last words you spoke to your brother were words of love?"

"How would you know?" Tommy asked in surprise.

A golden glow began to fill the room, shimmering like a veil around Monica. "Do you believe in angels?" she asked softly.

"Jesus, Mary and Joseph," breathed Tommy as, frightened, Rose reached for his hand.

"Don't be afraid," Monica said reassuringly. "I am a messenger, sent by God. He wants you to know that He loves you both, very, very much. But you must listen with your heart and not with your head. Can you do that? Can you put away the Protestant words and the Catholic words and listen to the word of God Himself?" Awed and speechless, the two nodded. "Why did God send an angel to you?" Monica continued. "Because to every generation the truth is born anew and with it comes the promise of peace. And this is your time and this is your chance, and I asked—I begged—the Father for the privilege of sharing this time with you because I love you, too. Because I love peace." Her eyes filled with tears. "Because I love Ireland . . . so much. You see, angels are created, not by human love, but by a simple whisper from the Father. And when God called me into being, I lived in His presence for an eternity until, one day, He said that I had work to do and it was time to begin it. And then He set me down on the greenest hill I had ever seen, where the first mist of creation still lingered in the valley, where the oceans crashed on ancient cliffs and the rich perfume of life itself filled my every breath. You see, I took my first steps on the soil of Ireland, and it was there that I first saw peace on earth. The peace that was meant to be and meant to stay. The peace that you are meant to keep."

"We?" whispered Tommy.

"Yes," continued Monica. "Your brother was not murdered. It *was* an accident and the peace is still intact unless someone like you, someone angry and still counting the dead, lashing out to take revenge one more time."

"Then I won't," Tommy avowed as he felt Rose squeeze his hand. "Of course I won't."

Monica nodded, tears still glistening in her eyes. "Good," she replied. "But God wants more from you, Tommy, and from you, too, Rose. I know that there is a romantic love that you feel for each other, and you mustn't be ashamed of it, for it is a gift from God. But there is other love, too. And God is asking you to put that love first. To love the country where you both were born, to love the peace that you've both been given, and to love the people—all the people, who are your brothers and sisters, who stand on the same hills and breathe the same air and thank the same God for making them sons and daughters of Ireland. If you'll do that, if you'll put away the pointing of fingers, the speaking of wickedness and the doing of evil, God will make you strong and He will make your love even stronger. You will raise up the broken foundations and you will be called the repairers of the breach and the restorers of the streets where the children of Ireland dwell. Will you do it? The love and peace you've found here, will you take it home with you? Or will you leave it behind?"

Tommy, dressed in a dark suit, stood before the coffin of his brother beneath the high vaulted dome of a Catholic church. He looked out among the assembled mourners for a long moment before clearing his throat and beginning to speak. Tess, Monica and Andrew stood to one side, listening with the others.

"Gavin loved this country," he told them. "He wanted peace for Northern Ireland more than anything. But he also loved me and he wanted me to have a future. He didn't want me to die for my country. He wanted me to live for it. So, he sent me off to America to find out what peace looked like." He stopped, remembering what he had experienced across the wide ocean. "I saw streets without barbed wire," he continued at last. "Neighbors of all beliefs and colors talking to one another. And, there I was, sitting down and breaking bread with Protestants." He pressed on, despite the scattered gasps of surprise heard from the pews at this revelation. "I know I'll see my brother again," he said, running his hand over the top of the casket. "But while I wait for that day, I'll be seeing my Protestant and Catholic brothers and sisters every day. Really seeing them, because I have learned that peace isn't just the absence of war. It's the presence of God. One God. The God of love. And from that love comes forgiveness."

A rustling was heard from the rear of the sanctuary as the doors opened and Rose entered, followed by Angus, Ian, Maggie and Bridie. Tommy smiled, choking back his tears.

"I know we've all lost someone," he went on. "But if everyone remains stuck in their hate, then no one will move forward. We all have to take a leap of faith together. And move forward together."

He took a deep breath and turned to look at the angels. "When I was in America," he said, "one of my new friends taught me a song. No, not a song. A prayer. I hope you will pray it with me now. For Gavin. For ourselves. For Northern Ireland."

Tess moved to the front of the altar and, in a clear, ringing voice, began to sing. "Let there be peace on earth / And let it begin with me." Slowly Tommy, Rose and the others joined in. "Let there be peace on earth / The peace that was meant to be." Kieran, Fiona and the other Catholic kids rose from their seats and joined their fellow volunteers in the aisles. "With God as our Father," they sang, "brothers all are we / let me walk with my brother in perfect harmony."

Together, Protestants and Catholics linked arms as, one by one, the whole church rose to join in. "Let peace begin with me / Let this be the moment now / With every step I take / Let this be my solemn vow." Monica and Andrew were singing now, too, as all the voices joined as one to reach up to heaven. "To take each moment and live each moment in peace eternally / Let there be peace on earth and let it begin with me . . ."

Flights of Angels

The painter sat dreaming before his canvas. It was a monumental work, a depiction of a huge skyscraper, suspended horizontally and textured in dark hues. Beneath the huge edifice small figures played—a father and his three sons. As he dreamed, the frolicking figures became more clear: it was the painter himself, romping with his three young sons George and Ray and John Henry, the oldest and, exuberant and sensitive, the most like their mother, Sally. As he watched, the small figures swooped and dove across the massive landscape of the painting until it seemed they had become a part of the artwork itself, a living breathing extension of his own vision.

A sudden, deafening clap of thunder awoke the painter. He looked around at his studio, silent now except for the sound of his own labored breathing. As he listened, rain began to fall on the roof, lightly at first and then in a steady pounding roar as the storm broke overhead. At his feet, an old golden retriever whined and licked his hand. William wanted to go for his evening walk.

With a groan, the painter slowly lifted his body from his chair and made his way to the door. Bending over painfully he attached the leash to William and together they stepped outside into the wet and windswept night. The painter walked along the side of his studio, leaning against the wall for support, but as William tugged at the leash, he lost his balance and went tumbling to the ground, the rain falling onto his upturned face. "Oh my God . . ." he cried in pain and fear, then shouted up to the house where he and his family lived. "Sally! Help! Help me!"

Inside the upstairs bedroom, Sally, a petite blond woman who seemed weighed down by burdens heavier than she could bear, heard a noise above the rain. Peering out the window, she saw her husband, the painter, lying in the backyard, as William paced back and forth, barking. With a sharp cry, she raced down the stairs and out the back door, praying desperately as she ran. "God . . . please, if you're up there . . . I need help. We're running out of time."

Three angels stood invisibly in the hallway, watching as Sally carried her husband in from the storm and helped him, one agonizing step at a time, up the stairs and into the bedroom.

"How much time is left?" Monica asked Tess.

"I don't know, baby," the elder angel replied. "But God is the maker of time and His timing is perfect." She turned to Monica. "I want you to work with Sally and the boys." Then gesturing to Andrew beside her, she added, "And you will be Richard's angel. But this is not a man who will go gently, Andrew."

"I never knew a great artist who did," the Angel of Death replied.

"This is not about saving a life or making great art," Tess told her charges. "This is about saving a great family and teaching them how to say good-bye."

"Saying good-bye can be the hardest thing in the world," Monica nodded.

"No," Andrew countered. "Dying without saying good-bye. That's worse."

Sally sat in the family's spacious and eclectically decorated living room interviewing the prospective help sent by a local agency.

Monica was applying for the job of helping with the three boys, freeing Sally to run the household while Richard finished working on a dozen paintings for an important upcoming gallery show. Andrew had come in response to Sally's request for an assistant to help her husband finish the work in time for the fast-approaching deadline. She had decided almost immediately to hire them both. Although money was tight, and would get tighter without the income from the exhibition, she had a good feeling about these two, a feeling that overlooked, for the moment, the financial strain the extra help would put her under.

"When can I meet Richard?" asked Andrew expectantly after handshakes sealed the agreement.

Sally took a deep breath. "There's something you need to know about my husband. He has Lou Gehrig's disease and, well . . . he's losing ground every day. I can see it. But he can't. Or won't. It's already affected his legs and pretty soon it will work its way up the rest of his body until . . ." She looked away, fighting back tears. "Well, let's just say his time is very precious."

While Monica was introduced to the boys, Andrew went back to the studio and tried to make himself useful to his new employer. He found Richard, his forehead bruised from his recent fall, staring moodily at another large canvas, this one showing the façade of a great building surmounted by granite angels. The two found much in common immediately, especially after Andrew began asking perceptive questions about the painter's work. "Why is it," he remarked, looking at the current canvas on the easel, "that you are so attracted to such immense structures . . . skyscrapers and ocean liners and monumental statues?"

"I like the idea of people making gigantic, seemingly impossible things," Richard replied. "The ambition to make something so grand, the sheer dedication . . . it makes me admire man." He smiled. "God, I understand. He can do anything. But the things human beings can do are overwhelming."

"Yes," agreed the angel, still looking at the magnificent paintings. "Some human beings are truly overwhelming." Turning to Richard he added, "Well, I'm just here to help. Your wife said you've got a deadline coming up and that—"

Richard grinned as he completed the sentence. "I have trouble finishing things?" He shook his head, then raising his finger, quoted, "God help me from ever completing anything."

Their conversation was interrupted by the sudden arrival of all three boys, led by John Henry who was carrying a package. "Special delivery!" he shouted as he handed the parcel to his father. Opening it, Richard pulled out a copy of *Moby Dick*. "I'm going to copy a chapter for your dream book, John Henry," Richard told his son. "I'll read it to you when we go whale watching next spring." Then, winking, he added, "But we won't use harpoons." Turning to Andrew, he explained, "I'm making books for each of my boys. Dream books. I started them the day they were born and I'm trying to fill them with places we'll travel to and things I think they ought to know."

Andrew nodded, then, picking up *Moby Dick,* flipped through the pages until he found the passage he was looking for. Clearing his throat, he began to read, "God keep me from ever completing anything. This whole book is but a draft—nay, but the draft of a draft."

The painter nodded, noting with approval, "An educated assistant. I think we'll get along just fine."

Richard hobbled painfully down the stairs, leaning heavily on Sally, listening to the excited chatter of the boys as they awaited his arrival downstairs. After his fall in the rainstorm, he knew what he had to do. First, he must admit to himself that he could not will away the devastating effects of his disease. He was going to die and the truth of that reality made it all the more important to accomplish his second goal: to tell his children what was happening and prepare them for what was to come.

"Here he comes!" shouted George, serving as a lookout at the bottom of the stairs, and he scurried off to join the others.

"The boys have been waiting all morning to show you their surprise," Monica said happily as Richard was slowly lowered onto the sofa with his wife's help.

"It took me that long to get here from the bedroom," Richard replied before his younger sons crept up behind him and clapped their small hands over his eyes. "No peeking!" cried Ray.

"Here we come!" shouted John Henry from the dining room and, a moment later, he came in on a motorized handicap cart, sitting triumphantly on Andrew's lap.

"Did you pay *Blue Book* for this?" Richard asked ruefully when he saw the cart and joined with his family in a chuckle that quickly turned to a wheeze as he struggled to catch his breath. Sally and the children watched with concern until his shallow breathing subsided while Monica and Andrew, exchanging a nod, quietly departed, respecting the family's privacy.

"Dad," asked John Henry, still sitting in the cart. "Why do you need this?"

Sally and Richard looked at each other. The time had come. As Richard gathered his children around him he spoke soothingly. "Now don't be afraid," he began, "because there's nothing to be afraid of. I have a disease and it makes my legs weak. That's why I fell down last night."

"Is the doctor going to do an operation?" John Henry asked.

"They can't," Richard told his son. "It doesn't work that way."

A crestfallen look came over the boy and the next question he asked was barely above a whisper. "Dad . . ." he said. "You're not going to die, are you?"

Richard looked quickly at Sally then, swallowing hard, answered, "Now, John Henry. Not for a long, long time." He brightened, turning to the younger kids and saying in a cheerful voice. "I think it's time for a doughnut. Who wants to get me one?"

The children scrambled into the kitchen, each wanting to be the one to fetch the prize, as Sally turned to her husband with a somber look on her face. "We're going to have to tell them the truth," she said, and leaning forward, fixed him with her eyes. "The whole truth. We're running out of time."

"I couldn't," Richard replied, with an agonized expression. "They're not ready to hear it yet."

"Or you're not ready to say it," Sally replied with unflinching honesty.

The painter sat in his modified wheelchair before his work, a vast unfinished canvas on which the early outline of an architectural edifice had been sketched in. He worked slowly and painfully, one hand supporting the other as he made one meticulous stroke after another. Next to a nearby table, Andrew cleaned a palate and watched as Richard tried desperately to wrap his stiff fingers around the brush. "This thumb's going funny," he said, gasping for breath. "Got to hold the brush different." Andrew crossed to him and helped place the brush between his middle and index fingers. "Not bad," Richard reported as he continued his work, but a moment later he was once again overcome by a spasm of breathlessness. When he could draw air again, he turned to Andrew. "I've only got two paintings done," he said in a weak voice. "If I can sell them, that won't even be enough to cover the bills for this month." He stopped, a light sparking in his eyes, as he looked around at all the unfinished canvases cluttering his studio. "But if I could finish all twelve . . ."

"Twelve paintings," Andrew replied dubiously. "That's a lot of work. A lot of time. It'll take everything you've got."

"Then that's what I'll give it," was the painter's response.

Andrew stepped closer and put his hand on Richard's shoulder. "And I'm ready to help you every step of the way."

Weeks passed in painful progression and Richard raced against his own failing body to complete the work that he was convinced would provide for his family after he was gone. Andrew, as he had promised, stood by him, helping when he could, and praying when he could see that it was only the raw determination of the painter that kept him going. As Richard's breathing became more difficult, the angle stood by with a respirator, ready to administer oxygen until, when it was clear that the breathing apparatus was needed all the time, he helped fashion a device that secured it over the top of Richard's head, keeping his eyes and hands free to continue painting. When his muscle control deteriorated to the point where he could not eat, the angel was there to feed him and, when his fingers cramped and his arms refused to move, it was Andrew who tied the brushes to his hands and mixed the paints to keep the painstaking artistry in motion.

But there was one thing no one, human or angel, could do for Richard: become a substitute father in the life of his sons. It was John Henry, the oldest and most sensitive, who was deeply affected by Richard's long absences in his studio. On those occasions when the boys, hoping to play, would venture into the studio, heavy with the smell of oil paint and turpentine, all Richard could do was sadly shake his head and return to the square of canvas over which he labored.

It was late one afternoon, and the three boys were gathered around the kitchen table for an after school snack. George grabbed the last doughnut off the plate, and the fragile balance that John Henry maintained suddenly snapped.

"That was mine!" he shouted at his brother, drawing concerned looks from Monica and Sally.

"We can get more tomorrow—" Monica began soothingly, but she could see that something much deeper was troubling John Henry.

"There's never enough for me," he shouted, his large eyes welling with tears. "Never enough of anything. Dad's always working. We never get to play anymore. He gets tired all the time." He clenched his fist in rage and frustration. "I hate painting! I hate doughnuts! I hate this stupid disease! I hate it!" He broke down sobbing as his mother gathered him in her arms. "Is Daddy going to die?" he asked through tears.

Sally took a deep breath. "Yes," she said quietly but clearly. "Not today. But, yes . . . Daddy's going to die."

"There's a time for everyone's Daddy to go and be with God," Monica added, kneeling down and looking the boy in the eyes. "And soon it's going to be your Daddy's time."

John Henry turned to his mother with a worried look. "Mom," he asked, "are you going to get the disease, too?"

"No," Sally said, fighting back her own tears. "It doesn't work that way." She hugged him again, tighter now. "I'm going to stay right here with you."

John Henry looked trustingly into her eyes. "If Daddy's going to die and go to heaven," he said thoughtfully, "maybe he won't hurt anymore and he'll be able to walk again."

"Your daddy's going to run in heaven," Monica promised.

It was late that same evening when Richard could no longer lift his arms to reach the canvas and finally had to abandon his work. Beside him, William slept peacefully as his master sighed and set aside his palate, prying the brush from his clenched fist. A wave of exhaustion suddenly overcame him and he flicked the power switch on his wheelchair and began moving toward the studio door. Before he rolled more than a few feet, he closed his eyes as sleep rushed up over him like a black wave and the edge of the cart bumped against a table where a can of turpentine fell over. It took only a few second for the flammable liquid to reach one of the candles Richard had lit to give his studio the proper atmosphere and lighting and, with a sudden sucking rush of air, the table ignited. As Richard slept unaware, the flames spread until they reached his precious canvases, which burned with an eerie light as the oil paint crackled and blistered.

It was William, barking loudly, who finally woke Richard, and he opened his eyes to find himself surrounded by the inferno. Desperately, he wheeled his cart around in a futile attempt to save at least one of his paintings, but the fire was spreading too fast and for a moment it looked as if he, too, would be engulfed, when suddenly, the door flew open and Andrew rushed in.

"The paintings!" Richard shouted between gasps, the scorching air blistering his throat as the angel grabbed him out of the chair and carried him from the flaming studio to the door. "Forget me! Save my paintings!" Andrew stumbled, nearly tripping, but managed to carry his load to the backyard lawn where they both collapsed, turning to look as the studio became engulfed in fire. "You should have saved my paintings," Richard groaned.

"Your life comes first," Andrew replied.

"My life's worth nothing now," came the grief-stricken reply.

Andrew stood alone in the dining room as late afternoon light flooded through the windows and across a large canvas, another of Richard's monumental compositions. It was the only piece that had survived the fire, the last painting in the life of an artist quickly drawing to a close.

The angel looked around him. He had done his best to convert the dining room into a temporary studio where Richard might continue his work, but even as he looked at the drop cloth and easel, he knew that the one thing he could not provide was time—time for the painter to bring to life his extraordinary vision with pigment and brushes and stretched canvas.

He approached the painting and moved his hand lightly, just above one of the sweeping lines that was so characteristic of Richard's technique. "An artist draws a line," he said, half-aloud, to himself. "It moves. It grows. It soars. It ends. It takes a journey. Each line has a life." He paused, then turned his eyes to heaven. "Father," he prayed, "please tell me when the line you've drawn for Richard will end." A slow minute ticked by as the angel stood motionless, as if receiving the answer to his question.

The silence was broken by the sound of labored breathing and the soft hiss of the respirator. Andrew turned to see Richard wheeling into the room, his face ashen and his body clenched with pain. Although several days had passed since the disastrous fire, he could still see the lines of regret etched on the painter's face—regret that it was he who had been saved, and not his work.

"Richard," Andrew said gently, "losing your paintings was a blow. But how would Sally and the kids feel if they lost you?"

Richard shook his head. "They *are* losing me," he replied without sentiment. "Sooner than later. And those paintings could have kept a roof over their head." He paused and looked up at the last, unfinished canvas on the easel. "I never really believed there'd be a last painting," he said, his raspy voice barely above a whisper. "But there it is. And it's got to count for so much." He turned back to Andrew. "I just pray it will sell. At least my family will have something."

"The prayers of a good man can do a lot," the angel said, as around him, a rich golden light began to break forth.

"That light . . ." gasped Richard, his eyes dazzled. "Oh my God . . . it's radiant. Where is it coming from?"

"From God," Andrew answered as the glory of the Lord surrounded him. "I'm an angel, Richard."

"An . . . angel," the painter repeated with a stammer. A look of wonder grew over his face, quickly followed by one of great sadness. "Oh, no," he cried. "Not now. Please, not yet . . . I've got to finish this. And . . . I still have so much to tell my sons. So much to show them."

"You just have tonight left," the Angel of Death told him, his face lit with love and compassion.

"But I've got to finish my work," Richard protested in anguish. "You know that. Tell him. Tell God that I've got to finish this or there's nothing left for my family."

Andrew smiled. "Don't put your trust in a piece of canvas or the work of your own hands, Richard," he replied. "Put your family in the hands of God. He is more than able to do beyond what you can even think or imagine or hope for them. God loves you, Richard. And He doesn't want you to worry about Sally and the boys."

"But I've let them down," sobbed Richard. "I could have left them so much."

"There's only one thing you can leave them now," was the angel's response. "And it's the most important thing of all." Andrew picked up the three dream books from a nearby table, the books into which Richard had poured his visions of beauty and truth as a legacy for his three sons. "God doesn't want you to spend this night working on a painting," Andrew continued. "He wants you to use your last hours finishing the work that really matters." He turned to the canvas. "This work is . . . beautiful, Richard," he said. "But it's a painting. It's a thing—it can burn, it can be stolen, or ruined. But the things that really matter can't be destroyed. Your love for your wife and children. Your dreams and your prayers for them. God's promise that He will keep your family safe—that is the real treasure, Richard. And where your treasure is, there your heart is, too. And it's your heart that needs to paint tonight." He paused for a moment as the light around him grew even brighter and he held out the dream books. "Finish these for your boys," he urged. "Leave them a scrapbook of your heart. A remembrance of what their father loved on this earth."

Richard stared at the angel, torn by the decision he faced. "I can't," he said at last. "There's not enough time." Desperately he tried to bargain. "I'll work all night," he said feverishly. "I'll finish the painting and the boys' books, too. I'll do both." Andrew only shook his head and Richard could see the truth reflected in the angel's eyes. "There's only time enough for one," he said, acknowledging the reality that faced him. "Which do you choose?" was the angel's inescapable question.

Richard, his eyes full of tears, turned back to his beloved painting. "I see it so clearly, Andrew," he told him. "I know where every brush stroke will go. I can see it so clearly . . . in my mind."

Andrew stepped forward and laid his hand on the painter's shoulder. "You've painted great ships and buildings and trains," he said. "All of them enclosed in your mind, waiting to be released." He, too, looked at the unfinished work. "This painting could be your masterpiece, if that's really the choice you've made." He held out the sketchbooks. "But you've already got three masterpieces, Richard: your sons. Give them this time. It's all that matters now."

The painter looked from his unfinished canvas to the three books in the angel's hands. Slowly, with trembling fingers, he took them and set them on the table. "God," he prayed, "give me the strength to move a pencil."

"His hand will hold yours," Andrew promised, "until you're finished." He reached over to remove the respirator as, suddenly, Richard began to breathe with renewed strength.

It was nearly dawn when, exhausted and drained, Richard put the finishing touches on the last page of the last book and turned to Andrew. "I'm finished," he said, weakly. "Is it time? Are you going to take me?"

"Soon," the angel replied. "But don't you want to say good-bye first?" He picked up the ravaged body of the painter and carried him upstairs, into the bedroom where his two youngest sons slept peacefully. With Andrew's help he slipped the books under their pillows and kissed them gently, murmuring a blessing into their dreams. The angel picked him up again and carried him into John Henry's room.

"You're going to be the man of the house now," he said, choking back tears as he leaned over his oldest son. "That's going to be tough on you." The tears began to flow now. The boy began to stir, his eyes opening.

"Dad?" he said sleepily. "What's going on?"

"I've come to say good-bye, John Henry," his father told him. "Don't be afraid. There are angels, son. They're here, and God is, too. I'm leaving, but God never will." A stifled cry was heard from the doorway as Sally rushed in and embraced her husband. "I came to say good-bye," he told her.

"Oh, no, Richard," his wife sobbed. "Please, no."

"It's okay," he reassured her, then turned to Andrew, who stood invisibly by the bedside. "Tell her, Andrew," he said.

Sally turned in the direction Richard was looking. "Andrew isn't here," she said, with a puzzled frown. "Richard, you're halluci-nating—" She stopped, awed by the peaceful smile that suffused her husband's face.

"I made the boys their books," he told her, as tears began to well in his eyes. "But I have nothing for you, Sal."

"I don't want anything, honey," she whispered in his ear. "I just want you."

Andrew stepped forward and touched the painter on the shoul-der. "Let's go," the Angel of Death said with a smile. "Let's walk to-gether."

Sally stood before her husband's last painting, a painting that, somehow, miraculously, had been completed in the course of a single night. A message had been carefully written across the top of the vast landscape, words that read: "Flights of Angels Sing Thee to Thy Rest."

"It's incredible," she said. "But how could he have finished it so quickly, and still have time to complete the dream books for the boys?"

"God never leaves anything incomplete," Monica replied. "Sometimes He finishes them through the hands of people like Richard, and sometimes He does it by Himself."

Sally stood for a long moment, gazing at the magnificent work. "It's hard to imagine, Monica," she confessed after a moment, "that there won't be any more paintings. I just can't believe that."

As she spoke, John Henry walked into the room carrying a small, blank canvas in his hands. Setting it down on the drop cloth, he picked up one of his father's brushes and, daubing it in the paint, began to sketch a tentative line.

Monica smiled. "There will be many more paintings. Sally," the angel said smiling. "Many more . . ."

Beautiful Dreamer

Calvin Gibson, a ten-year-old black child in worn-out sneakers and hand-me-down clothes, stood in front of his class at Abraham Lincoln Elementary School in the heart of one of the poorest neighborhoods in the nation's capital. There was a smirk on his face as he began reading his class report on the subject of "What I Want to Be When I Grow Up."

"When I grow up," Calvin began, his voice heavy with street-wise sarcasm, "I want to be a hit man." Immediately the class broke into nervous giggles and scandalized murmurs until the substitute teacher, a woman with expressive eyes and a ready smile who had introduced herself as Miss Tess, called for quiet and gestured for Calvin to continue. "Probably for the CIA," Calvin ventured. "The pay is real good and you get to keep all your cash in Swiss bank accounts. You don't have to go to the same stupid office every day and you don't have to worry about paying electricity bills because you stay in hotels and when you retire you get to live on a beach in South America."

"And where exactly in the library did you look all of this up?" Tess asked dubiously.

"I saw it on the TV," the youngster replied, as the class erupted in laughter again.

"Sit down," said an exasperated Tess and turned to the rest of the class. "What's the name of this school?" she asked, and the children responded in unison.

"We learned all about him last year," a studious girl in the back of the room told her.

"Well," Tess replied, "I'm glad to hear that. Because he deserves to be learned about." She paused. "So I guess you also know all about the 'hit man' who assassinated President Lincoln?"

"His name was John Wilkes Booth," Calvin piped up proudly.

"That's right," Tess replied. "Well, this morning I'm going to tell you a story—a true story about John Wilkes Booth and the man he murdered. Maybe it will help Calvin make a new career choice, and maybe not. We'll just have to see." As she settled at the edge of her desk, her voice began to paint a picture as she took the children back with her, beyond the names and dates in their history books, to the drama of men and women standing at the crossroads of great events that shaped the destiny of our country, when brother fought brother in a war that would bring freedom and liberty to an enslaved people. "It was right here in Washington, DC," she told them, "on April fourteenth, eighteen sixty-five . . ."

Andrew, his face bewhiskered and dressed in a high buttoned jacket, straw boater and spats, stood on a dusty street outside Ford's Theatre as a horse and carriage pulled to a stop in front of a gas-lit lamp post. A familiar face leaned out of the carriage window—it was Sam, who supervised heavenly caseworkers in this region of nineteenth-century America. The senior angel, with his spats and side-whiskers, fit right into the time and place. "Right on time," he said with a smile. "I like that in an angel."

"Glad to be here," Andrew replied, looking around. "It's been a while since I've had a case in Washington. It's quite a different place." He looked approvingly. "Amazing what peace can do to people's spirits."

"What you feel in this city is victory," Sam cautioned. "There is no peace. Not yet. Especially not in the hearts of the angry and vanquished."

"And there's one heart in particular, I presume?" Andrew asked.

Sam nodded. "There'll be another angel working on this assignment," he explained. "Her name is Monica, from Annunciations. She's here to pass along a certain message, in the event that you should fail."

"I can't remember ever failing before," Andrew responded with surprise. "I've always had the truth on my side and that always seemed like enough."

Sam put his hand on the angel's shoulder. "Angels fail, Andrew," he said. "Humans fail. Only God does not fail. And this time He will not fail to offer the truth to someone who desperately needs to hear it. But if that man—that very angry man—refuses to listen, it will be his choice." He frowned. "The problem is, it will be a choice that will change the world."

The conversation was interrupted by an excited commotion outside the theater. "Have you heard?" one of the stagehands asked another as they put out a sidewalk display announcing the evening's performance of the play "My American Cousin." "The President is coming to the evening show!"

The First Lady, Mary Todd Lincoln, a stout woman with a determined air, bustled into her husband's office, wringing her in hands in distress. "Mr. Lincoln, what are we to do?" she fretted. "General Grant and his wife are unable to attend the play this evening. We simply must have a full box to show our support."

Mr. Stanton, the Secretary of War, stood at a table reviewing the latest dispatch with the Commander in Chief. "But surely, Mr. President," he protested, "you don't intend to go out tonight." Turning to Mrs. Lincoln, he warned, "Every time your husband shows himself in public, he risks his life."

"The war is over," replied the headstrong woman in a firm tone. "For four long years, the President hasn't been able to have a moment's peace. He needs—and he will have—an evening of entertainment."

The Secretary pursed his lips. "Do you think an evening at the theater will rid him of his bad dreams?" he asked pointedly.

"You told him about the dreams?" Mary asked her husband in a stricken tone.

At that moment, a figure appeared at the door, carrying a seamstress basket and dressed in a long muslin skirt and a lace-trimmed blouse. "Excuse me," she said, brushing back ringlets of hair. "My name is Monica. I was sent by the dressmaker." She smiled at Mrs. Lincoln. "I was told it's a very special dress for a very special occasion. I have certain . . . experience that might be useful."

President Lincoln rose from his seat. "Please ladies," he said. "Use this room. It's much warmer and Mr. Stanton and I have a meeting down the hall."

The First Lady slipped behind a screen to change into an emerald green evening gown and, as Monica began to pin the hem, the careworn woman began to speak, slowly at first, but with more animation as she sensed a compassionate ear. "I wanted a special dress for him," she explained. "I know I'm not so young anymore, but after so many years and the loss of our two dear boys in this dreadful war, I wanted to remind Mr. Lincoln of our wedding day." She looked down at Monica. "Do you think that was foolish?"

"I think it's lovely," the angel replied.

"We had so many dreams back then," Mary continued with a sigh. "Good dreams." She frowned, her voice catching. "Not like that terrible nightmare he had. He thinks God sent it to him."

"A dream?" asked Monica, her ears perking up. "Sent by God?"

"Maybe it *is* a warning," the First Lady continued fretfully. "But why would God want to punish Mr. Lincoln . . . a man who puts all his trust in the Almighty?"

"God doesn't want to punish your husband," replied Monica with conviction. "I'm sure of it."

Back in the classroom, Calvin broke Tess's storytelling spell with a derisive snort. "This is stupid," he declared. "Nobody can just walk into the President's office."

"Well, back then you could," retorted Tess. "As a matter of fact, Mr. Lincoln didn't even let them lock the White House door." She shook her head sadly. "It was a different world back then."

At a table in the back of a dark and dingy tavern down a muddy side street, a man of dashing good looks sat before a half-empty bottle of brandy. In his hand he held a knife and with the tip of the blade he carved the words SIC SEMPER TYRANNIS into a wooden plank.

"Death to all tyrants," Came a voice from the shadows. "The state motto of Virginia, I believe."

"You, sir," replied the man in a drunken slur, "are a gentleman and a scholar." He held out his hand. "Allow me to introduce myself: John Wilkes Booth, at your service."

The angel stepped from the shadows to shake the man's hand. "The name's Andrew," he said.

"Always nice to meet a fellow sympathizer," Booth continued with a gracious flourish. "What fine Southern state did you say you were from?"

"I like to think of it as the state of grace," Andrew replied, taking the chair that Booth unsteadily offered him.

"You know," Booth continued, leaning forward and fixing the angel with a hazy eye, "if there were more men like you and me,

Atlanta wouldn't be a pile of Yankee rubble." He spat bitterly on the floor. "And all because of this tyrant, Abraham Lincoln!"

"What sort of tyrant champions equal rights for all men?" Andrew countered.

"What about my rights?" the man demanded, pounding the table. "The right to own slaves? Why, it's in the Bible, in black and white."

"The Bible acknowledges that slavery existed," Andrew argued. "But God never made anyone a slave. People make people slaves. And slavery, sir, is an abomination."

Booth poured another drink and leaned expansively back in his chair. "You're a gentleman," he said reasonably. "We can agree to disagree. I can go my way and you can go yours."

"I suppose so," Andrew replied doubtfully.

"Well, then, sir," Booth cried triumphantly. "Why can't the state do the same? If the South can't agree with the North, then let's just be gentlemen and call it a day."

The angel shook his head. "It's not that easy," he replied. "If every disagreement dissolved a union, there'd be no marriage, no friendship, no contracts, no countries. There'd be nothing but anarchy. And *that* is how tyrants arise."

Booth seemed disinterested in Andrew's words, his attention drawn instead to the figure of Sam, who had just entered the tavern. "You and I are both gentlemen," he said, turning with an oily smile back to Andrew. "You obviously come from the best. As do I. And we will tolerate nothing less. Which is why—" his voice rose quickly to a shout, "—I will not drink in the company of niggers!" The tavern grew silent, all eyes turned to the boisterous man in the corner. Booth rose on wobbly legs and staggered toward the front door. "Lincoln's nothing but a tyrant," he said defiantly, as he turned back to glance at Andrew. "And we all know what happens to tyrants, don't we?"

As he lurched from the tavern, Andrew hurried up to Sam. "I think he just threatened the President's life," he said grimly.

Sam only nodded. "Sooner or later, the hatred in a man's heart finds its way into his words and then into his hands until he becomes a creator of evil itself."

"I thought this story was about assassins, not presidents," Calvin objected, once again disrupting the flow of Tess's narrative.

Tess sighed deeply and threw up a silent prayer for patience. "It's about both, Calvin," she finally said. "There are two kinds of people in this world—the kind who tear down and the ones who build up. And before you decide which one you want to be when you grow up, I want you to have all the facts. Now . . ." she paused, "where was I? Oh yes, the President was alone in his study that afternoon . . ."

Spring sunlight flooded the windows of Lincoln's office as he looked through a large pile of papers on his desk. Stopping to rub his eyes wearily, he sensed a presence in the room with him and, looking up, saw the little seamstress Monica standing in the doorway.

"Ah, Madame Dressmaker," he said with a smile. "I'm afraid my wife has just left."

Monica stepped into the room. "It's you I've come to see, Mr. President," she replied. "I believe you've been having a bad dream."

The President frowned and waved his hand dismissively. "It's nothing," he demurred. "Just the self-inflicted tortures of a weary mind."

"The dream did not begin in your mind, sir," Monica responded. "It came from the mind of God."

As Lincoln stared at her with increasing wonderment, a soft golden glow began to illuminate her face, and then the entire room.

It felt as if he were standing on holy ground. "You're an angel," he said in an awestruck whisper, and as Monica smiled and nodded, he thought for a moment, then continued. "There was many a night these past four years, Angel, when I prayed for a heavenly visit. And now that the war is over, the Almighty has a message for me?"

"He has always answered when you sought His counsel," Monica replied as she took another step closer. "But I'm here to ask you about your dream, Mr. Lincoln. Please, tell it to me."

The President's face darkened as he remembered the nightmare that had awakened him in a cold sweat a few evenings before. "There seemed to be a deathlike stillness about me," he told her in a low and somber voice. "Then, I heard subdued sobs. I left my bed and went downstairs until I arrived in the East Room where I met a sickening surprise." He shuddered. "Before me rested a corpse in funeral vestments. Around it were soldiers and a throng of people weeping piteously. 'Who is dead in the White House?' I asked one of the officers. 'The President,' was his answer. 'He was killed by an assassin.' " Shaking himself from the dark reverie, he asked the visiting angel, "Has God sent me an angel to prepare me for death?"

"Mr. Lincoln," Monica replied softly. "I believe that your faith in God has long ago prepared you to leave this world and meet your creator. But until that day comes, God wants to reward your faithfulness by bringing you a measure of peace now." The glow around her grew brighter as she continued. "I cannot see into the future, Mr. Lincoln. But I know that God loves you very, very much. He wants you to know this about your dream: no matter what happens, what is most important is that, in this dream, you are walking the halls of the White House. And for generations to come, children and presidents, citizens and legislators, average Americans and world leaders will stop in those very halls and listen for the echo of your footsteps, hoping to catch one distant, reassuring sound of honesty and goodness and genuine sacrifice. The people of this county in the centuries to come will not simply honor your memory, they will *need* it. They will cling to it in the days when heroes are hard to find. When little boys and girls wonder if there was ever a time when principles mattered more than politics. When parents search for an example of courage to point to. They will need you, the men and women of every race and religion, who will struggle to continue what you have begun, who will fight for freedom and fairness, who will even sacrifice their own lives one day; the fighters and the dreamers . . . who will follow you to the mountaintop."

The President looked down humbly and, after a long moment, spoke in a voice tinged with sorrow. "I suppose," he said, "that if God sends you an angel to bring peace, it's because you're going to need it."

John Wilkes Booth carefully bored into the wood of the door to the large box seat in the Ford's Theatre already decorated with red, white and blue bunting in anticipation of the President's arrival. He knelt down and peered through the peephole he had made, giving him a perfect line of sight to where the President would be sitting that night, in his favorite black walnut rocking chair. Rehearsing his actions, he slowly crept into the box, the knife still in one hand. It was at that moment that Andrew appeared in the doorway.

"What in blazes are you doing here?" the startled assassin cried.

"I might ask you the same thing," the angel replied.

Booth's eyes narrowed. "Who are you, Andrew?" he asked suspiciously. "I believe you are what we refer to in the theater as 'the mysterious stranger' who enters to complicate the plot. But it's too late for that, my friend." His voice rose. "This bearded gorilla, this butcher from Springfield, this Lincoln has the idea he wants to emancipate the slaves . . ." His voice was trembling now with rage. "Well, I say it's time somebody emancipated the country from Mr. Lincoln!"

Andrew could only stare, shocked at the depth and intensity of

Booth's hatred. "If you disagree so violently with the President," he asked at last, "why didn't you join the Confederate army and fight for what you believed?"

Booth only smirked. "They also serve who only stand and wait," he quoted, adding with a sinister gleam in his eye, "for the right time."

"There is never a right time for this, John," protested the angel, who was brushed aside as Booth took a swig of brandy from a pocket flask and departed with frightening determination.

"Okay," Calvin exclaimed, back in the classroom, startling the spellbound children. "Here comes the good part. John Wilkes Booth sneaks in back and *pow!* Just think what he could have done with an AK-47."

"Stop it!" demanded Tess. "This is not a movie, young man. This really happened. A real man lost his life and shed real blood and his little boy cried himself to sleep that night because his daddy was never coming back. Can you understand that?"

Calvin, unsettled by Tess's intensity, sat back in his seat. Next to him a classmate called out, "Calvin's daddy's not coming back, either!"

"Shut up!" shouted Calvin. Then, with a knowing look toward heaven, Tess resumed her story.

In the midst of a sudden spring downpour Andrew hurried through the darkness of an alley to the stage door of the theater. Once there, his face tense and pale, he put his ear to the wet wood straining to hear what was happening inside. Suddenly, the sound of a gunshot rang out and Andrew stiffened, tears welling in his eyes as a muffled voice from inside the theater cried out, "Sic Semper Tyranis!"

A day and a night later, in a pine thicket deep in the Virginia woods, Booth and his accomplice, a dull-eyed youth named Davey

Herold, huddled under a blanket as the drizzling rain continued. Both legs broken as he jumped from the theater box to the stage, Booth was bound in a crude splint, but a feverish light of triumph burned in his eyes. The men were about to remount their horses when a lone figure approached them across the wet landscape and, a moment later, Andrew emerged from the darkness.

"So," the relieved assassin remarked. "You want to help us now, do you, Andrew?" The angel nodded. "What news do you bring us?" Booth inquired.

"The President is dead," Andrew informed them solemnly.

"And I shot him," Booth crowed as he turned to the boy beside him. "We will be remembered a hundred years from now, Davey," he exulted. "When school children read about the heroes of the South, they will see our names next to the likes of Jefferson Davis and Robert E. Lee."

Wordlessly, Andrew handed over a newspaper that he held clutched in one hand. "What's it say?" asked Davey. "Does it call us heroes?"

Booth, opening to the front page, read the banner headline—LINCOLN ASSASSINATED: SHOT IN BACK OF HEAD BY A COWARD. Enraged, he ripped the paper to shreds, as in the distance the sound of barking dogs and men on horses could be heard. "There's coming, Cap!" Davey hissed.

"Then we must go," Booth ordered. He turned to Andrew. "Are you with us, Andrew?" he asked.

"Yes, Mr. Booth," sighed the angel as they set off through the underbrush. "Until the bitter end."

In the elementary school classroom in the poor neighborhood not far from where history had been made that dark day, a bell rang and class was over. As the children hurried out after getting a promise from Tess that she would return to finish her story, the angel looked up to see Calvin, sitting alone. "What was the bitter end like?" he asked in a quiet voice.

"Are you sure you want to know?" Tess asked. "It could change your career plans." The boy nodded and the angel, sitting down beside him, continued.

In a tobacco shed on the edge of a farmer's field, Booth and his trembling accomplice listened as the Commander of Federal Troops surrounding them shouted out a last warning. "Booth," he demanded. "Surrender! We'll give you five more minutes and then we're going to set fire to this place and smoke you out like rats."

"You said we were going to be heroes . . ." whimpered Davey.

"Shut up," Booth snarled and with a shove, pushed him out of the shack. "Here's a man who wants to surrender," he shouted back with defiance, then winced in agony as his broken leg throbbed. Tense minutes passed until, with the shattering of glass, a flaming bundle of straw was hurled inside. Within seconds, the tobacco shack was ablaze and Booth huddled in a corner, sipping from his brandy flask and awaiting the end. It was then, silhouetted against the flames, that Andrew appeared. "My friend," Booth exclaimed. "You have not forsaken me." He peered through the smoke. "Strange, but the light from the fire . . . illuminates you like some sort of avenging angel. Quite theatrical, actually."

"I am an angel," Andrew stated calmly. "Sent by God."

Booth smiled cynically. "No doubt God wishes to congratulate me. I am an instrument of His punishment, Andrew. I have done what He wished me to do."

Andrew shook his head sadly. "No," he said. "What you have done was not ordained by God. What you did was to murder a human being in cold blood. There was no glory in it, no providence in it, only shame." He stepped closer. "And yet, by the grace of that same God, John, there is still time to trade that shame for mercy, time to beg for it from the only One who can give it to you now."

Booth struggled painfully to his feet. "No!" he shouted. "There is no shame and I need no mercy. I have avenged the glorious South!"

"You have avenged nothing," replied the angel. "You have achieved nothing but the wrath of God. And yet, now, even now, He offers you a choice. Forgiveness and peace or separation from Him, forever. Think, John. Listen with the ears of your spirit. The only thing that will truly kill you today is your anger and your rejection of God's love and forgiveness." He stepped back. "It's your decision."

"Your God can keep His forgiveness," screamed Booth in a frenzy. "I have my revenge." A shot rang out as a sharpshooter, drawing a bead on the figure lit by the fire, did his deadly work.

As Booth's limp body was pulled from the raging inferno of the shack, Andrew walked away through the darkness into the woods. There, standing in the path, he saw a familiar figure.

"You did your best," said Sam.

Andrew could only shake his head. "You knew I would fail from the beginning."

"No," replied the elder angel. "Hearts can change in an instant. And they must be given a chance. But some hearts have already died long before the man has." He looked back at the lurid scene in the field. "It's over for him," he continued. "But there is something left for you to do." He pointed down the path, where the first rays of dawn lit the heavy mist on the ground, revealing another familiar figure, wearing a long black coat and a stovepipe hat. "I have new work for you to do, Andrew," Sam said.

"You mean . . . an Angel of Death?" Andrew asked, then smiled. "It will be a privilege." He walked up to the spirit of Abraham Lincoln.

"So," Calvin asked as he and Tess sat alone in the classroom, "did John Wilkes Booth go to hell?"

"Well," replied Tess thoughtfully. "He made a decision to separate himself from God and that's just about the worst kind of hell you can imagine. A lot of angry people do that." She paused, looking down at the child. "Are you angry, baby?" she asked. Calvin was silent, unwilling to allow her to touch the pain he felt. "I think you are," Tess said, after a moment. "I think you're angry about a lot of things. You're angry that your daddy went away and you're angry that your mama has to work nights and that your house is so cold every time it snows." She leaned close, gazing at him with her large brown eyes. "And you know what else?" she continued. "I don't think you really want to be a hit man at all. I think you're just so angry that you think that's all you *can* be. But that's not true, baby. Now, tell me, Calvin. What do you *really* want to be when you grow up? Tell Tess the truth."

"No," the boy said stubbornly.

"Why not?" asked Tess.

"Because you'll laugh at me," he replied. "Like everybody else."

"I won't," Tess promised. "Whatever it is, I won't laugh."

Calvin paused for a long moment before deciding that he could trust this unusually kind substitute teacher. "Okay," he said at last. "When I grow up, I really want to be . . . the President of the United States."

"Glory Hallelujah," Tess cried as she looked toward heaven, then back at Calvin. With a reassuring smile, Tess put her arm around the child, and they walked out of the classroom and into the bright light of day.

Buy Me a Rose

The black Mercedes wound its way up the steep mountain pass, the scenery white from a recent snowfall. Behind the wheel, Ellen Sawyer, an attractive woman in her mid-forties, drove distractedly, her eyes on the road but her mind a million miles away . . . and her heart aching with a dull but constant pain of neglect.

As the spectacular scenery rolled by unnoticed, Ellen's despondent thoughts returned to the events of the past few days. In retrospect, it seemed inevitable that this moment would come, a moment when she had to confront her unhappiness and make the choice she had avoided for almost twenty years.

Twenty years . . . that's how long she had been married to Greg, a handsome, ambitious man who had become one of the most successful real estate developers in the state of Oregon. But his success did not come without a price—the price of their marriage. It seemed that with every new deal he closed, every highrise financing package he put together and every development project he envisioned, another piece of their relationship was sacrificed on the altar of endless hours at the office, weekend business trips and cocktail parties where Ellen was required to smile and nod and play the gracious hostess to Greg's prospective clients.

And now, the biggest deal of all, the crowning achievement in

Greg's portfolio, was hanging in the balance and, with it, the future of their marriage. He had worked hard to assemble the investors necessary to purchase a large section of waterfront property in a depressed area of the city. Although at one time it had been an elegant and historic district, it was now a prime target for a massive redevelopment scheme. While it would, of course, mean relocating families and businesses that had existed there for generations, Greg stood to make a killing on the sale of the property.

But that's where the problem lay. Her husband had already managed to obtain deeds to nineteen of the twenty lots in the area, but a newcomer, a young man named Andrew, had swooped down and snapped up the last property and was refusing to sell . . . at any price. Greg, consumed by his work at the best of times, was now completely obsessed with getting the last piece of the puzzle to fall into place and, as a consequence, seemed hardly aware of his wife. What was once a loving and mutually nurturing relationship had grown cold and distant. Even as Ellen tried to rekindle the flame, Greg drifted in and out of her days like a ghost—a ghost with a cell phone glued to his ear.

Maybe, at any other time of the year, it wouldn't have mattered so much. After all, Ellen had grown accustomed to living her life in solitude, even as she yearned for the connection that had once been so strong between them. But for months she had been looking forward to the weekend they had planned together in the cabin at Lake Bearclaw to celebrate their twentieth anniversary. Only now, she found herself driving through the magnificent mountain scenery by herself. Ever since the waterfront project had become jeopardized, Greg could think of nothing else and, when his investors threatened to pull out unless he could secure the final property, he had scheduled a weekend meeting—the same weekend as their anniversary. It was Greg who had suggested she go up to the cabin herself, "for a little rest and relaxation," is how he put it, but she couldn't help but wonder if her presence was just one more distraction he could do without. That very morning, on her way out the door, he had interrupted a conference call long enough to hand her an anniversary present—a certificate for a thousand shares in the new development. She knew he meant well, but the gesture was about as romantic as a handshake and a pat on the back.

The yearning Ellen felt deep within her had only become stronger in recent days. She had hired a bright young woman named Monica to help her around the house, and the two had been cleaning out a spare room when Monica accidentally knocked over a box containing old scrapbooks and her high-school annuals and parcels of letters from another time and place.

The time was her first year in college and the place, a coffee shop off campus where she worked as a waitress while she dreamed of a career as a fashion designer. It was there that she first met Denny Blye, a good-looking young man with a brush of reddish hair and a gift for singing and writing songs. He had composed one on the spot for her that day, in lieu of a tip, and as she read again through his letters, she could almost feel the warmth of his smile. She loved the way he looked at her, as if she were the most beautiful, most special creature he had ever seen. Later that afternoon, as she sat alone in her sewing room, she had read one of his letters and the words brought tears of remembrance and regret to her eyes.

"You have taken me up like one of those garments you make," Denny had written, "you've cut me out of rough cloth and made me into something comfortable. For the rest of my life I will live as a different man because of you. These days I dream of a small but good life, a little tone—maybe I'll finally build that tree house in Oregon City and we'll live together in the clouds, forever."

That dream, in the end, hadn't come true. Ellen and Denny had discovered that they wanted different things from life and, in many ways, it was Greg's ambition that had drawn her to him in the first place. But as she read over Denny's letters she could feel the ache in an empty place he had once filled—a place that made her feel safe and cherished . . . and loved.

As she piloted the big car up the steep incline she saw a fork in the road approaching. One direction led to Lake Bearclaw and the well-appointed cabin where she would be spending her anniversary weekend alone. The other led to Oregon City, the last place she had received a letter from Denny. She stopped in the middle of the road while, inside of her, a battle raged.

Standing at the crossroad, invisible to human eyes, three angels watched with concern as Ellen Sawyer struggled to decide which road to choose.

"Twenty years is a long time for two people to be married," Tess told Monica and Andrew. "And Greg and Ellen are going to need our help to make it to the next twenty."

"Oh, dear," fretted Monica. "You know I don't have that much experience in marriage, Tess."

The senior angel smiled. "That's okay, baby," she replied. "Marriage is God's way of giving human beings a chance to practice loving one person completely, without strings attached. When they learn how to love each other like that, then they get a better idea of how God loves them. But sometimes they forget and give up before they get it right. And that's when their love dies."

The angels watched sadly as Ellen's car began to move down the road toward Oregon City, in the direction of her long-lost love.

"I know that look," said Tess, as she stood behind the bar in the hotel lobby as Ellen entered and, searching for a payphone, made a call. A troubled look came over her face as she hung up and crossed to where Tess was waiting. "Kind of glazed, kind of tired, kind of cold. You need coffee, don't you?" She put her forefinger to her lip, thinking. "Let me guess. Sugar, no cream."

Ellen smiled wearily. "How did you know that?" she asked.

"You're dealing with a professional here," a beaming Tess replied. "And as a professional, I'd have to say that phone call wasn't all you expected it to be. Was it something he said, or something he didn't say?"

Ellen put her head in her hands as Tess poured a cup of coffee. "I just lied to my husband for the first time," she admitted. "I told him I was at our cabin. Instead . . . I'm here." She looked up. "I guess this is the part where I spill my guts to the bartender."

"I guess it is," Tess agreed with a nod.

Ellen sighed. "I can't remember why I married my husband," she explained to the kindly stranger. "I loved him. I still love him. But things have changed and we don't have a life together. There's just his life and I'm one small part of it." She looked into Tess's wise brown eyes. "What should I do?" she asked.

In response, Tess topped off her coffee cup. "You're going to have one more for the road," the angel said decisively, "and you're going to follow it home, baby. That's the only direction that will lead you not into temptation." Ellen began to speak, but Tess held up her hand. "Don't say anything," she commanded. "Just nod."

Ellen hesitated a moment before acknowledging the truth of what Tess was saying. She nodded and, slipping off the stool, began to walk across the lobby. It was then that she heard a strangely familiar voice coming from a small lounge at one end of the hotel. "Good evening ladies and gentlemen," it said, in a warm and welcoming tone. "I hope you're having a good time in Oregon City. My name is Denny Blye and I'm going to sing a few songs for you."

Ellen stopped dead in her tracks. "On, no, baby, no . . ." murmured Tess and she watched the lonely woman move, as if drawn by a magnet, toward the voice.

Andrew sat across from Greg at an elegant downtown restaurant, doing his best to resist the practice pitch of an accomplished entrepreneur. "I control nineteen properties on the waterfront," Greg was telling him. "You control one. I want you to sell it to me. What do you want?"

"I want you to give me your nineteen," Andrew shot back. "The waterfront area is historically significant and a neighborhood for generations of families. It should be restored to its original state." He leaned forward. "But I've got a hunch you want to sell it to retail stores and businesses, make a killing and get out."

Greg's eyes narrowed. That was exactly his plan. "So you want to save the waterfront and all the little people who live there?" he asked sarcastically. "Come on, Andrew. I'm not my brother's keeper."

"Yes, you are," Andrew answered evenly.

"Look," countered the frustrated developer. "If I put profit aside and become a do-gooder, do you know what that would make me?"

"Happier?" asked Andrew bluntly.

Entranced by her own memories, Ellen sat in the back of the room as Denny performed for a small audience in the lounge. When he asked, "Anybody out there ever been in love?" she wanted to jump up and proclaim that she had, once, but it was all too long ago. And as he sang his next song, she felt as if he were reading words written on her heart. "This is the house that love built / Memories of you, built in each wall / Still haunt my dreams . . ."

As he closed out the set and moved to a small table by the side of the stage, she stood and walked over, hardly daring to trust her feelings enough to call out to him. But it was Denny who looked up and, recognizing her immediately, rose, walked over to her and said simply, "Ellen. It's you." It was the look in his eyes that brought tears to hers and in a moment she was in his arms, sobbing, as he stroked her hair and whispered. "It's okay. Whatever it is, it's okay."

He led her back to the table and over the next half hour, as she dried her eyes and tried to calm her pounding heart, they caught up with the twenty years that had separated them. "Did you ever get married?" she asked. "Ever build that tree house for two?"

"Tree house, no," he replied with a smile. "Married, yes. For about fifteen minutes." He shrugged. "But that's all right. These days I spend most of my time with Abby. She's sweet and gentle and very understanding."

"Abby," she asked. "Is that . . . ? "

"My black Labrador," he explained. "We go camping on the weekends." He leaned forward. "But what brings you here, Ellen, after all this time?"

She lowered her eyes, avoiding his question. "You still sound wonderful," she said at last. "You were always such a good song-writer."

"I wrote them all for you," he replied, seeking her eyes. "I've never stopped thinking about you, Ellen," he confessed. "And I promised myself that, if I ever saw you again, you wouldn't get away from me a second time."

"I'm a married woman," she told him in a voice barely above a whisper.

"You didn't say 'happily married,' " Denny observed earnestly. "One thing I'll always be proud of, Ellen. I made you happy." He took her hand. "Didn't I?"

"Yes . . ." she said. "Yes, you did."

Above them came the loud sound of a throat deliberately being cleared. "Less talk," Tess commanded. "And more singing."

Denny grinned. "That's Tess's way of telling me that it's time to get back to work. Will you wait for me?" He paused. "We can go back to my place after the show."

Ellen hesitated. "Everything's happening so fast," she said. "I . . . think I'll just check in here tonight."

Denny nodded. "Then how about breakfast tomorrow and a walk with Abby?"

Ellen smiled wanly. "I'd like that," she replied.

Greg slammed down the phone in his home office just as Monica, dusting the house, entered the room. "That was my number one investor," he told her, giving vent to his frustration. "He wants to bail on the project." Thinking quickly, he snapped his fingers. "Wait a minute," he continued. "Ellen does charity work with his wife. Maybe she can put in a good word for me." He rapidly punched up the number of the Lake Bearclaw cabin and was surprised when the caretaker, and not his wife, answered. After a brief conversation, he hung up, a scowl on his face. "She never got to the cabin," he told Monica, anger rising in his voice.

"I'm sure there's an explanation," Monica said, trying to calm him.

"Yeah," he replied bluntly. "She lied." He picked up the phone and hit the caller ID button, connecting him immediately with the payphone in the Oregon City hotel. Connecting to the switchboard, he made a terse inquiry, then hung up the phone, his jaw clenched. "I found her," he scowled, then slammed his fist on the desk. "The biggest deal of my life and she pulls a childish stunt like this. What is she thinking?" Rising quickly, Greg grabbed his car keys and rushed from the room.

Ellen and Denny walked down a tree-lined path where a fresh snowfall had painted the landscape a pristine white. As Abby, Denny's frisky Lab, romped around them, the two spoke in low, earnest tones.

"I've never been unfaithful to my husband," Ellen told Denny.

"I'm not asking you to be," he replied. "But you're sure not happy, either, Ellen, or you wouldn't have come here."

"Are you happy?" was Ellen's simple question.

"I've got a good life," Denny answered thoughtfully. "You in it would make it that much better." He paused, turning to her. "But do you remember why we broke up? We wanted different things. And we got them." He smiled, with a trace of sadness. "The truth is that I love seeing you and we'd probably have a good time together for a while but, in the end, people don't change."

"I don't believe that," was Ellen's retort. "I want a simple life again. I want . . ." she looked around "this."

Denny shook his head. "You didn't come here looking for me. You came to visit your past because you've been having trouble with the present."

Ellen thought for a long, slow minute. "He's not a bad husband," she said at last. "And let's face it, he had all the ambition that I kept trying to find in myself."

"And in me," Denny added, with a knowing nod of his head.

"We have a good life," Ellen continued. "But what I want most is just for him to . . ." her voice broke, "notice me again. To write me a love letter . . . like you did once."

Denny stopped and turned to face her. "You've got to go home to make that happen," he reminded her gently. He reached out to brush away a stray lock of hair. "Stay in touch, okay?"

"I will," she replied and leaned forward to kiss him good-bye.

At that moment, a familiar voice sounded loudly in the cold air. "Get away from my wife!" shouted Greg as he charged down the path. Grabbing Ellen by the arm he pulled her aside and took a swing at Denny, connecting squarely to his jaw. The singer reeled back, but stayed standing as Ellen screamed for Greg to stop.

"Did you hit me because you love her," Denny asked his assailant, "or because you hate to lose?"

"I'm sorry," Greg replied, shocked by his own behavior. Then turning to his wife he said, "We're going home. I'll wait in the car."

Ellen turned to Denny with a stricken look. "I'm okay," he reassured her as he rubbed his jaw. "Go on home." He smiled and winked. "It's not a love letter, exactly. But, in a weird way, it's a start."

"Nothing happened," Ellen insisted for the hundredth time as they entered the front door of their spacious home. "You've got to believe me, Greg."

"If you have nothing to hide," he asked between clenched jaws, "then why did you lie to me?"

Ellen struggled to put her feelings into words. "I . . . don't know . . ." she stammered. "I found some letters of Denny's in a box and started reading them and I just . . ." she fought back tears. "I haven't been happy for a while, Greg," she managed to get out at last.

"How can you not be happy?" he demanded. "Everything I've done I've done for you."

"Give me a break!" Ellen shot back, her anger rising now to match his. "You're a workaholic who just needs a wife to show up at the parties and charity dinners. You dumped me on our anniversary for some business deal! I always come in second and I'm tired of it."

"I've always tried to give you everything you wanted," Greg insisted.

"I don't think you know what I want," was her terse reply.

"Tell me," he said.

Her eyes brimmed with tears. "It . . . doesn't count if I have to ask for it."

Greg heaved a heartfelt sigh. "So now what?" he asked in frustration. "Do I have to guess? I suppose Denny would know the answer, right? Denny, the fully evolved sensitive male, has it all figured out, right?"

Ellen's tears flowed freely now. "All I know, Greg," she replied, "is that for the few hours I was with him. . . . I was happy."

Ellen sat alone in her sewing room, reading over Denny's packet of letters, cherishing each word and every loving phrase. "Greg?" she said, turning as she heard a sound behind her.

"No," replied Monica, emerging with a teapot and cups on a tray, "It's me." Entering, she sat down and poured out two cups of the fragrant brew. "My friend Tess always says that a good cup of tea helps when someone is hurting," she continued, pausing a beat before adding, "but the truth will do a lot more good." She turned to see a questioning look on Ellen's face. "The truth is," she said gently, "those love letters don't belong in your life anymore, Ellen."

Ellen looked down at the packet of letters on her lap, unwilling to acknowledge the reality of what Monica was saying. "Every so often I read one of these when I feel a little blue," she explained. "They remind me that there is someone out there who used to think the sun rose and set with me." She began to cry. "But he's not my husband . . . and all I want is my husband."

"Ellen," Monica responded intently, "you have your husband. God gave him to you, to have and to hold. But you can't hold on to him and these letters, too."

"Thank you, Monica," replied Ellen. "But you're not married, so you don't understand."

"No, I don't," Monica agreed. "But God does. He is your friend. And I am His angel." An unearthly golden light began to shine around her, filling the small room with a brilliant glow.

"What's happening?" asked the awestruck Ellen.

"You're receiving a 'love letter' from your Creator," was

Monica's reply. "God loves you, Ellen. He knows every lonely night you've spent waiting for your husband to come home. He knows the longing in your heart for the romance and excitement that you think is missing in your marriage now. There is nothing in a woman's heart that God does not understand. He made you, Ellen, just as he made Greg. And He made you for each other."

"Then why am I so unhappy?" Ellen asked in a quavering voice.

Monica pointed to the letters. "You've been asking your husband to compete against a memory. The memory of someone who is not a better man than Greg, but who was simply able to write on paper what your husband had written in his heart."

"Is it wrong to want that from Greg?" the tearful Ellen implored. "To want romance and love letters?"

"No," replied the angel. "But ask yourself—when was the last time you wrote a love letter to *him?*" She reached out to put her hand over Ellen's. "Love is not a line you draw in the sand and then dare someone to step over. It's not a feeling you have that comes and goes. Love is a choice. And God is asking you to make that choice now."

Ellen looked back down at the letters. Slowly, she picked them up and, one by one, tossed them into the glowing embers of the fireplace, watching as they burned, turning to ash and drifting up the chimney.

Greg sat at a table in the lounge of the Oregon City hotel, awaiting the arrival of Denny. He had a score to settle, but even as he pondered his next move, he could feel a knot of doubt and guilt tightening in his stomach. Ellen had said that he didn't really know what she wanted. Did he? Had he ever asked?

A figure approached and Greg was surprised to see Andrew take a seat next to him. "What are you doing all the way up here?" he asked.

"I'm here on business," the angel replied and leaned forward to look directly into Greg's eyes. "As you may have guessed, I represent Someone with an interest in your properties. And He wants to be your partner."

"Forget it," Greg snarled. "I don't need a partner. Whoever you are, and whoever you represent, I just need to know one thing: Are you in a position to sell or not? Because if you are, I'm prepared to double my offer. And if you're not, then we have nothing further to discuss."

Andrew rose, taking a deed of sale from his jacket pocket and tossing it on the table. "The property is yours, Mr. Sawyer," he announced. "But let's be clear about something. You didn't win. It's a gift. God has given you many gifts and He expects you to take care of them. You start by accepting the greatest gift of all—the love that He has for you. And then you share that love and you work harder at that than anything else. Because, in the end, when you and I meet again, that love will be your only hope. And it will be all you need."

A dumbfounded Greg stared at the deed on the table. Unable to find the words to say, he turned back to Andrew only to find that the angel had vanished into thin air. Staggered by the strange events of the past few minutes, with the words of the angel still ringing in his head, he didn't notice as another familiar figure approached his table.

"She's not here," Denny informed him, then asked, "Are you planning to hit me again?"

"No, no," replied the startled Greg, then pursed his lips and confessed, "Well, to tell you the truth, I was planning on it. But once I got here . . ." He looked over to the place where Andrew had been "I changed my mind." He turned back to Denny. "Look," he continued hesitantly, "I don't . . . quite know how to ask this. I mean, after twenty years you'd think I'd know my wife and what she wants, but . . ."

"Roses," was Denny's one-word reply.

"What?" asked the puzzled Greg.

"That was the secret," Denny explained. "Once a week, I'd give her a rose or a daisy or whatever I could afford. I wrote her a note every once in a while for no reason at all. I made up songs about her, pretty terrible ones, but that wasn't the point. I just made sure she felt like the most important thing in the world to me."

"Do you still love her?" Greg asked seriously.

"Enough to want to make sure she's loved by you," was Denny's determined answer.

"She is," responded Greg. "But I don't know how to write a love letter."

Denny smiled. "Sure you do," he said. "It's not about finding the words, my friend. It's about finding the time."

Greg entered the house just as evening was falling and, in the gilded glow of twilight, saw his wife standing at the foot of the stairway, unsure of how to approach him or what to say. He crossed to her and, with all the gallantry and grace he could muster, he produced a beautiful bouquet of roses from behind his back. Attached to the flowers was an envelope and inside, in words he had taken the time to write, was a letter that expressed to his wife of twenty years the love he had for her, yesterday, today and for all their tomorrows.

Trust

The squad car pulled to a screeching stop outside an old brick tenement house in a dilapidated neighborhood on the outskirts of Cleveland. The officers jumped out in time to see a man clamoring down a fire escape and running headlong down an alley.

Zack Bennett, a fifteen-year veteran on the force took off after the suspect, followed closely by his new rookie partner, a young woman named Monica, who wore her rich auburn hair tied tightly in a bun. Pursuing him through the railroad switching yard they plunged headlong into an abandoned warehouse, through twisted piles of debris, until, at last, the suspect was cornered.

Zack stood, breathing heavily, sweat covering his face and his vision blurry. He fumbled at his utility belt for handcuffs, but his trembling hands dropped them onto the concrete floor. The would-be burglar tried to make a break for it, but at that moment, Monica, her gun drawn, arrived breathlessly on the scene. "Hold it," she shouted authoritatively. "Right there." The criminal halted as Zack, recovering his composure, slapped on the cuffs.

"Go check on the backup," he told his partner. "I'll read him his rights."

Reluctantly, Monica began to move off, but she turned back to watch silently from the shadows as Zack frisked the suspect, who whined the whole time about his constitutional rights. "What have we here?" Zack said, pulling out a small baggie of pills from the back pocket of his prisoner. "A little speed, some downers . . . you're a regular pharmacy." As Monica watched grimly, Zack slipped the drugs into his own pocket as he manhandled the suspect back through the warehouse.

"This cop took my stash!" the criminal shouted as he caught sight of Monica. "He's got it. He must be a doper."

Zack shoved him violently, then turned to his partner. "First lesson, rookie," he growled. "The perp's always going to lie, always going to try to get between you and your partner. Never give him an inch."

Monica followed silently as they made their way back to the squad car. The angel had had some tough assignments before, but the case of Zack Bennett promised to be one of her most challenging. Her new role as a cop, wielding a weapon and chasing bad guys, was taxing enough. The real test would come as she tried to help Zack escape from a corner he had backed himself into and could find no way out by himself. She found herself more grateful then usual for Tess's support, as the senior angel had taken on duties as a police radio dispatcher back at the station. As she and Zack hustled their suspect into the back of the car and sped away, she remembered what Tess had told her at the very beginning of this assignment: "This is a man in great danger . . . to himself and to everyone who knows him."

It was a danger that had begun, ironically enough, with a narrow escape from death. Three months before, Zack Bennett, one of the force's most dedicated and conscientious officers, had faced every cop's nightmare when a desperate criminal had pulled a gun and, with one squeeze of the trigger, had brought Zack's world crashing down around him. The bullet had missed his spine by a mere inch and, during the course of a long and painful recovery, he had kept the .38-caliber slug on his nightstand as a reminder of how near he had come to finding out whether or not God really existed.

But the bullet wasn't the only reminder of Zack's close call. For the first time in his career, fear had begun to gnaw away at his confidence and self-esteem. A man's life could be extinguished in the blink of an eye and that reality had lodged itself deep into his consciousness. Nothing seemed to take it away, nothing, that is, except for the sedatives and pain killers the doctor had prescribed to make him more comfortable during his long recovery. At first Zack had used the pills as they were intended, to help him sleep when the pain in his wounded shoulder became too intense. But he quickly learned that the drugs also helped to ease another kind of pain, the pain that came from being afraid to face the uncertainty of life and the danger that was inherent in his chosen profession. By the end of three months, when he reported back to active duty, nothing, from outward appearances, had changed. He was still the same ruggedly handsome cop, and he still exuded the fearless attitude and natural leadership that had seen him through his years as a star quarterback on his college football team and his early training at the academy. But now Zack Bennett was dealing with a full-blown addiction the only way he knew how—by denying it to himself and trying to hide it from those closest to him.

It wasn't easy. His wife, Jill, who operated a small pastry and coffee shop in front of the couple's apartment, knew something was wrong with her husband—something terribly wrong that seemed to drive him further away from her with every day that passed. And his former partner of five years, Ben Rivera, had also picked up on the changes in Zack's personality and professional demeanor. That is until Zack abruptly requested to be assigned a new partner when he returned from medical leave, alienating and angering a long-time friend who would have easily seen the troubling signs of Zack's addiction. Isolated and facing a problem much bigger than he was, Zack had run out of the prescription drugs the doctor had provided and now, against every principle and value this good cop stood for, he was reduced to shaking down the local lowlifes for whatever stash they had in order to feed his habit. It was time for some heavenly intervention, and Monica prayed she would have the courage and wisdom to help a good, but proud, man reach out to God when he needed Him most.

"Knock it off," snarled Ben Rivera, as Zack, coming up behind him in the police locker room, gave his former partner a playful punch on the shoulder. The out-of-breath, disoriented cop of a few hours before had been replaced by someone fast-talking and full of nervous energy, as the uppers Zack had taken from the street punk cranked him up on an artificial high.

"What's your problem?" he asked Ben, bobbing and weaving like a boxer in the ring.

"We've been partners for five years," Ben replied angrily. "I thought you trusted me, until you hooked up with that rookie. I guess you must blame me for taking that bullet."

"It wasn't your fault, Ben," Zack assured him as his eyes flicked nervously from side to side.

"Then how come I've lost a partner and a friend?" Ben asked bitterly. "Something's wrong, Zack. Nobody knows you like I do . . . and you can't keep me away forever."

From across the room, Peterson, a brash newcomer on the force, shouted "Head's up!" as he tossed a ball across the locker room toward Zack, the star pitcher on the precinct's softball team. Zack turned quickly, but in a drug-fueled flashback saw a bullet instead of a ball racing toward him. With a strangled cry of fear, he dropped to the floor as, around him, the room fell into an uncomfortable silence.

Watching invisibly as Zack got to his feet and pushed his way into the squad room, Monica and Tess shared a concerned expression. "I just want to shake him," said the young angel. "He's got to understand what he's doing to himself."

Tess shook her head sadly. "That's not going to happen until he hits bottom," she warned. "And hitting bottom is the only thing that's going to get him on his knees." She turned to Monica. "Let's just hope he doesn't hurt anyone else on his way down."

It was nearly dawn when Zack, coming off the powerful stimulants, finally arrived home, carefully opening the front door and tiptoeing into the apartment. "I'm not asleep, Zack," came a voice from the darkness as his wife, Jill, turned on a small lamp by the table where she sat. She was an attractive woman in her early thirties, but Jill's open honest face was now etched with worry and exhaustion as she confronted her husband. "What's wrong with you, Zack?" she asked desperately. "It's five-thirty in the morning. You've got to be at the station in a half hour."

Zack seemed surprised by the news. "Really?" he mumbled. "I . . . couldn't sleep. I guess I'll just shower at the station . . ."

"Zack!" Jill said sharply. "I want some answers. You owe me an explanation. You're acting weird and I want to know what's going on."

"I don't need you looking at me like that," was Zack's accusing reply.

"Like what?" responded Jill, truly confused.

"Like you think I'm going to get shot again," Zack said, giving unwitting voice to his fears. "Like you think I'm not a good cop."

Jill rose and crossed the room to her husband, standing face to face with him. "Great cops get shot, Zack," she told him, trying to break through the walls he had erected around him. "Getting shot doesn't mean you're not a good cop."

Without answering, Zack turned and left. Outside, in the predawn darkness, he reached into his jacket pocket for the bag of pills he had confiscated. For a long moment he stared at them and then, with a sigh of disgust, he threw them into the storm drain of a nearby gutter.

Later that same morning, Zack and Monica cruised along the city streets on the first patrol of the day. "We're running a bit late this morning," Monica observed and, when she didn't get a reply, continued, "What's on the agenda? Same as yesterday?" Still, no answer came. "Are you all right, Zack?" the angel finally asked bluntly.

"I'm always all right," he snarled, avoiding her eyes as the dispatch radio crackled to life and Tess's voice came over the loudspeaker. "Fifteen-Alpha-nine," she transmitted, "where in heaven's name are you? You're supposed to be at the courthouse for the pre-arraignment hearing for your arrest yesterday."

Zack ruffled frantically through the papers next to him on the seat. "Where's the schedule?" he demanded. "Did I pick up the schedule?" Without waiting for an answer, he turned the car around in the middle of the block and, with a screech of tires, headed full-tilt down to the courthouse.

Rushing through the imposing front doors, Zack and Monica hurried to a bank of elevators just in time to see their suspect walking away with a spring in his step. "Well," he said with a sneer, "looky here. It's the cop and copette. Running a little late today, huh?"

"You're not going anywhere," Zack replied, unwilling to believe what was happening.

"Sure I am," the criminal shot back. "I'm walking away. If you guys don't show up to tell them I'm the bad guy, there's no case." His lip curled with contempt. "I love the Constitution. I love America." He began to move toward the front doors, then he stopped and turned back for one last parting shot. "By the way," he said to Zack, "thanks for taking care of the 'evidence.' Hope you enjoy it."

Zack began to lunge at the suspect, but Monica held him back, as a harried looking Assistant District Attorney came down the stairs and Zack turned on him with the full brunt of his outrage. "How could you let that piece of slime walk?" he demanded.

"If you wanted him arraigned, you should've shown up," came the DA's terse reply. "My job is not to wait around for you. Do you have any idea how many felons walk because you guys can't take ten minutes to show up?"

"I've never missed a hearing," Zack retorted.

"You just did, buddy," was the DA's angry response as he moved down the hall.

A dejected Zack walked slowly from his Captain's office, still smarting from the weight of their exchange. Zack had always prided himself on his spotless record, but now that all seemed like a cruel joke as the craving for drugs began to consume his will power. Sweaty and shaking, he moved to a corner of the squad room and stuck his hand in his pocket, forgetting for the moment that he had thrown his supply away that same morning. With a sudden desperate look, he moved rapidly out the front door and into the city streets he had sworn to protect, walking past the unseen angels who stood in silent witness.

"He's coming down hard," Tess said, with a resignation tinged with compassion. "His body's going crazy."

"At least he quit," Monica remarked hopefully. "Once he goes through withdrawal, he'll be fine, won't he?"

"It's not always that easy," Tess cautioned with a shake of her head. "Getting rid of the pills doesn't get rid of the problem." She turned to Monica with a somber look. "This isn't over yet."

As if in prophetic fulfillment of the angel's words, an hour later, Zack found himself in a seedy downtown neighborhood shaking down yet another hapless drug dealer and coming up with a handful of assorted pills. Popping three at random, he waited for the chemical rush that brought with it the temporary release from his fear and anxiety. Calmer now as the drugs pumped through his veins, Zack got back in his squad car and returned to the station.

As he entered the squad room, Monica rushed up to meet him. "Zack," she pleaded, "I have to talk to you."

"Don't start on me," Zack snapped back, his distorted perceptions making him instantly defensive. "You don't need to know where I am every minute—" He stopped, seeing the grim look in the rookie's eyes.

"They just brought an attempted rape victim in," she explained in a low voice. "She made a positive ID. It's our suspect. The one who walked today."

The blood drained from Zack's face as he heard the news, and the shock was compounded a moment later when Tess arrived, carrying a clipboard.

"Listen up," she announced loudly. "The following officers will report to the locker room for random drug testing." As she ran through a list of names, she turned with a quick glance to Monica as she read off the last: "Bennett."

Zack emerged from the drug test, his face still pale but with a determined stride. Signaling to Monica, he moved out to the parking lot and climbed into the squad car. "Where are we going?" asked Monica as she got in next to him.

"We're going to catch us a rapist," was his reply, spoken through clenched teeth. "That creep is free because of me. It's my fault and it's going to be my collar."

"You can't, Zack," Monica said, then drawing a deep breath, she continued, "You're a cop on drugs."

Startled, Zack turned to her, seeing the truth reflected in her eyes. He sighed. "You know I don't have much time," he said in a low voice. "They'll get those test results in twenty-four hours. I'll lose my badge." His jaw clenched. "But at least I can do something about that scum in the meantime."

"You're in no condition," protested Monica. "You have an addiction, Zack, and that's the only thing you can do something about right now."

Zack sat silently for a long moment before answering. "I lay in that hospital bed for a month," he said at last, "and then another two at home. First the pills were for killing the physical pain, but the closer it got to getting back to the job, the more they became about killing the fear. All I could see was that bullet coming at me. The only thing that made it disappear were the drugs."

"And now there's hardly anything left *but* the drugs," Monica added urgently. "You've pushed away everyone you love just to protect a secret that you hate."

"It's not going to be a secret when those tests get back," he remarked ominously.

"I want to help you, Zack," the angel pleaded.

Zack turned to her with a look of fierce resolve. "If you really mean that," he said, "you'll help me find this guy." As he spoke, he pulled up next to the warehouse into which they had chased the suspect earlier that day. "Ten to one this is where he crashes," Zack explained as they got out of the car and moved toward the door with their guns drawn. Stepping inside, he gestured for Monica to stay behind. "You cover this exit," he told her. "And call for backup. I'm going in."

"Maybe I should go with you," the angel suggested, but Zack had already moved off into the gloom of the interior, trying to clear the effects of the drugs from his brain and concentrate on the job at hand.

At the far end of the large, littered room, a figure stepped out of the shadows, a gun tightly held in both hands. The rapist took careful aim as Zack, unaware that he was a target, moved stealthily along one wall.

"Hey!" a voice hissed from behind the criminal. "Over here!" Spinning around, he saw Monica standing behind him and in the next split second the warehouse echoed with the deafening sound of gunfire. Monica reeled back against the wall, looking down at the bullet hole in her chest as she slumped to the floor. A stunned Zack arrived moments later and, yanking his radio from his belt, shouted out a message. "Officer down!" he cried. "Officer down!"

At that moment, Ben Rivera and another officer appeared at the door of the warehouse, and the rapist ran breathlessly out to the street. "Freeze!" Ben shouted as he and his partner converged on the desperate criminal and, in a few moments, had him on the floor and handcuffed. Pulling out his radio, Ben radioed to Zack. "We got him," he reported. "We were in the neighborhood when we heard the backup request." His voice sounded tense as he asked, "Who's down, Zack?"

But Zack wasn't listening. Right before his eyes, Monica had straightened up and sat with a peaceful smile on her face as all around her a golden glow began to shine forth into the dark confines of the warehouse. "Who is it, Zack?" Ben asked again over the radio. "Is it the rookie?"

Fearful that he was hallucinating, Zack answered, slowly, trying to keep his voice from trembling. "It's okay," he said. "Bad call. We're fine. Get him out of here."

"Zack," Monica began in a voice full of compassion. "I told you I wanted to help. I am an angel." A look close to terror came over him at the words. He backed away, sheer panic on his face. "Don't be afraid," the angel continued. "I have a message for you from God. He wants to help you."

Zack, wondering now if the drugs really had driven him insane, took another step backward. "I'm going out of my mind," he muttered and, turning, ran staggering from the warehouse.

"Zack!" Monica shouted after him, then turned to see Tess standing next to her.

"He's not ready yet, baby," she told the junior angel. "He's still not on his knees."

It was after closing time when Zack, still badly shaken, returned home, entering his wife's shop by the front door and jumping back with fear when he saw a figure appear in the doorway leading to their apartment. "Freeze!" he shouted, whipping out his gun only to realize, a moment later, that he had drawn a gun on his own wife.

"Zack," cried a frightened Jill. "What's the matter with you?"

Shaking like a leaf, his skin slick with sweat, Zack holstered his gun. "What's the matter with me?" he said, defensively. "It's dark, it's late, you come sneaking up on me . . ."

"I'm not the one who's been sneaking," Jill replied, taking a step toward him.

"What's that supposed to mean?" her husband snarled.

"What's wrong?" she persisted. "You look like you've seen a ghost. I'm scared, Zack."

Unnerved by her questions, Zack unbuckled his holster. "You're being ridiculous," he insisted. "Everything's fine." As he tossed the gun belt on the counter, his service revolver accidentally fired, shattering a jar of penny candy and sending the brightly colored balls rolling loudly across the floor. Instinctively, Zack grabbed Jill, covering her with his own body to protect her.

"Oh, God," he cried. "I'm sorry. I'm sorry."

"Why wasn't the safety on?" Jill demanded, beginning to cry with fear and confusion. "You always put your safety on . . ."

It was at that moment that the light of realization dawned in Zack's eyes. He could have killed his own wife . . . the person he loved most in the world. He was out of control and no one was safe around him. Turning without a word, he left the store.

"Zack?" a frightened Jill called after him. "Zack, please!"

Returning to the warehouse, inspired by the vision of a glowing Monica, Zack carefully inspected the site where the point-blank shooting had occurred. There was not a trace of blood. "He shot her," the strung-out cop murmured to himself. "I saw him shoot her. Right here." Shaking almost uncontrollably, he pulled out his stash of pills and, opening the bags, tried to pick them up with numb and sweat-drenched fingers. Instead, he dropped them on the floor and with a cry of despair, got down on his hands and knees and picked through the filth and rubble to find the drugs he had spilled.

It was then he caught a reflection of himself in a dust-stained window nearby—a desperate junkie crawling on the dirty floor to find his fix. Furiously sweeping the pills out of his sight, he rose to his knees and, looking up, spoke with a voice trembling but utterly sincere. "God," he said, his eyes filling with tears. "Help me. Please . . . bring back the angel . . ."

Opening his eyes again he looked down and saw the bullet he had carried with him since his near-fatal shooting, lying close to him on the floor. Reaching out to pick it up, he was amazed to see it roll out of his reach and into another hand, waiting to retrieve it. Slowly his eyes looked up and there, dressed in dazzling white robes, was Monica, the golden glow around her even more brilliant.

"Didn't I say not to be afraid?" the angel reminded him. She opened her hand to show him the bullet. "You carry this with you to remind yourself of how close you were to death," she continued. "But you're a lot closer now than when this bullet was three inches from your spine."

"Am I hallucinating?" Zack asked in a hoarse whisper.

Monica shook her head. "No," she told him. "I'm very real. I'm here because God sent me to help you. There's a reason why you survived that bullet." She pointed to the pills scattered over the floor. "And it wasn't for those. This bullet ripped through your body, and your body survived. But your spirit is still bleeding. That's because you weren't wearing your armor." He gave her a quizzical look and she smiled as she explained. "There's only one thing in this world that is truly bulletproof, Zack. It's faith. Not faith in a gun that shoots or a radio that works or even your cop's instinct. It's the faith you wrap yourself up in every day of your life. Faith that, no matter what happens, you won't lose God's love. And all the bullets in the world can't pierce it. And all the pills in the world can't replace it."

"But I'm scared," confessed Zack. "I'm scared all the time. I'm scared to live like this."

"God loves you, Zack," Monica told him with complete conviction. "And if God is on your side, what is there to fear? Nothing. Now or ever."

She reached out to give him back the bullet. Taking it in the palm of his hand, he stared at the small metal slug for a long moment then, tipping his hand, let it drop to the floor.

Ben drove Zack, sitting next to him in the squad car, to a stop outside Jill's coffee and pastry shop.

"Glad we can be partners again," Ben said with a grin. "Just as soon as you get out of rehab, we'll be back on the streets, catching bad guys."

Zack returned the smile gratefully. "Thanks for the support," he said humbly, as he looked through the store window to where his wife was counting up the day's receipts. "She was always afraid I wouldn't come home after work," he explained with chagrin. "Now I think she's afraid I *will*."

"Go get her, tiger," Ben urged with a smile. "She's a good woman. She'll understand."

Zack got out of the car and, as he crossed the street, passed two invisible angels, sharing their own grateful smiles.

Tess and Monica watched from a distance as Zack slowly approached his wife, took her in his arms and began, carefully and lovingly, to explain all that had happened.

"Sometimes," Tess observed, "the simplest things are the hardest to say."

Monica nodded in agreement. "Things like 'I'm sorry.' Things like 'I didn't mean to hurt you.' Things like 'We'll get through this.' " She turned to Tess. "I think Zack Bennett is out of danger," she said confidently.

"And so is everyone else who loves him," replied Tess, adding with a twinkle in her eye, "Good job, 'partner.' "

Into the Light

James Block stood before the altar in the small chapel of the county hospital, while alongside him, his longtime girlfriend and about-to-be-wife, Rachel, beamed with joy. This was a day that she had been waiting to arrive for over eight years—eight years when she had heard every story, every excuse and every stalling tactic in the book. No one was more surprised than she was when James, out of the blue, called her up and asked her to marry him, right then and there, that very day.

James smiled smugly to himself as the preacher read the wedding vows. No one could ever say that James Block didn't know how to get himself out of a jam when he had to. And this was one jam that took all his practiced skills as a hustler to squirm out from under.

Thirty-two-year-old James Block, tall and thin with a receding hairline and charm to spare, had a lot of experience getting himself out of tight spots . . . almost as much as he had getting himself into them in the first place. He was a con artist extraordinaire, a man with a silver tongue and slippery fingers who had been in and out of trouble with the law for most of his life. But for all his run-ins with authority, James had never spent a single night in jail. He'd made sure, years ago, to find himself the best lawyer in the business and to keep him on retainer for any kind of legal emergency.

And then there was the sob story about his bum ticker. James had been diagnosed years before with a heart condition and the doctors had told him he'd be lucky if he lived past thirty. Determined to make sure he squeezed each and every ounce of high living out of those years, he also made sure to squeeze tears from any jury that sat in judgment of him. A man living on borrowed time, just trying to get ahead before the grim reaper caught up with him: He'd sold that story a dozen times and, every time, those twelve suckers had bought it.

This time was no different. Caught red-handed in a bribery scheme, James had trotted out the old heart condition story, complete with violins, and had gotten away with a six-month suspended sentence and community service. It was a sweet deal, considering that all he had to do to repay his debt to society was to mop a few floors and clean a few windows at the local hospital. With a little luck, he figured he could probably even scam his way out of that.

But he found out there was no such thing as luck when he met the formidable head nurse in the hospital to which he'd been assigned. She was a real dragon lady named Tess who seemed wise to his tricks even before he tried to pull them. She wasn't about to let him get away without performing every last minute of his community service, and she let him know as much in no uncertain terms.

And then came the news from that high-priced lawyer of his. The cops, it seemed, weren't quite ready to give up on their bribery case and, in an attempt to gather more evidence, had subpoenaed Rachel—the same Rachel to whom he made the promise that he'd get out of the rackets and cons after this one last job. Poor, sweet Rachel . . . she'd believe anything.

And she did, too. Knowing that a wife could not legally be required to testify against her husband, James had put in a call right then and there, cajoling her into coming down to the hospital and getting hitched. There had been a lot of talk about mending his ways and not being able to live without her and James even meant some of it . . . as long as it got him what he needed. Which, in this case, was a wife who couldn't say a word against him in a court of law.

He had even taken care of finding a witness for their instant wedding, a sweet nurse with red hair and an Irish accent named Monica, whom he'd talked into coming to the chapel, just as the preacher got to the part about, "Do you take this man and do you take this woman?"

The trouble was, someone else showed up right about then, too—an uninvited guest who wore a white suit and seemed to stare at James as if he were looking right into his soul. No one else seemed to notice the man in the white suit and when James demanded to know who he was, the stranger only fixed him with that eerie gaze that sent a chill down his spine.

But there was more than one unwanted guest in the chapel that morning. Just as James and Rachel had finished their I do's, the door burst open and a squad of cops rushed in, waving that subpoena for Rachel. "Rachel Carson?" they demanded, and it was all James could do to keep from bursting out laughing.

"Wrong," he crowed. "It's Rachel Block. And unless I'm mistaken, and I know I'm not, you can't force a legally married woman to testify against her own husband."

Rachel turned to him, a cold fury burning in her eyes. "So that was why you were in such a hurry," she hissed. "This is without a doubt the most narcissistic, egotistical—are you getting the picture?—arrogant, manipulative—"

James was sure he could sweet-talk his way back onto her good side, but right about then he had other things on his mind. The stranger in the white suit had moved down the aisle and now stood very close, his eyes burning, and he had a somber look on his face. As James watched with growing dread, a sudden sharp pain shot down his left arm and he suddenly felt as if an elephant was sitting on his chest. He crashed to the floor as a heart attack sucked the breath out of him and the commotion in the chapel suddenly seemed very distant and indistinct. He could hear Rachel screaming his name, and he saw the face of the nurse Monica leaning in very closely as she took his pulse. "I'm sorry," he heard her say as she felt him sliding into a long dark tunnel. "I'm afraid he's gone."

When James awoke he found himself alone in the empty chapel. Confused and disoriented, he rose to his feet and looked toward the altar. It was then that he saw the man in the white suit, standing silhouetted against a bright white light. Unsure of what, exactly, was happening, but attracted to the brilliant glow, James began walking toward the light, only to see the figure of the man recede farther and farther away, the harder he tried to reach him. Soon, James found himself running as hard as he could to reach the light and felt a panic rising in his throat as the darkness began to thicken all around him. Exhausted by his efforts, he stopped and, for the first time, turned around. A huge engulfing blackness rushed at him and with a terrified scream, James covered his face to hide from the fiery horror that was about to overtake him.

When he opened his eyes again, he saw the ceiling fixtures of the chapel swimming in and out of focus and a swarm of nurses and doctors crouched over him. "I've got a pulse," one of them said. "I think he's coming back." The next face that came into view was that of Rachel and he could feel her warm hand gripping his. "Please, Rach," he croaked. "Don't leave me."

"I'm right here, James," she replied, fighting back tears. "Right where I've always been."

"The guy in the white suit," he asked as he was hoisted onto a gurney. "Where did he go?"

"Just close your eyes," his new wife pleaded. "Try and rest."

It was late the next morning when James tossed and turned in his hospital bed, groaning as the vision of the man in the white suit returned to him in his dreams. As the darkness once again enveloped him, he let out a strangled yell and opened his eyes to find a young girl of thirteen sitting by his bed, her hands folded and her eyes closed.

"Who are you?" he asked, his voice still heavy with fear. "And what are you doing here?"

The girl opened her bright blue eyes and gave him a dazzling smile. "My name is Amy Ann," she said. "I'm in the room next to you. I heard you yelling in your sleep, so I came over to see if there was anything I could do."

"Is that why you were praying?" James asked, his eyes narrowing suspiciously.

"You . . . sounded scared," Amy Ann replied. "And you didn't look so good." She paused, then began to cough, a harsh rattling sound from deep inside her chest.

"I was having a bad dream," James admitted. "I was in a tunnel and there was this white light. It was so real I could almost touch it. But then . . ." he stopped, unwilling to describe the terror of the darkness that was overtaking him, ashamed to admit that, as hard as he tried, he couldn't reach the light that was beginning to disappear.

"Maybe it wasn't a dream," ventured Amy Ann. "They say when you die, you see a beautiful white light." She paused. "I heard the nurses talking. They said you were gone. Your heart stopped beating . . . for almost a minute."

James lay silently, trying to absorb what he was hearing. "Man," he said at last. "I always thought that that afterlife stuff was just a big scam."

"You don't believe in heaven?" Amy Ann asked in surprise.

"No," he replied. "Because if I did and there was someone up there keeping score, I'd be in trouble. Serious trouble."

"Maybe," Amy Ann ventured, "it's not too late to change things."

James considered this for a moment as they both listened to the soft bleeping of his heart monitor. "I wonder what it would take?" he said finally, half to himself.

At the nurses' station later that afternoon, Tess was surprised to see James pushing Louise, a cancer patient, down the hall in a wheelchair.

"James Block," she announced. "You just had a heart attack. You're supposed to be resting."

"No time for that," he replied as he pulled a black notebook from his bathrobe and made a quick notation. "Helped sick lady in wheelchair," he muttered as he wrote, then looked up at Tess with a broad smile. "What can I do?" he asked. "Who can I help?"

"Well," replied Tess doubtfully, "since you're up, I think Amy Ann could use a visit. She took a turn for the worse last night. I'm afraid her cystic fibrosis is advancing faster than the doctors thought."

A troubled look came over James as he turned and made his way down the hall. Turning into Amy Ann's room, he found the young patient sitting with Monica.

"James," she said happily as he entered. "We were just planning my birthday. I'm going to be fourteen tomorrow. Will you come to the party?"

"Sure thing," he replied. "And I'll bring my new wife, Rachel, along. She bakes a mean chocolate cake." The smile on Amy Ann's face was quickly replaced by a look of pain as she began to cough uncontrollably. As James watched helplessly, Monica quickly turned her over, strapped on an oxygen mask and began rapping sharply on her back. "Hey," protested James. "Is it really necessary to hit her so hard?"

"It's the only way to clear her lungs," Monica explained as Amy Ann's coughing continued relentlessly.

Uncomfortable at the sight of the young girl's condition, James backed out of the room and walked back toward the nurses' station, pulling out his notebook and reviewing it in the process. "There's got to be something else I can do," he said when he reached Tess. "I oiled the wheelchairs, emptied the bedpans, delivered all the Jell-O and read to the kids."

"Don't you think you've done enough?" asked Tess, between pursed lips.

"Not even close," responded James as he headed off down the hallway looking for more good deeds to perform.

A moment later, Monica arrived at the station. "Amy Ann's resting now," she told Tess as she noticed James farther up the corridor. "I can't believe it," she marveled. "It's like James is a new man."

Tess shook her head, setting her salt and pepper curls in motion. "More like an old dog trying to convince God that he's learned some new tricks," she countered. "He's doing all the right things . . . for all the wrong reasons." Suddenly an alarm began to blare at her desk. "It's Louise," she said. "She's in cardiac arrest." Switching on the PA, she sent out an urgent call. "Code blue, room one–two–two–four." Turning to Monica, she gestured. "Come on, baby. We've got work to do."

Louise, pale and weak, was resting comfortably after the emergency team had finished their work. She had made it through the crisis and Tess stood by her bedside, stroking her forehead. "You just relax, baby," she said soothingly. "You had a close call there." She looked up to see James standing in the doorway. "James recently had a close call himself," she continued. "Didn't you, James?" She smiled and rose, leaving the two alone to talk about their shared experience.

"So," James asked cautiously. "Did you . . . see the light?"

Louise's eyes widened in surprise. "Yes," she replied. "It was so warm. So comforting." She smiled. "It was all around me. I can still feel it. And that wonderful man . . ."

"The guy in the white suit?" James probed, a sinking feeling growing in the pit of his stomach. Whatever Louise's experience had been, it sure wasn't the same as his. "About thirty? Quiet? Kind of just stares at you?"

"Oh, no," replied Louise. "He spoke to me. He was so kind and he was with me every step of the way."

Deeply troubled by what he was hearing, James backed out of the room and, turning, hurried down the hallway. It was then that he saw Andrew—the mysterious man in the white suit—turning down a nearby corridor, and James hurried to catch up. "Hey!" he shouted. "Hey, you! Wait up!" Patients and nurses watched, curious about this frantic man yelling down an empty hallway.

"You were there, weren't you?" James demanded as he caught up with the angel. Andrew nodded wordlessly. "She said it was wonderful in the light," he continued in an urgent tone. "That you were with her every step of the way. What about me? Will it be wonderful for me next time? I've been doing all these good deeds."

Andrew shook his head, with a look of pity. "James," he said, "even if every one of your good deeds was a step to heaven, it would never reach high enough."

"You mean I'm not going to heaven?" the hustler asked with a crack in his voice.

"That's not up to me," Andrew replied. "It's up to you."

"Don't give me that line," James spat bitterly. "You can't con a con," he declared as he turned on his heel and stormed away.

The next morning Rachel stepped into James's hospital room, Amy Ann's freshly baked birthday cake in her hands. She stopped dead in her tracks when she saw the angry and frightened look on her husband's face as he methodically tore one page after another out of his black notebook. "Shredding documents again, James?" she joked uneasily.

He looked up at her, a wild expression in his eyes. "It doesn't matter," he muttered. "Nothing matters."

"James," she said with concern. "What's wrong with you? I spent all morning baking this cake like you asked me. I thought this birthday party was important to you. Don't disappoint this little girl."

James glared at her. "When she grows up she'll find out that life is just one big disappointment," was his answer.

"She's not going to grow up," came a voice from behind them, and they turned to see Tess standing in the doorway. "She doesn't have much longer to live," Tess continued bluntly. "It's only her faith in God that's sustained her this long."

"Her faith in God?" James echoed cynically. "You mean her fantasy."

"God is not a fantasy, James," Tess responded in fervor. "You should know that better than anyone. You saw His light. Most people are never given that gift."

"Gift?" James repeated. "You mean curse. What was the point of seeing that light? To torture me? To tell me that God exists but not for James Block?"

"You can't blame God for the choices you made in your life," Tess shot back.

"What about Amy Ann's life?" James snapped. "She's probably never done a bad thing in her life, but you know what? It doesn't matter. Good deeds count for zip. There's light and there's dark. And which side you end up on is just a crapshoot."

Tess glared at him. "Whatever is going on in your world," she said at last, "you can put it aside long enough to help a young girl who's dying."

"Oh, I'll help her, all right," James responded ominously as he barged out of the room with Tess and Rachel, still holding the cake, right behind him.

Amy Ann, sitting up in bed with Monica by her side, lit up with delight when she saw James enter her room. "James," she cried. "Now it really *is* a happy birthday."

"I'm here to tell you the truth, Amy Ann," he said, his voice trembling on the edge of hysteria. "You need to know . . . that you're going to die."

"Stop it, James," a shocked Rachel whispered.

"Why?" he asked in a seething rage. "It's God's truth. And it's also the truth that God doesn't even care. I know. I've seen the 'light.' "

"I thought God was watching over me," Amy Ann whimpered, her young face suddenly full of doubt and fear. "I thought He was going to be with me." She sobbed and suddenly began gasping for air as Monica grabbed the respirator and placed it over her mouth.

"Leave," Tess commanded with imposing authority as Rachel pushed James back out into the hallway.

"How could you do that?" she demanded. "How could you tell her that there is no God?"

"God's the biggest con artist of them all," James replied. "He's nobody to put your faith in. He's a jerk. And only a loser puts their faith in a jerk."

Rachel just stared at him for a long moment. "Maybe you're right," she said at last. "After all, I put my faith in you for eight long years, hoping that one day you'd become the man I knew you could be. But that's never going to happen." She began to weep. "I pray to God I never see you again." Sobbing, she ran down the hallway.

"Rachel!" James shouted as he hurried after her. It was at that moment that the figure of Andrew appeared from around a corner and began to move inexorably toward Amy Ann's room. "No!" he shouted in rage and utter frustration. "You can't have her! I won't let you take her." Diving for the angel, he tackled thin air instead and went crashing into a cart of hospital supplies. Groaning, he got to his feet and charged a second time, once again passing right through the angel where he stood.

"Are you okay?" asked the Angel of Death.

Slowly and painfully, James got to his feet. Turning, he saw Andrew and Monica standing before him, both bathed in a brilliant heavenly light. In her hand, Monica held his black notebook. "How'd you get that?" he asked in amazement. "I tore it up."

"Anything is possible for an angel," Monica replied and began to read from the pages of the pad. "Pushing a woman in a wheelchair. Reading to a blind child. Getting a cake for Amy Ann's birthday." She looked and, with an ironic glint in her eye, said, "My. It's no wonder you're angry. All these good deeds and it still isn't enough. I suppose you think you deserve bonus points for being 'good' enough to tell a little girl she's dying."

James narrowed his eyes suspiciously. "So," he said, "if you're both angels, suppose you tell me why Amy Ann has to die in the first place."

"Dying isn't what you think, James," Andrew answered softly.

"I know what it is," the con man insisted. "I saw it all. The light and the dark. And I know where I'm going. Into the darkness. Into hell . . ."

"Hell is separation from God, James," Monica explained. "It's an eternity without light. If you are on your way there, it's not God who is sending you. You're sending yourself." She held up the notebook. "You haven't done these things to honor God. You've done them to get yourself into heaven." She smiled compassionately. "People are always trying to build themselves a stairway to heaven. Some are like towers. Some are only a few steps high. But there's never been one that's high enough to reach all the way to God. That's when a soul has to stand on the top step and say, 'Here! Here

I am. Please lift me up the rest of the way!' And God hears you, James. He reaches down and takes you home."

"That's what God's mercy is," Andrew added. "He doesn't give you what you deserve. He gives you what He wants you to have. Because God loves you. All you have to do is sincerely ask for His forgiveness. Ask Him to live in your heart and make you new. It's up to you."

"Then," James asked in awe, "there really *is* a heaven?"

The angels nodded. "More beautiful than you can imagine," Monica assured him. "And you can get there." She paused. "Who do you think God is?" she asked.

A bewildered James shook his head. "I don't know," he admitted.

Monica smiled. "God knows that," she told him. "He knows you weren't ready to walk into the light. That's why He gave you a second chance to know Him. When you stand before your Creator, don't you want to see the face of a friend, not a stranger?"

Andrew reached out and put a hand on his shoulder. "That light you saw?" he reminded him. "It's just the beginning. Wait until you see what comes after that." He smiled. "God gave you a second chance, James. Take it."

The chapel was empty with soft afternoon light shining through the stained glass windows as James entered and made his way slowly to the altar. Slowly and softly he began to speak, awkwardly trying to find the words for the first prayer he had ever uttered. "Look," he said, swallowing hard, "I've used everybody my whole entire life. I've even tried to use You. I've taken Your name in vain." He shook his head in shame. "But I guess I don't have to tell you." The lump in his throat grew larger. "I've been trying . . . to build a stairway," he stammered. "I think I got maybe two steps on it. Must look pretty pathetic from where You sit. But the angel, she says that

prayers reach higher than stairs, so if You can hear me . . . I'm calling. Come and get me, God." Tears filled his eyes as he dropped to
his knees. "Because I can't go any higher. Not without You. I know
that now." A long moment passed as he summoned his courage. "I
know I'm no good," he continued at last. "But if there's anything I
can do, then please, God, use me. Starting now." Rising, he turned
to see Rachel standing in the chapel doorway, the tears in her eyes
matching his own. "Rachel," he said, his voice choked with emotion. "What are you doing here?"

She smiled. "Just having my prayers answered," she whispered
and in the next moment they were in each other's arms, weeping
with joy for the renewed love and commitment that God had
sparked between them.

"There's someone else who deserves to have her prayers answered," James said, as he held her in his arms. "I don't know what
I'm supposed to do, except to go and be with her." Kissing his wife,
he left the chapel, leaving her to marvel at the amazing transformation that had just taken place.

James entered Amy Ann's hospital room as Monica tried her
best to make the young girl, weak and barely conscious now, as
comfortable as possible. "Amy Ann," he said softly as he stepped inside. "Amy Ann, I've made a terrible mistake."

She opened her eyes and smiled wanly. "No," she said, her voice
barely above a whisper. "You were right. I'm going to die." She
raised her hand to summon him closer. "Can I tell you a secret?" she
asked as he leaned in closely over her bed. "All my life I've been
praying to God, James. All my life. And I believed. I really did. But
now, when I need Him most. . . . I'm scared. I mean, what if there
isn't a heaven? What if I die and there's no God? What if there's
nothing but darkness, after all."

James exchanged a meaningful look with Monica. "God is waiting for you, honey," he promised her. "There *is* more. I know. I've seen a little piece of heaven myself."

Amy Ann looked up at him, her bright eyes dimming. "You know, James," she said. "You can't con a con." A violent coughing fit suddenly wracked her fragile body. Monica began pounding her back to clear her chest, but stopped after a moment. It was too late now. All she could do was try and make these last minutes as peaceful as possible.

"Amy Ann," James said intently. "Listen to me. I'm telling you the truth. God loves us. I know that now. If you can't hold on to Him, ask Him to hold on to you. Ask Him, sweetheart! Ask Him!" Amy Ann continued coughing uncontrollably. "Isn't there anything we can do?" James asked helplessly.

"You're doing it," replied Monica with a smile.

Amy Ann reached out to hold his hand and he leaned forward again, whispering in her ear. "There's a beautiful light," he told her. "All you have to do is walk toward it."

"I'm so tired," the girl said in a fading voice. "I can't make it all the way."

"You don't have to, honey," James told her as tears streamed down his face. "Just go as far as you can. He'll take you home from there."

A soft golden light suddenly filled the room. Amy Ann opened her eyes and, along with James, looked up at the smiling face of Andrew.

"Hello, Amy Ann," he said as he stepped toward the bed. "Are you ready? Let me show you the way."

James reached out to stroke her hair, touching her face one last time. "I love you," he said and the smile on her face let him know that she had heard what he said and would carry that love with her as she went to meet their Father.

Lost & Found

Evil can be compared to a weight, bound tightly around the heart of a man. The more evil he experiences, the more he encounters, the heavier that weight becomes, until, at last, he is paralyzed by the burden of it. Without help, without a way to lift that accumulation of evil, he will sink beneath his own despair. But with help—the help of God and the angels He sends to do His will—a man tormented has a choice to make and a chance to be free. Angels can bring him to that point of decision. But it's the free will of every human that must decide whether to fight the evil of the world . . . or succumb to it.

For Frank Champness, that evil was chronicled in the pages of a large, red leather scrapbook he kept hidden away in a drawer of his modest bachelor apartment. Frank never took the book out, never looked at the pictures of innocent children or read the heartrending accounts of their abduction. He didn't need to. He knew their stories all too well. Some of them had concluded in joyous reunions, when he had been able to hand a little boy or girl back into their mother's arms. Then there had been the ones that had ended in tragedy and horror, the ones that added yet another weight to the groaning burden of guilt and anguish that was the constant companion of Frank Champness.

As a missing persons officer on the St. Louis Police Force, Detective Champness had had a hand in each and every one of the cases now commemorated in the yellowed clippings of his scrapbook. His zeal for his work was matched only by the sense of crushing defeat when a missing child was never found . . . or worse. He couldn't help but blame himself when he had failed, and when the accusing voices became too loud to bear he had quit the force, moved to New York and become a full-time investigator for the city's Center for Missing Children. There was no more-dedicated member of the Center's staff than Frank Champness; none more professional in his work or proud of the victories he shared with the other staffers. And there was none whose secret suffering was more painful when, as too often happened, a vanished child could not be found, no matter how hard he worked or how many sleepless nights he spent turning meager clues and scanty evidence over in his mind.

Today was no exception, promising to be as hectic and harrowing as any in the busy Center for Missing Children. It had been the new receptionist, a silver-haired woman with an engaging smile and a no-nonsense manner named Tess, who had first given him the urgent message that a young boy vanished from the men's room in a local mall. Frank and his partner, another ex-policeman named Don Dudley, were ready to move out immediately, stopping just long enough to brief the Center's newest employee—a redheaded administrative assistant with sparkling green eyes named Monica, who had been hired to help with the ever-increasing case load. Thanks to additional funding allocated to meet the growing epidemic of cases, Monica had arrived along with a computer tech named Andrew, who was working on a special program that would reconfigure the photographs of children and artificially age them, depending on how many years they had been missing, to aid the investigators in their work. Frank, of course, was grateful for any help he could get, but no matter how many new staffers were recruited, he always took each and every case as a personal responsibility. Finding missing children was his job to do . . . and his burden to bear.

Yellow police tape cordoned off the crime scene in the bustling mall when the investigators arrived with Monica. The angel watched as Frank immediately headed toward a distraught woman, standing lost and alone in a corner.

"That's the mother," he said as Monica hurried to catch up with him.

"How can you tell?" she asked.

"I've seen that look a thousand times," was his grim reply. Monica sensed the inner turmoil in the investigator, something simmering just below the surface that was threatening to boil over in the brightly lit confines of this mall.

As Frank introduced himself to the mother, Monica saw Don Dudley cross to the door of the men's room and begin to interview a tall teenager with sandy blond hair who was wearing a janitor's uniform. He'd been working in the bathroom when little Craig Cooper—the missing boy—had seemingly vanished into thin air. But she knew simply by looking at him that this young man had nothing to do with the crime. There were some things an angel could tell about humans with a simple glance.

"This is my fault, isn't it?" Craig's mother was saying, her eyes filling with tears as she looked up into Frank's face.

"This happens in malls all over the country," Frank replied with a distant voice, and then, as if noticing for the first time the pain in the woman's eyes, added with compassion, "Don't blame yourself. That won't do you or your boy any good. Now, do you have a picture of your son?" Mrs. Cooper quickly produced a snapshot showing a freckle-faced eight-year-old with a missing front tooth. Slipping it into his jacket pocket, Frank pulled out a business card and handed it to her. "Call me anytime," he said, his voice now soft and reassuring. "Day or night." He smiled, as Don Dudley approached. "I'm going to get your boy back for you, Mrs. Cooper. That's a promise." Ignoring the scowl on his partner's face, Frank turned to leave. "Take her statement," he ordered, then moved off quickly, yet not so fast that Monica couldn't see his suddenly heavy breathing and the sheen of sweat that covered his face.

Seeking out a hidden corner of the mall, Frank leaned against the wall. His breathing had now become a harsh panting, and he gripped his chest as wave after wave of panic swept over him. From a place deep in his memories, the voice of newscasters began to surface, harsh and accusing. "Brian Grayson disappeared two weeks ago from a local mall . . ." began one, only to fade into another report; "Investigators have failed to locate the child who was abducted over a year ago;" and then a third, "It's been ten years since Brian Grayson was last seen in this mall . . ." Brian Grayson. The name itself caused a shudder of dread to rack his body, even as he saw his partner and Monica approaching, concerned looks on their faces. Pulling himself together, he turned and headed for the exit without waiting for them to catch up.

"What the hell was that all about?" Don demanded angrily when they returned to the Center's crowded office. "You know better than to make promises." He jabbed his finger at the other man's chest. "What if you can't make good on it?"

Frank knocked his hand away. "Back off," he snarled, as he stormed into his office. "Just back off."

Don shook his head, more concerned now than angry. "Something's going on with him," he said to Monica. "He never drops the ball like that." In the lobby the elevator bell sounded and, as the door slid open, Don's face broke into a smile. "Of course, with a distraction like that, who can blame him?" Monica's heart sank as she turned around and saw a familiar figure stepping from the elevator and through the doors of the Center. "That's Frank's new girlfriend," Don continued as he cast an anxious look at Tess behind the reception desk. The senior angel shook her head ruefully, as if to say that a tough assignment had suddenly gotten a lot tougher. The slinky and impeccably dressed woman who had suddenly appeared on the scene was none other than Kathleen, the fallen angel whose sole purpose, Monica sometimes thought, was to undo all the good work she and Tess tried to accomplish among humankind. An agent of the enemy, a walking force for evil, wrapped in a beautiful package, Kathleen created havoc wherever she appeared, and her arrival clearly signaled that the stakes of this mission had just gone up.

"Well, well, well," the fallen angel purred. "We meet again."

"I wish I could say I was happy to see you, Kathleen," Monica replied.

"Well, somebody's happy to see me," Kathleen answered coquettishly as Frank emerged from his office and, seeing her, rushed over, his face lighting up as she gave him a kiss, long and a bit too personal.

"Frank," Monica said, clearing her throat. "I still have some paperwork you need to—"

"Hasn't he had enough of this depressing job for one day?" interrupted Kathleen. "You've probably had seventeen missing children calls since lunch."

Turning to Tess, Frank asked, "How many have we had?"

"Seventeen," Tess admitted grudgingly.

"Isn't she amazing?" beamed Frank. "Sometimes I think she must be psychic or something. She's just too good to be true."

Tess and Monica watched with deep misgivings as Kathleen hooked her arm around Frank and led him out the door.

"Talk about someone going to the devil," remarked Andrew, coming up behind them. "I can't believe this."

"Happens every day," replied Tess, shaking her full head of hair.

"Every chance she gets she tries to destroy the good in people," said Monica, as she sat in the empty office after hours with Tess and Andrew. "Now she's going to hurt Frank. I just know it. But why?"

"Trying to make sense out of evil will just get you a headache, Miss Wings," warned Tess. "Evil is for evil's sake. Period. It's only goal is destruction."

"All I know is that you can't let Frank Champness get dragged down." interjected Andrew, adding grimly, "This is one of the toughest assignments an Angel of Death can get. Attending the murder of any child . . ." He shook his head as if trying to dislodge a haunting memory. "But I can't tell you how many times I've been ready to go, when Frank gets there in the nick of time. I don't know how he does it."

"Sure you do," smiled Tess as she glanced heavenward. "The miracle is that there isn't more evil let loose on the world."

Meanwhile, across town, the evil that had been let loose in Frank's life had just finished making him a delicious dinner. "All my favorites," he marveled as he polished off the last bite on his plate. "Maybe you really are psychic."

Kathleen turned on her most radiant smile. "I just feel so comfortable around you," she said, then let a small frown cross her face. "That's why I worry about you and that job." She leaned closer, letting him get a full whiff of her heady perfume. "It's too much pressure for one man, Frank," she whispered. "You've got to get a break. You've done so much for those children. Now it's time to do something for yourself."

Frank stood up and held out his hand. "Come with me," he said. "There's something I want to show you." Leading her into the living room, he pulled an old red leather scrapbook from the bottom drawer of a cabinet. Sitting down on the sofa with her he began slowly turning its pages, where one newspaper clipping after another told the story of a missing, abducted or vanished child. "I first started keeping this when I got assigned to Missing Children," he explained, as Kathleen assumed a mask of care and concern. "Sometimes we'd find them before it was too late." He stopped as terrible memories began to stir. "And sometimes we didn't. So I cut out these articles from the paper. Successes and failures. But I'd never look at them again." He shrugged. "I guess it was a way of cutting the darkness out of me and locking it away."

Kathleen looked deep into his eyes as she stroked his face. "Those poor little children," she said. "The guilt you must feel when you're too late to help. It's no wonder I worry about you." Her carefully chosen words resonated, leaving a mark of pain etched deeply on his face. She leaned over to kiss him. "I want you to go straight to bed after I leave. You need a good night's sleep."

Frank smiled, saying, "It's good to have someone looking out for me."

An hour later, as he lay in restless sleep, a brief but violent thunderstorm passed over the city, bringing with it flashing lightening and lashing rain. In the sudden lurid glare of a thunderclap, the figure of Kathleen could be seen, a chilling smile on her face and the scrapbook in her hand. She opened it, seemingly at random, to a clipping with a headline that read RUNAWAYS FOUND IN WAREHOUSE. A photograph of the dark interior of an abandoned storage facility seemed to waver and blur before her as its image was suddenly transferred into Frank's sleeping mind.

In the surreal dreamscape of the warehouse, he felt himself moving through a maze of broken glass and rusting machinery until the beam of his probing flashlight fell on two motionless shapes beneath a dirty blanket. The nightmarish vision was accompanied by a voice that intoned the terrible fate of the abducted runaways. "They froze to death," it said. "If only we could have gotten here sooner." With a stifled cry, Frank awoke. He was alone in his room

. . . alone with the guilty conscience of a man who could do nothing to restrain the evil that took innocent lives.

It was when Frank and Kathleen got together for breakfast the next morning that the fallen angel launched the next phase of her plan—a plan that depended as much on Frank's loneliness as it did on the desperate guilt that gnawed at his heart.

"Remember when you said I might be psychic?" she asked with a sly smile. "Well, I think you were right. There's a real connection between us."

"What do you mean?" asked Frank unsuspectingly.

"Well," she continued smoothly, "I seem to have this picture in my mind of something bright red. And there's a feeling that goes with it . . . that you should reach out and grab it. If you don't, something really bad is going to happen."

"I'm supposed to grab something bright red?" asked the puzzled Frank.

Kathleen shrugged. "I know it sounds strange, but that's not all." She reached out and touched his hand. "That little boy you're looking for. I keep seeing him with animals."

"What kind of animals?" was Frank's next question.

"Lions and tigers and bears," she replied, to which Frank added, with a laugh, "Oh my . . ." They both giggled, the strange tension that accompanied Kathleen's words dissolving in the bright sunlight pouring through the window.

They were words that Frank vividly recalled later that morning when he arrived at work to find the building's elevators shut down for servicing. With a frustrated sigh he headed for the stairs and began the long climb to the fifth floor offices of the Center. But by the time he had reached the third floor, his breath was coming in short gasps and he could hardly lift one foot in front of the other. Surprised at how suddenly out-of-shape he felt, as if a strange weakness had overcome him, Frank struggled against a dizzy spell, reaching out to steady himself and feeling the stair railing break off under his hand.

Reeling backward he flailed at the edge of the stairs, grabbing the first thing he could find, unaware that his pager had dropped from his coat pocket and clattered down the landing. Recovering his balance, he stared at the object bolted to the wall that had stopped his fall: a bright red fire extinguisher.

"Something red," he muttered to himself as he tried to catch his breath. "She did it again." Moving unsteadily up the remaining flight, he was unaware of the dark eyes with the uncanny crimson tint that watched him from the shadows of the stairwell. Frank safely out of sight, Kathleen stepped forward and, with a satisfied smile, picked up the pager and tossed it from hand to hand.

Entering the lobby of the Center, Frank was about to return Tess's cheery greeting when the headline of the morning paper caught his eye: CIRCUS COMES TO TOWN, it read and underneath, in words that jumped out at him, "Lions, Tigers, Bears to Perform."

He turned quickly to Tess. "I've got a lead on the Cooper kid," he announced excitedly. "I'm going to check it out now. Beep me if anything comes up."

Three hours later, a dejected Frank returned to the office where Monica, with a worried look on her face, met him in the lobby.

"Where have you been?" she asked with a tinge of anger in her voice.

"Following a lead," replied Frank as he headed for his office, adding under his breath, "It didn't pan out."

"We got a call from somebody who spotted Craig Cooper downtown," Monica informed him as she followed, uninvited, into his office. "But by the time we got there it was too late. We found his cowboy hat . . . but that's all."

Now it was Frank's turn to get angry "Why didn't you beep me?" he demanded.

"We did," Monica replied evenly. "Eleven times."

Frank reached into his coat pocket and, realizing his pager was missing, sank into his desk chair with an air of utter defeat.

Monica felt compassion for this overwhelmed man, who seemed to be carrying the weight of the world on his shoulders. "You mustn't blame yourself," she said softly.

"Oh, mustn't I?" he responded bitterly. "Then who should I blame?"

"If you must lay blame," the angel replied, "then blame evil. It's not you who loses them, it's evil who takes them. Satan works every day of every year to destroy what is good in this world."

"Monica," Frank said, "I know you mean well, but I don't believe in Satan. It's people that are evil and the bottom line is that Craig Cooper is still missing because I screwed up." He put his head in his hands. "I can't believe this is happening again." Noticing Monica's questioning look, he sighed deeply before continuing. "Brian Grayson," he said, by way of explanation. "Three years old when he disappeared from a mall. I was a rookie back then, had this idea of being a hero and personally returning Brian to his mother." He paused, swallowing hard. "So I held out. I had two leads, but instead of passing one along to another cop to follow up, I took them both." A wave of pain and recrimination passed over his face. The first one didn't pan out. By the time I got around to the second . . . it was too late. Brian was gone. That was fifteen years ago, and I'm still looking for him." He shook his head and pointed to his chest. "If evil exists, it's not some outside force. It's in here."

Later that afternoon, as Tess was leaving the office, she noticed a tall, sandy-haired teenager with a confused look standing in the lobby. With a quick glance of acknowledgment heavenward, she walked over and said boldly, "You're trying to decide whether to go upstairs or not, aren't you, Ryan?"

"How do you know my name?" asked the startled teen.

"I know a lot of things," replied Tess with a smile. "Like I know you're the janitor from that mall, and you might have some information about the missing boy."

"I feel kinda dumb," Ryan admitted. "What if I'm wrong?"

" 'If' is the saddest word in the history of language," Tess responded. "You hang on to 'if' long enough, it'll eat a hole in your heart. But if you let it go, tell people what you know, even if it seems dumb, that little word loses its power."

Five minutes later, Ryan was sitting in Frank's office relating a small but telling detail of the abduction to the officers. "There was a man in the bathroom before me," he was saying. "He was acting kind a funny, but I didn't think much of it. Then later I noticed some tags in the trash. Like from new clothes. I figured it was probably a shoplifter."

Frank straightened suddenly. "Do you remember what store they were from?" he asked.

Ryan nodded. "Kelly's Men's Store," he replied. "They've got a shamrock on their tags."

Frank was already on the phone, summoning Don, Monica and the rest of the team into his office. "You did real good, Ryan," he smiled with his hand over the receiver.

Frank, with Don and Monica in tow, moved quickly through a dirty and debris-strewn storefront in a ramshackle neighborhood on the edge of the city. Their flashlight pierced the gloom as Monica shouted out Craig Cooper's name over and over again. Suddenly, a faint and trembling voice could be heard behind a locked door in one corner of the room. Grabbing a crowbar from the floor, Frank smashed through with a single powerful blow and shined his light on the dirty face of a small boy, hungry and frightened, but safe . . .

With the lead provided by Ryan, Frank's well-oiled investigative machine had been able to break the Cooper case open within a day. Even as the entire Center gathered to watch the child being re-united with his mother, Frank stood off to one side, still unable to shake the haunted feelings of guilt that stayed with him always, even in the midst of such a joyful reunion.

"I wish I could do something to help him," Monica lamented later as she sat with Andrew at his computer terminal. "Kathleen is getting to him, but I can't interfere. He's got to make the choice himself." She paused, looking at a faded yellow newspaper clipping in her hand. A caption under the photo of a small boy read BRIAN GRAYSON. "It's an unsolved case of Frank's," Monica explained in answer to Andrew's query. "He thinks it's his fault the boy was never found. That was fifteen years ago and it's been torturing him ever since."

A moment passed as Monica could almost hear the wheels turning in Andrew's mind. "Stop the presses, Angel-baby," he said at last, taking the clipping out of her hand. "This may be a long shot," he added, as he slipped the picture into the computer scanner. "Fifteen years is a long time, but you never know . . ."

They both watched intently as the computer aging program slowly did its work on Brian Grayson's features. As a new, more ma-tured face began to come into focus, Monica gasped sharply. She could hardly believe what she was seeing.

Frank walked dejectedly through the twilight rush hour of the big city, the alienation he felt isolating him from the throngs of peo-ple that passed by. Today should have been a good day—they won one for a change, but all that the return of Craig Cooper did was to remind Frank of those other children who hadn't come back . . . and maybe never would.

As a he turned the corner of his block, a little girl holding her mother's hand looked solemnly into his face. "It's all your fault, Frank," she seemed to be saying and as he turned away in horror he saw another child, staring at him from a ground floor window. "It's all your fault," the boy mouthed and, consumed with the very real fear that he was losing his mind, Frank lurched into his apartment building and unlocked the door with trembling hands.

An unearthly apparition awaited him when he entered. Every surface of the room was covered in newspaper clippings, as if the contents of his secret scrapbook had been displayed for all to see. Reeling back, he closed his eyes and, when he opened them again, the clippings were gone. Blinking back the vision, his face dripping with sweat, he fell to his knees and, in a hoarse whisper, began to pray. "Please, God, help me."

Along with a pure golden light, a sudden sense of peace descended into the room and, as Frank looked up, he saw Monica, dressed in white robes and surrounded by a shimmering light. "I'm an angel," she told him, "sent by God to help you."

"An angel," Frank stammered. "This can't be happening."

"It's not," said a voice behind him, and when he spun around he came face to face with Kathleen, her own body lit with a dark glow and her eyes burning like embers. "She's just your hallucination," the fallen angel cajoled. "Your job has finally pushed you over the edge. You can't take the pressure anymore. You've done enough good deeds for one lifetime. It's time to take care of yourself."

"What a perfect plan," Monica said evenly. "Destroy a man who repairs families." She reached out to touch Frank's hand. "Think," she urged him. "When did things start to go wrong for you? When did the nightmares begin?"

Frank threw a quick look at Kathleen then turned stubbornly away. "No," he insisted. "She loves me."

"It's a poor imitation of love," Monica insisted. "If you look at her with the light of God, you will see her for what she really is."

Kathleen hissed and took a step back. "The pain and terror of those children is on your shoulders," she cried. "They're paying for your mistakes. God has abandoned you."

"No!" Monica shouted. "Never! She's telling you lies!"

"God," Frank pleaded. "Help me! Who's telling the truth?"

"Come on, baby," coaxed Kathleen. "You said yourself I was too good to be—" she stopped, realizing too late what she had let slip.

"Too good to be true," Frank said, finishing her sentence, then adding in a tone of righteous indignation, "Get out!"

With a look of pure evil, Kathleen backed away, fading into the darkness until all that could be seen were her glowing red eyes. After a moment, they too were gone.

"My God," Frank murmured in a shaken voice. "What was she?"

"She used to be an angel," Monica explained. "But she traded the power of love for the love of power. And she almost stopped you from doing what you were born to do . . . save children."

"I don't save them," Frank replied sadly. "I lose more than I win."

Monica nodded. "Some of them you will carry home in your arms," she said. "The others, God will carry home in His. You were overcome by feelings of guilt, Frank. But God wants to take away that guilt and replace it with His grace and forgiveness. You've always done the best you could. God knows that and He wants you to know that He is proud of you."

The entire staff at the Center had gathered in the lobby when Frank arrived at work the next morning. In their midst was a tall teenage boy with sandy hair, the janitor who had helped break the case of Craig Cooper. Monica stepped forward. "Frank," she said, "I'd like you to meet someone very special. His name in Brian Grayson, the boy you've been looking for all these years. He needs someone to take him home."

Great Expectations

The silence in the doctor's office was deafening as Bill and Joanne McNabb, a married couple in their early forties, stared in disbelief at the physician that sat across the desk from them. Her words still rang in their ears—"amnio results" . . . "extra chromosome" . . . "Down's syndrome"—but neither could quite believe what they were hearing.

Instinctively, Joanne, an attractive woman with dark hair and a warm smile, laid her hand on her belly. They had waited so long, tried so hard, for this baby and when, at last, she found out she was pregnant it felt like their last chance. At her age, she had almost given up hope, but then, a miracle had happened and the dream of a lifetime was about to come true. News that her son—another fact the amnio test had determined—would be born with Down's syndrome was devastating, but even as she heard it, she held on firmly to the hope the doctor offered. There was no way, the obstetrician insisted, to know how this condition would affect the life of her son. "Every child is different," she said with an encouraging smile, "and every day we find new ways to help them. Knowing early also helps us to help him reach his highest potential." It would be difficult, there was no question about that. But she and Bill loved each other and that love would be strong enough to overcome

275

any obstacle their child might encounter. Together they could do it.

She reached out to squeeze her husband's hand and was surprised when she didn't feel a response. Turning, she saw an expression of dark despair clouding Bill's open and expressive face. "Our baby's going to be . . . retarded?" he whispered hoarsely.

"It's impossible to tell how far he will develop, Bill," the doctor replied soothingly. "Let's not make assumptions. Down's syndrome is—"

"Don't talk down to me," Bill snapped back. "Just because I don't have a diploma on my wall doesn't mean I'm dumb."

"The chances of a woman Joanne's age having a Down's syndrome child are about one in sixty," the doctor reminded him. She rose. "Look, you two need some time to let this sink in. I'll come back in a while."

"Sixty to one odds," Bill muttered bitterly as the doctor left. "And we lost." He looked at his wife, trying to find the words to express the thought that was forming in his mind. "Knowing early also gives us . . . other options."

"What other options are you talking about?" she asked quietly.

"We . . . don't have to have this baby," he replied, watching her face carefully to gauge her reaction.

Joanne shook her head, as if trying to clear away a thick fog. "You're going too fast for me, Bill," she said. "An hour ago, we were having a baby. A few minutes ago, we were having a baby with Down's syndrome. Now you're talking about not having a baby at all." She stood up. "We'll talk about this later. Let's just go to the shower now."

Bill shook his head. "I can't face all those people now. Besides, I don't want anyone else to know about this. Not until we've decided . . . . what to do."

"We have to go," his wife replied. "We're hosting it. Besides, even if we're not going to celebrate having our child, our friends want to share the joy of having theirs." She reached out for his hand. "I know this is a shock," she said gently. "For both of us. But we can get through this, Bill. I know we can." His anguished look was the only reply she received.

Juliano's Coffeehouse, a cozy and comfortable downtown hangout for young couples and their kids, was buzzing with activity as Bill and Joanne walked through the front door, smiles pasted on their faces to hide their heavy hearts. Their friends, holding their newborn daughter, rushed up to meet them and, in a moment, they were swept into the happy swirl of the baby shower.

Among the familiar faces in the crowd were three strangers to the small town, all quick to share in the warmth of this blessed event. Behind the counter, expertly creating frothy coffee concoctions, was Andrew, who, as he explained to the new arrivals, had temporarily taken over management of the shop while its owner was away. A redheaded woman with an Irish lilt and a sunbonnet introduced herself as Monica, the town's new Lamaze instructor, teaching birthing classes for expectant parents. An exuberant woman with a broad smile and a mane of salt-and-pepper hair completed the trio of newcomers.

As Bill, who sold cappuccino and special coffee blends, discussed business with Andrew, Monica and Tess sat in a booth, deep in conversation. "Bill and Joanne are facing the most important decision of their lives, Angel Girl," Tess was saying, as she filled the angel in on her new assignment. "And it could go either way. You're going to need all the help you can get, which is why there's been a specialist called in. You remember Taylor, don't you?"

"Of course," replied the delighted Monica. "He's a wonderful—" A loud crash from the kitchen cut off her words.

"Hold that thought," Tess said with shake of her wise head as she rose and headed for the kitchen.

Monica sat silently for a moment, reflecting on her new case. "Dear God," she prayed, after a moment. "Sometimes you arrive with a whisper. Sometimes you—" there was another loud crash from the kitchen. Monica smiled, then continued, "fall into our lives. But whatever you bring us is beautiful." She sighed. "Please God, help this couple to accept the beauty you are about to bring into their lives."

It was then that a small boy, spinning in circles with a toy airplane, ran directly into a busboy who was emerging from the kitchen with a tray full of cups and saucers. The crashing of china brought the party to a sudden halt as everyone turned to look at the accident. "That's okay," the busboy said, as he knelt down to pick up the broken pieces. "Accidents happen to everybody." He turned, smiling, and looked directly at Bill and Joanne, who were sitting nearby. While both immediately saw the distinctive features that indicate the presence of Down's syndrome, it was only Joanne who seemed to notice something else as well—a reassuring look from his bright eyes that seemed to reach deep into her soul with a wordless but comforting message.

"This is Taylor," said Andrew who had arrived to help with the clean up. "He started yesterday. We work together a lot . . . on special events."

Taylor smiled, his whole face lighting up. "I'm kind of a specialist," he said.

"Did you see the way everyone looked at that poor kid," Bill remarked to his wife as, around them, the noise of the party resumed. "I don't want anyone staring at my kid like that." His eyes followed Taylor as he happily bussed tables. "That's the best job he'll ever have. I wanted more for my son."

"Bill," Joanne replied. "I know you're hurting, but we're going to have to tell everyone what the doctor said before our shower."

Bill recoiled. "We can't have a shower," he protested. "How can we celebrate this?"

"We're still going to have this baby," was Joanne's unwavering response. "And he's still going to need things."

"No one can buy him what he's going to need," was Bill's bitter retort.

Monica stood in a large, open room. Around her was a circle of pregnant women, each with an attentive husband by her side, including Joanne with Bill right next to her. "Now that you've all mastered breathing," the angel explained, "let's move on to step two: communication. Moms, you need to tell Dads what you need. Let's take a moment right now to try it."

Joanne took a deep breath, summoning her courage. "I need to tell people, Bill," she said at last. "We'll both feel better if we do, honey."

"Sure," was Bill's terse reply. "Looks of pity always make me feel better." Now it was his turn to summon his courage. "Joanne," he began, "I think it's time we faced reality. If you have this baby—"

"*If?*" Joanne echoed. "If . . . ? "

"*We* will have a mentally retarded child," her husband continued stubbornly. "A little bit or a lot, he still won't be the perfect, bright baby we dreamed of." He paused. "The baby we could still have someday."

"Someday?" Joanne protested. "Bill, it's a miracle we got pregnant at all."

"This is no miracle," Bill replied darkly. "This is a mistake. We can correct it and move on."

"I can't believe you're seriously considering this," Joanne whispered while around them, happy couples murmured and cooed. "Do you know what you're saying?"

"Of course I do," Bill snapped. "I'm saying there's no hope for our kid to be like others. I'm saying he'll need round-the-clock care for the rest of his life. And I'm saying our lives will become dedicated to our retarded son. Is that your idea of a family? Because it sure as hell isn't mine!" As Monica watched, trying with all her might not to interfere, Bill stood and gestured for Joanne to follow him to a far corner of the room. "I'm saying what you're thinking," Bill continued as they huddled together for privacy. "I'm saying we can't have this baby. His life would be miserable and our lives would be ruined."

"You want me to get rid of it, don't you?" Joanne said, her eyes flooding with tears. "Even if we could have another baby, what if it doesn't have the right color eyes? Are we going to abort that one, too?"

"I know it's awful to think about now, but in a year, you'll be glad we did this." Bill said as he reached out to gently stroke her face. "That's why we did the amnio, honey. Remember. To know what was coming."

"Yes," replied Joanne in anguish. "So that if there was anything wrong we could do something to fix it."

"And there is," Bill answered, quietly. He brought her close, resting her head on his shoulder. "It's going to be okay, honey," he promised her. "You believe that, don't you?"

She nodded meekly, but there was no way to stop the tears.

It was later that afternoon that Bill and Joanne stopped by Juliano's for a late lunch and a chance to calm their raw nerves after the emotional turmoil of the past few weeks. While his wife picked at her food, Bill's eyes once again fell on Taylor as he moved from table to table, picking up dirty dishes and chatting with the customers.

At that moment, the door opened and a young couple entered, followed by a skipping young girl with thick glasses and the same Down's syndrome characteristics as Taylor. "Olivia!" the angelic busboy cried. "Good to see you!" Joanne brightened immediately at the sight of the small girl, even as Bill stood up, preparing to leave.

Andrew, seeing the developing situation, hurried over. "I'm having a problem with the steam nozzle on that cappuccino machine," he told Bill. "Could you have a look at it?"

"Go ahead, honey," Joanne said, already kneeling down to where Olivia was happily playing with Taylor. "I'm fine."

For the next few minutes, Bill watched with increasing discomfort as his wife and Taylor joined Olivia on the floor, laughing and talking together. "Come on," he snapped at last, pulling his wife to her feet. "We've got to get going." As he hurried her through the front door, Andrew and Taylor exchanged a disappointed look.

"Couldn't you have at least said hello to that little girl?" Joanne asked, breaking the angry silence in the car as they drove away.

"The whole thing just creeped me out," Bill snarled. "We're supposed to be getting over this and that didn't help."

"Maybe it did," Joanne replied hopefully. "Olivia had Down's syndrome and she was adorable. She seemed like such a happy little girl."

"What's she got to be happy about?" demanded Bill. "And what about her poor mother. If that woman had a choice, don't you think she'd have wanted a healthy child?"

Joanne blinked back her tears. "I saw a mother who loved her little girl," she said at last, then turned to face her husband. "I can't keep going back and forth about this. It's too painful."

Bill nodded vigorously. "That's what I've been trying to say. Let's stop talking about it. Let's just do it. Now." Without waiting for her answer, he made a sudden U-turn and sped back into town while Joanne looked forlornly out the window as life passed them by.

Joanne, feeling vulnerable and exposed in the flimsy hospital gown, turned around as she walked through the swinging door of the local family planning clinic. Bill, seated in the waiting room, put on a brave smile and waved at her but could see from the look on her face that she hardly noticed.

Moving down the corridor, Joanne was directed to an examination room and numbly followed along until, at the threshold, she came face to face with a young woman, a radiant glow in her eyes. "It's wonderful," she gushed. "The most incredible thing I've ever seen. You can make out her head! Her whole body! Right there . . ." She pointed to the fuzzy but unmistakable image of the baby in her womb, captured on an ultrasound screen. For a long moment, Joanne just stared. Then, suddenly, decisively, she turned on her heels and walked away.

"I couldn't do it, Bill," she told her husband when she returned to the waiting room, wearing her street clothes and an excited expression. "I was going to do it, but for you—not for me. We've tried so hard to have a baby. What if this is our only chance?"

"We can have another baby," Bill insisted as they walked together into the parking lot. "I know we can."

"Even if we could," Joanne countered, "there would always be an empty chair at our table. Whoever he is, whatever he is, I would miss him."

"Listen to yourself," Bill snarled. "This isn't a him. It's not even a viable human being. You're the one preaching pro-choice all these years. What happened?"

"I got pregnant," Joanne replied evenly. "I'm still pro-choice . . . and I just made one. I'm going to have this baby."

"She's so obsessed with this baby . . . it's like *we* don't even exist any more." Bill sat at the counter of Juliano's, pouring out his woes to a sympathetic Andrew. Months had passed since Joanne had made her decisive choice to keep their baby, but, even as the child continued to take form inside her, Bill's anger and frustration had lodged deep in his heart. He'd stopped going to the Lamaze classes, with Tess volunteering to take over as his wife's coach, and now, more and more often, he seemed to seek the lonely sanctuary of the coffeehouse.

"A new baby changes everything, Bill," Andrew replied. "That *we* is about to become three." He poured his customer another cappuccino, but could see that Bill wasn't listening. Instead, his eyes were fixed on Taylor as the angel went about his cleaning chores.

"That's all he's ever going to be, isn't it?" Bill remarked, with a mixture of pity and *self*-pity.

"Taylor?" answered Andrew. "He's very happy with who he is. If you got to know him, you'd find that he's funny and insightful and he gives himself one hundred percent to whatever he's doing."

Bill snorted derisively. "He's a busboy." He turned back to Andrew. "Look, I never went to college. I'm always going to be just a salesman. I want more for my kid." Swallowing hard, he leaned forward. "Andrew," he confided in a low tone. "Joanne's baby is going to be . . ." he looked at Taylor.

"I know," was all Andrew could say. He took a deep breath. What he was about to say wasn't going to come easy. "Bill," he began, "you spend more time here than anywhere else. In my line of work you learn to recognize when people don't want to go home."

Bill slammed down his cup on the counter. "Fine," he said between gritted teeth. "You want a confession. Here it is. All I wanted was a normal family." The bell above the door rang, announcing a new customer and both men turned to watch a tall, good looking teenager in a letter jacket enter the shop. "A kid that would grow up straight and true," he said, without taking his eyes off the teen. "Maybe the captain of the high-school football team. Might even get a college scholarship . . . be an architect or a lawyer." Glancing back at the teenager, he added, "That's the kid I wanted."

Suddenly, with a flash of cold steel, the teenager pulled a gun from his jacket and leveled it at the nearby customers. "Nobody move!" he shouted. "Do what I say and you won't get hurt." With a wild look he swung the barrel at Andrew and Bill. "I want all the money in the register!" he shouted.

"No problem," Andrew said trying to calm the thief. "It's yours. Just take it easy." He began to move toward the register, but was waved away.

"Not you," the thief hissed. "I don't want any tricky stuff!" He gestured toward Taylor. "Get the moron to do it."

As Taylor emptied out the cash, the doorbell rang again and Joanne, her stomach distended by her seventh month of pregnancy, entered. In a panic, the thief spun around and pointed his weapon in her face.

"No!" shouted Bill and with nearly superhuman speed leaped up and began to grapple with the gun. A sudden deafening sound echoed through the coffeehouse mixed with screams while Bill watched in horror as his wife slumped to the ground, a red stain spreading quickly over her maternity blouse.

"Joanne!" Bill screamed, rushing to her side as the teen ran out the door and disappeared down the street.

"The baby," she murmured weakly. "The baby . . ." Her husband scooped her into his arms and held her tightly as Taylor knelt down beside them.

"No," the angel said urgently. "Keep her flat. Put her feet up. It's the best thing."

"Get away," Bill snarled. "Leave us alone!" He looked down to his wife. "Everything's going to be fine," he said, trying to keep the tremor from his voice.

She looked up at him, her eyes clouded. "If something happens to me, I want you to keep our baby." She clutched at his shirt. "He's us. He's the best part of us." In the distance, the wail of a siren could be heard.

The gurney rattled through the brightly lit hospital corridor as a paramedic tried desperately to hold Bill's attention long enough to gather vital information. "How many months pregnant is your wife?" he shouted, as they rushed toward the operating room.

"Seven!" Bill managed to answer. "But don't worry about the baby! Save my wife!"

A nurse stepped in his path as automatic doors opened to swallow his wife into the harsh glare of the operating room. "You need to stay out here, sir," she said firmly. A moment later a doctor in a surgeon's gown emerged. "Your wife is critical," he said tersely. "But if we move fast we can save the baby. You did the best thing for her and got her feet up. Not many people can think that fast in a crisis."

Almost before Bill could absorb this information, the doctor thrust a clipboard into his hand. "We need your permission for an emergency C-section," he said as he heard his name shouted from beyond the doors. "I can't promise anything, but we'll do our best."

Then, suddenly, Bill found himself alone. Sinking to a chair he stared at the paper on the clipboard for a long moment. "God help me," he groaned.

"That's why I'm here," replied a voice and he looked up to see Taylor, his eyes sparkling with wisdom and compassion, standing close by in the hallway. A long moment passed. "You don't want a son like me, do you?" he asked in quiet and steady voice.

Too upset to be anything but honest, Bill replied, "No. I'm sorry. But I don't."

"There is something worse than Down's syndrome," Taylor continued. "It's called fear."

"Don't talk to me about fear," Bill growled.

"Why not?" asked Taylor, a strange golden light beginning to form around him. "That's what angels do."

Bill watched in utter amazement as the light grew brighter. "Are you trying to tell me," he stammered, "that you're . . . an angel?" He shook his head. "God sent me a retarded angel?"

"No," Taylor replied. "God sent me. To tell you not to be afraid. He created you in love. He created your baby in love. He will give you the love you need. And then your son will give it back to you . . . for the rest of your life."

"I don't have a son yet," Bill insisted stubbornly. "And I may lose my wife."

"What we do in love is never lost," the angel replied, and the words seemed to echo in Bill's mind. He grabbed the pen, scribbling his signature on the C-section consent form and when he looked up again, Taylor had vanished.

Unable to sit any longer in the claustrophobic confines of the waiting room, Bill began aimlessly wandering the hospital hallways, finding himself at length at the large plateglass window that looked upon rows and rows of newborn infants in the maternity ward.

"Every one of them is perfect," he said, his voice tinged with sorrow as he pressed his face against the glass. He could feel a helpless frustration welling from deep inside, combined with the shattering events of the day and the anguish he felt over Joanne's life-and-death struggle on the operating table. Raising his eyes to heaven he began, for the first time in his life, to pray. "I . . . uh . . . don't know if You're up there, God," he began. "I hope You're not, because You won't like what I'm going to say. But the doctor says that Joanne's in bad shape. She may have damage that can't be fixed . . . in her brain . . ." Overwhelmed now, he buried his head in his hands. "I can't do this God," he whispered. "I can't take care of this kid and then take care of Joanne, too. Help me, Lord! I don't know what to do."

"Yes, you do," came a voice from behind him. "And you're doing it. It's called prayer."

Bill spun around, surprised and embarrassed. "I didn't know anyone was listening to that," he muttered.

"You'd be surprised Who's listening," Tess replied, stepping forward with a smile. She laid a kindly hand on his arm. "God isn't taking anything away from you, Bill," she continued. "The world takes things away. God restores them. And a thousand times better, too!"

"Thanks," Bill responded, the doubt evident in his tone. "But it doesn't look that way today."

"You love Joanne with everything you've got, don't you?" Tess continued. "And that baby is part of her . . . and part of you. A part of your love for each other." She gestured toward the cribs on the far side of the window. "That's why your baby is as perfect as any one of these. He was born of love." She gave him an appraising look. "Can I ask you something? If Joanne did have brain damage, would you leave her?"

"Of course not," Bill answered instantly. "She's family."

"So is that little boy of yours," the angel replied with a beaming smile. "So maybe you should pray for your wife *and* your baby. Not for the one you wanted . . . but for the one you're about to receive." She stepped back. "Nothing is impossible," she concluded. "You can do all things through Him who gives you strength. Just ask."

It was dark in the hospital room, the only sounds the soft clicks and whirs of the medical machines attached to the motionless form of Joanne, lying in bed. On a chair beside her sat her husband and, in his arms, a tiny bundle.

"You have the most wonderful mother in the world," Bill was saying in a soft and tender voice to his newborn son. "She's smart and she's beautiful and she loves you very, very much." He held the bundle a little closer. "And so do I."

In the same soft voice, he turned to his wife. "Joanne," he said, gently coaxing, "we're waiting for you to wake up. We know you've had a hard time, but we also know that nothing is impossible if you just ask." He held up the baby. "So Taylor and I are asking." He paused and smiled. "I hope you don't mind. I went ahead and named our son after our friend Taylor, so he would grow up proud. He will, Joanne. And you'll be there to see it." Leaning forward, he stroked her forehead. "You're going to get better, honey. One day at a time. We can do this. We *are* doing this. Aren't we, Taylor?"

The baby made a tiny cry as his father held him close. "It's okay," Bill whispered. "Daddy's here."